D0337738

Roulette

ALSO BY MEGAN MULRY

A Royal Pain (Unruly Royals)
If the Shoe Fits (Unruly Royals)
In Love Again (Unruly Royals)
R is for Rebel (Unruly Royals)
Bound to Be a Bride
Bound to Be a Groom
The Wallflowers

Roulette

MEGAN MULRY

WITHDRAWN

Montlake
Romance

This is a work of fiction. Names, characters, organizations, places, events, and incidents are either products of the author's imagination or used fictitiously.

Text copyright © 2014 Megan Mulry
All rights reserved.

No part of this book may be reproduced, or stored in a retrieval system, or transmitted in any form or by any means, electronic, mechanical, photocopying, recording, or otherwise, without express written permission of the publisher.

Published by Montlake Romance, Seattle

www.apub.com

Amazon, the Amazon logo, and Montlake Romance are trademarks of Amazon. com, Inc., or its affiliates.

ISBN-13: 9781477826706
ISBN-10: 147782670X

Cover design by Mumtaz Mustafa Designs

Library of Congress Control Number: 2014943174

Printed in the United States of America

For J.

CHAPTER ONE

I'm walking home from the beach, carrying my surfboard under one arm, and I realize I'm feeling pretty content about life in general. I finished grading all my student papers in time to leave the office early. I've got two weeks of spring break in Russia ahead of me, and I'm actually looking forward to spending some time with my father, for once. I even made it from USC to Venice faster than usual, with plenty of time to squeeze in an hour of surfing before meeting up with Landon.

I'm not feeling cocky or anything, just grateful. I'm enumerating, I guess:

I have a boyfriend.

I have a house.

I have a job.

I have friends.

I have parents.

Thinking about it like that, in a list, gives me a momentary weird feeling that I shouldn't be so sure. About the parents. About any of it. Hubris or something.

I hose down the board and store it in the shed behind my house. I take a shower and get dressed for my farewell dinner with

Landon, pulling my thick blond hair back into a tight ponytail, the way he loves.

A little later, there we are, having fun, drinking margaritas and eating killer Mexican food at our favorite place on La Cienega, but I get that creeping anxiety again. I'm always nervous before I go see my father in Russia—the flight, the language, the awkward nature of my family dynamics.

My *family dynamics* are more like a classic episode of *Dynasty*. Cue scene: big-money/big-hair summer of 1984 at the Hôtel du Cap on the Côte d'Azur. Russian mogul seduces young French starlet. *Et voilà!* Nine months later, I enter stage left. Mikhaila Voyanovski Durand, love child. That pretty much describes how I *don't* want my life to turn out—and Landon is the obvious antidote to all that.

Landon and I have been dating for about a year. And lately, he's started getting what I think of as The Look. (The Look that means he is entering Phase Two: You Are Wife Material.) I've known this about him from the beginning. He's driven. He has long-term goals. As such, he lives his life on a schedule.

He's a really successful cardiologist at UCLA Medical Center, though I'm no slouch—as his dad kindly pointed out, on our recent visit to Ohio, that I, at the age of thirty, was going to be one of the youngest tenured professors at USC. But it's no exaggeration to say that Landon's high expectations are usually met. Having accomplished all he has in his thirty-five years, he's never really had an unrealistic expectation. He makes shit happen. He saves lives. Literally.

I manage to avoid the subject a couple of times over appetizers, when he gives me those extralong I-know-you-know-what-I'm-thinking looks. But by the end of the fajitas, I can't put him off any longer. He's got things to say and he's going to say them.

"Do you know, I think this might be our anniversary . . ." He's holding his margarita halfway to his lips, like he does when he's trying to seem like he's just remarking casually on some random thing.

I'm messed up, probably, because he's basically the perfect guy and I'm still wrestling with my marriage phobia. I don't have much to go on, as far as marital role models are concerned. *Much*, in my case, equals nothing. I have nothing to go on. My parents never got around to marrying each other. In fact, I'm not sure they ever got around to liking each other.

My father is an emotional iceberg but a really good person—loyal and honest. My mother is flamboyant and loving and all that, but she never met an indiscretion she didn't like. She raised me on her own in Bel Air. I use the term *raised* very loosely.

I am not about to get into any of *that* with Landon the night before I leave for Russia for two weeks, so I try to keep it light.

"Anniversary of what? We never really had a first date or anything. Did we?"

"You know what I mean. That night at the Pearsons' house? That was definitely the first time we weren't just hanging out. Remember, by the pool? It was the Friday of your spring break, just like tonight."

I smile and nod, because of course I remember making out by the pool that night and of course Landon avoids saying the phrase *making out*.

"And then we went out the next night . . . and then . . ." He winks.

I remind myself to tell him—at some future, less-important-feeling time—that he needs to quit it with the winking. It irks me.

Instead, I smile to let him know that I, too, have happy memories of the first time we went out for dinner, just the two of us, and ended up back at my place, having sex on the couch in the living room. At the time, I loved how having sex not in a bed was his idea of over-the-top, wild-and-crazy sexual mayhem. But since then, we always have it in bed. It's just easier that way. Which is fine.

Anyway.

I can tell Landon is working himself up to something, and I try to cut him off at the pass.

"Will you—" he starts.

"Landon—" I interrupt.

"Move in with me?"

We sort of talk over each other, but I think he realizes I thought he was going to propose, and for a split second he also realizes that I am clearly relieved he only asked me to move in with him. Even though I have my reservations—he is so intractable, so fixed in his opinions—I tell myself those are minor flaws, or even points in his favor, part of what people mean when they talk about compromise, part of what it means to be a *mature* person. And mature people live together . . . and eventually get married. Unlike some parents, who shall remain nameless.

There is a great big part of me that wants everything a life with Landon promises: stability, a normal routine, a house, a dog, some kids eventually. I truly believe I want all of that. And it is right there. I know I should just say yes—because what more could a girl ask for? What kind of damn fool says no to Landon Winslow Clark III, MD? But something holds me back from giving him the full-on, 100 percent *yes*! I tell him he's so sweet to bring it up, but I'm too preoccupied with my trip tomorrow. I tell him I need to focus on getting through the next two weeks in Saint Petersburg, and then we can deal with logistics. That seems to satisfy him for now—he likes that I'm talking *logistics* and that we've broached the subject, that moving in together is on the table. I picture him checking it off his mental to-do list.

This is what it must feel like to be a grown-up. This is how it must *feel* to be a thirty-year-old functioning adult and make adult decisions to move in with your doctor boyfriend, to have conversations and make plans. I am building a real life, one that doesn't rely on distant Russian billionaire fathers or flighty French movie-star mothers who passed their kid around the globe like a relay baton.

CHAPTER TWO

The day I arrive in Saint Petersburg, intending to spend my spring break convincing my father that I will not, under any circumstances, be taking over his Russian manufacturing business, the poor man is laid up in the hospital with pneumonia.

My uncle Alexei meets me at the airport and takes me to see my father. He's kind of drowsy and out of it when I arrive, but it doesn't really occur to me to worry, because he's always been really fit and healthy in that gruff way of his. For a few seconds, he seems really happy to see me when I kiss his cheek, but then he falls back to sleep without saying much.

Alexei and I agree to meet back at the hospital in the morning, so I head over to my hotel. I figure my father will be rested up by then and the three of us can still spend a few days at the lake house about two hours west of the city as planned. I fall asleep from a combination of jet lag and the strange comfort that being in Russia always brings.

When I get to the hospital the next day, I'm still jet-lagged and don't really understand what's happening. But I do. Nurses are scurrying around the far end of the corridor, and the closer I get to his room, it becomes overwhelmingly evident that they're freaking out and it's about my dad.

Alexei comes barreling out of the room, and then sees me and pulls me into one of his signature bear hugs, and I can hardly breathe. And then he's telling me in Russian that my dad died unexpectedly in his sleep, and he's using words like *awful* and *incomprehensible* and *it's just us now*. I get it, I do, but it's also a barrage of syllables and noise, and I think I'm not really here but still on the plane from LA and having one of those weird long-haul-flight anxiety dreams. But I'm not.

My dad died.

I'm still holding a paper coffee cup in my hand, and I don't really know why. And then a whole bunch of Official Death Business goes down for a couple of hours, and I wade robotically through them. Once it's over, Alexei and I go back to my father's apartment and Alexei is pretty much a wreck. He's talking a mile a minute about everything from some factory deal to my mother to a whole bunch of minutiae I haven't a clue about.

He and my father were two of the closest people I've ever met: best friends, brothers, business partners. I finally convince him to go home and make the arrangements for the funeral, and that seems to motivate him. So here I am, alone in my father's apartment on a sunny Sunday afternoon. Alone.

Some people see this sort of thing coming: hints, signs along the way. I analyze data for a living. I'm a statistics professor; I am paid to be observant. I'm also physically observant: I surf, I go rock climbing, I like to pay attention to the world around me. But in this case, it is as if I am not looking at *anything*, am not even remotely aware of something as obviously unavoidable as death.

I try to tell myself he was only my biological father, nothing more, but even I know it for a lie. My father and I were practically clones; our brains clicked in the exact same staccato rhythm.

An hour later I'm still standing in his apartment, when I finally realize the ringing phone isn't coming from one of the flats down the hall or from outside the window. I cross into the bedroom to answer it.

"*Da?*" I'm fluent in Russian—both from my father and from taking it at MIT—but I still need to focus on the phone when I'm out of practice. I press the old-fashioned receiver hard against my ear in preparation.

"Miki, is that you? It's Landon. What's happening? Is he okay?"

About thirty minutes ago, I left one of those it's-kind-of-a-family-emergency messages with Landon's answering service.

"No." I relax because the person is speaking English; then I tense a bit because it's Landon and Landon likes answers. And I don't feel like I have any.

"Aw, Mik, I'm really sorry. Do you want me to fly over there . . . I could try . . . I'm not sure I could get away from the hospital without a fight, but I—"

"No," I interrupt. "No, that's totally not necessary. He died"—I look at my watch, as if I'm the coroner declaring time of death—"about two hours ago. We're doing a quick private funeral. My uncle Alexei's hoping to make it happen tomorrow. And he usually can make things happen, I guess. Given the length of time it would take, it wouldn't be worth it for you to fly all this way . . ."

Landon sighs into the phone, somewhere in a corridor of UCLA Medical Center. "All right." He sounds relieved but like he knows he shouldn't let on too much about the relief. "I feel kind of shitty not being there. Are you sure?"

"Sure. I'm sure. It's not like my father and I were really close."

"He was still your dad . . . but I know what you mean. I guess you're right. You barely knew him."

I stare out the bedroom window, thinking how I need to get some Russian Windex and clean the smudges near the handle, where my father must have last lifted the frame. Then I look down and notice the pale-blue bedroom carpet; it is old, and especially worn where my father must have stood up each morning, next to his bed. I stare at the spot while Landon talks about some opportunity to start a private practice or something.

I have a flash of a childhood memory, of my father doing his morning exercises—those antiquated at-home calisthenics—raising his hands to the ceiling, then bending over and touching his toes. Then up again. It must have been one of my first visits, when I was seven or eight, because I remember feeling small. He was vividly large when he extended up like that. And he smiled at me, quickly, once.

I didn't know my father very well, and Landon didn't know him at all. There is no point in his coming to be with me.

I have the terrible, unbidden follow-up thought that Landon doesn't know me at all, either, and that there is no point to the two of us even being together. I stuff that thought right into my imaginary I'm-freaking-out-only-because-my-dad-just-died box. Because those are just crazy thoughts. Landon is top-grade husband material, and I do *not* need to be picking apart whether or not he *knows* me.

"Hey, Lan, I should go and deal with all this stuff." Proper relationship-crushing thoughts, begone. Landon is good. Solid. My father is gone. Vapor. "I'm going to stick to my original flight back, the Sunday after next. Alexei and my dad are—were—still riding me hard to come work for Voyanovski Industries . . . so I need to deal with all that."

"That's ridiculous. You can't do that—you're a professor, not a businesswoman."

Well, now. When he says it like that, I kind of want to prove him wrong. "It's not that I *couldn't* do it, Lan, but obviously I'm not moving to Saint Petersburg because—"

"Because you're moving in with me, remember?"

"Right," I answer slowly, but what I want to say is, *Whatever, dude. Priorities? Dead father? Selfish much?* Then I just exhale, because he probably means it as a comfort, that I have a life waiting for me back in LA. A good life.

I can tell he's already flipping open a medical chart, since he's doing that quick "mm-hmm, mm-hmm" thing to pretend he's still mentally there.

"Okay," he continues. "Call me if you need anything; otherwise I won't bug you." He's obviously ready to end the call, and I don't resent it. We both have a shared dislike of lingering on the phone.

"Thanks for calling, Landon."

"You're welcome, Mik. Hang in there."

Click.

Alexei is able to get everything done for the funeral. He is always able to get things done. He is a jovial older man who talks too much and appears to be doing nothing more than chatting all the time, but meanwhile, everything is "taken care of" by the time he finishes telling the same old story about his great-uncle in Mexico who once had dinner with Trotsky or his great-grandfather who wrote epic folk poetry in the nineteenth century.

While my father was cool and hard to reach until I was old enough to understand a spreadsheet, Uncle Alexei always loved me in that crazy, doting way that only a relative who isn't your parent can. Alexei was always laughing and squeezing my cheeks and telling me Russian fairy tales while we grilled fresh fish over an open fire during our summer holidays in Sardinia.

Alexei was widowed four years ago and never had any children, so we serve as a tiny receiving line of two for the twenty or so people who have been confidentially notified about my father's death and invited to the private funeral. Everything in Russia seems like it has to be a secret, or at least that's how Alexei operates. I don't think it's really necessary, but he's always had a dramatic nature.

I recognize one man in particular, mostly because he is a bit loud and makes a stink when Alexei won't allow his bodyguards into the private room we reserved for the small reception. He is Pavel Durchenko, infamous in Moscow and Saint Petersburg for his exorbitant wealth and his questionable means of acquiring it. His home on Sardinia is near ours, and I've met him a few times before, very briefly, when he came to visit my father there. He's probably in his early forties, physically fit and wound up tight, looking like his suit was sewn onto him that morning. Impeccable.

Now, I've met a few charismatic people in my day—my mother, for one—and I've seen this before, at close range. This man has *it*, that thing that makes you shiver when he grasps your hand in his. The bits of silver in his hair and his silvery-gray eyes make me feel like he is made out of some type of gleaming iron ore.

He looks straight into my eyes, giving his condolences. "Your father was a very good man. Sharp. We did business together."

"Thank you." I don't really know if there is a right thing to say, so I've resorted to a lot of thank-yous over the past few hours.

"He and I understood one another," Durchenko says cryptically.

I nod because I have no idea what else to do. I don't want this guy to murder me in my sleep. Nodding seems like a safe bet.

"My deepest sympathies," he says, but it's like he's trying to communicate with me using telepathy. He's saying something about sympathies, but his eyes are boring into mine and it's starting to freak me out.

"Thank you," I repeat. When he releases my hand, I feel like one of those cartoon characters who fly backward after extracting a finger from an electrical socket.

"Please call on me if you ever need anything," he adds, pressing a small business card into my palm. "That's my private number."

I nod again, say thank you again, and wonder briefly if he and I will be stuck in some infinite loop of thank-yous and nods.

"Very well." He pats my upper arm and moves on to pay his respects to Alexei. I have the distinct feeling he wanted to say more about his business with my dad, but decided it wasn't the appropriate thing to do under the circumstances. I can tell without turning to look that Alexei is straining to remain his cheerful self as he accepts the man's supposedly kind words, when they are so obviously enigmatic warnings of some sort. I don't know if Durchenko is a murderer or just a billionaire businessman, but in Russia, lately, they are often two sides of the same coin.

After everyone has taken a shot or two of vodka and a few bites of caviar, the small party breaks up and Alexei asks if I want to go for a late supper. I decline—I'm sick of being around people, even sweet and caring ones like Alexei—and promise to meet him at the corporate offices the next morning to deal with the business side of things.

By noon the next day, my head is spinning out of control. Alexei is under the absurd impression that, now that my father is dead, I *will* take over Voyanovski Industries, his and my father's thriving company, with paper factories and timber holdings across Russia, Ukraine, and Belarus.

"This is what your father wanted! This is your legacy!" He's not yelling at me, exactly, but it sounds like yelling in his guttural Russian.

"Alexei." I try—and fail—to stay calm. "You are not listening to me! I have a PhD in information and operations management! I'm supposed to be sitting in an office in the IOM department at the Marshall School of Business at the University of Southern California! I'm a teacher!"

"You must have known this is what your father wanted, Miki. How can you say you didn't know that?" Alexei is beginning to sound desperate.

"I came here specifically to tell you *both* that I'm about to get tenure at USC and this is *no longer* up for discussion. I'm a professor; I am *not* a businesswoman!" I recoil as I realize I sound like Landon. Alexei crosses his arms and purses his lips. He looks like a caricature of a disapproving maiden aunt far more than he looks like the COO of a very large company. He and my father worked together their entire lives. The Voyanovski brothers built everything from scratch, through all those years of political upheaval.

"Stop looking at me like that," I snap.

He raises his eyebrows and pretends to be accommodating. "Very well. So let me ask you, then: Why *did* you get a business degree? Just to *talk* about business? Or to actually *do* it?"

I roll my eyes. "Quit trying to bait me. Of course I *could* do it, if I wanted to. But I don't want to."

"You're lying to yourself. You were born to do this."

"All right, look." I lower my voice a bit. "I'll do what I can about restructuring the Segezha deal, but that's it." He's been fixated on this factory deal in a small town called Segezha. There's a financing issue, and I'm actually kind of looking forward to seeing if I can sort it out. It's all very contained, not like I'm taking over the whole company or anything.

He claps his meaty hands together and stands up to go. "Excellent!"

Now, I may be confused about my boyfriend and family dynamics and a whole slew of other Big Life Issues, but I am a serious whiz when it comes to finance, and Alexei knows he just scored a major point.

"Where do you think you're going?" I stand up, too, and follow him toward the door of my father's office. We've been sitting in the two chairs across from the big desk, neither one of us willing to sit in the dead man's chair.

The office is still bright, despite its old-fashioned, dark paneling. The crisp sunshine of early spring highlights a glorious midday view across Saint Petersburg through the tall windows. The roof of the Hermitage and the sparkling waters of the Neva should be having at least a slightly mollifying effect on my nerves.

No such luck. I am totally keyed up. Excited. Not that I am going to tell Alexei, but there is that whirring part of my brain that can't wait to dig into the bones of my father's business. He was a spectacular businessman, and I want to see how he did it. And in a weird way, it makes me feel as if my father and I are still connected somehow.

"I'm going to let the shareholders know that you've agreed to stay on—"

"Alexei! I have not—"

"Temporarily."

I sigh. "Okay, fine. Let them know I'm here this week and next to sort through some of the most pressing business."

After he walks out, I turn back to look at the office. What a nightmare.

In addition to my PhD, I have an MBA in mergers and acquisitions. Ostensibly I am interested only in theory, but that's like saying someone who plays poker with imaginary money feels exactly like someone who walks into a casino with $100,000 cash in her pocket.

It's not the same thing.

I sit down in my father's seat and open the Segezha file. As much as I hate to admit it, I love it. I chose a career in academia because it was safe. I don't want to live on the edge, like both my parents—in their own ways—did.

But Alexei doesn't miss a trick. He knew I'd bite.

CHAPTER THREE

By the Tuesday of the following week, I *am* feeling kind of superhero-ish. Maybe I could swoop in once a month, clean up the occasional corporate mess, and swoop out.

That idea comes to a screeching halt when Alexei suggests I actually call on some of Voyanovski's larger clients and introduce myself.

"No way."

He gestures at the piles of paperwork I've already gone through, the myriad minor problems I've already solved in just over a week. "But, Miki . . . you are the very good one at it." He's been brushing up on his English with me, and I smile at his funny grammar.

"That's different. That's just numbers. And paper. I get numbers. I don't get people."

He shakes his head. "That is not true. Look at you. You're lovely."

"Oh my god." I burst out laughing, then almost start crying. "You are so sexist you don't even know you're being sexist! What does being *lovely* have to do with the net present value of the financing you think we can get from Kriegsbeil? You're a nutball."

"A what?"

Alexei is fluent in English, but he always loves learning these quirky turns of phrase.

"Nut. Ball. You know? A ball made of nuts? Crazy? Cuckoo?"

He smiles. "Ah, but you say I am *nutball* when I first ask you to do all this corporate problem solving, and now look at you." He folds his arms and nods his head, like he's just proven Fermat's theorem.

He is irresistible. "Okay, I'll grant you I've enjoyed getting to understand the company. But, trust me, I am *not* a people person. I am a numbers person. I know this about myself. Please believe me."

He shakes his head from side to side. "No."

"What do you mean *no?*"

"I don't believe you. You are people person!" he declares in his slightly stilted English.

"Oh, dear. Fine. Believe what you want, I'm not in the mood to argue. In the meantime, I think I can finish the cost analysis on the Segezha plant, and then *you* can call Kriegsbeil and Clairebeau to let them know what we're aiming for."

"Ack! Kriegsbeil! They should get nothing, the dirty Germans." With that, he turns and leaves the office. I laugh at his decades-old political hostility and turn my attention back to the spreadsheet on the computer screen in front of me.

Alexei is right. I am happy to get lost in numbers. There are solutions. Clarity is possible. Definition. Finality.

I work for a few more hours, figuring out the best way to sort out the Segezha deal. Basically, my father wanted to gradually offload the plant over the next few years by letting the German company Kriegsbeil be the lead investor and eventual owner. Alexei, on the other hand, believes Voyanovski Industries should retain control and find financing from multiple investors instead. Preferably non-German investors.

One of the potential alternative investors is a French company called Clairebeau. I've followed its success in the business trade magazines: it's a classic case of a young, ambitious CEO who turns a company around by taking needless risks. Just last year, I used Clairebeau as a case study for what *not* to do during a large-scale corporate restructuring.

I open the file on the desk in front of me and pull out Clairebeau's annual report. I stare at a picture of the cocky CEO, Jérôme Michel de Villiers. He's your run-of-the-mill smoking-hot media mogul. Risk on a stick.

Luckily, I won't be the one dealing with him; Alexei will.

I go through the file, make a few notes on a separate piece of paper. It looks like Alexei is probably right. It makes much more sense, financially, to spread out the risk of the plant renovation among multiple investors, German or otherwise. The long-term returns will be huge.

On the other hand, there are a few scribbles in the file that make me think my father wanted to sell the plant outright, though his notes are vague. Some more digging shows Kriegsbeil has very close ties with one of Pavel Durchenko's holding companies, and I remember the way he looked at me at my father's funeral, with that stare of his. Still, there's nothing anywhere to indicate that my father and Durchenko had an actual agreement, and I'm not about to strike up a conversation with an oligarch like Durchenko about an under-the-table one.

When in doubt, I go back to the financials.

I create a cost-analysis report, study different exit strategies, do more research into Clairebeau and Kriegsbeil, run more numbers, and after changing a few of my expectations, I decide I might as well lob some ridiculously high numbers to Clairebeau and see if they bite. They'd be idiots even to start a negotiation on these terms, but at least I can rest knowing I technically offered them the chance to bid. I send an email from my father's account to Monsieur de Villiers and decide to call it a night. It's late, and Mr. Parisian Playboy probably won't get it until tomorrow anyway.

I print a copy and save the file, then make a quick call to Alexei to let him know that I'm finished with the report and have sent an offering memorandum to de Villiers. I don't bother telling him the outrageous nature of what I offered. I can hear the smile in his voice. "That's my girl."

I don't think he's going to be so merry when he reads my recommendation, but I'm not in the mood to get into it right now. Despite the financial advantages of keeping the factory, a greater part of me wants to respect my father's wishes—even if I don't really understand them—so that's what I am going to advise we do in my final report to the board.

"Honestly, Alexei, if you don't cut it out with the *girl* and *lovely* nonsense, I'm not going to do another thing for you or this blasted company. I am a number cruncher. I evaluate data and performance models. I am so not your *girl!*" I hang up on him and can hear his deep laugh from down the corridor after I end the call.

The phone rings right away, so I assume it's Alexei calling back to rib me. Instead, I've got an angry Frenchman perforating my eardrum.

"Alexei! What the hell?" the voice booms in English before I can even say hello. "This offering is outrageous! Are you trying to bankrupt me?"

"Who's calling, please?" I ask, kind of stunned at the audacity of someone who can just *launch* like that. Of course, I know perfectly well who it is; I'm just stalling for a few seconds to think about my options.

"Who the hell is this?" he barks.

"I'm Mikhail's daughter."

"No, you're not," he snaps back.

"Yes," I say, pausing for effect, "I am. I'm Mikhaila . . . Voyanovski." It isn't technically a lie; Voyanovski's my middle name. Kind of. My legal name is Mikhaila V Durand. Just V. No need for a period.

"Is this a joke? Mikhail never mentioned any children."

"I'm sorry—who's calling?"

"Jérôme Michel de Villiers." He says it definitively, but with that silky accent coiling around the *r*'s. He says it as if the whole world should recognize his voice over the telephone. His arrogance is bizarrely appealing.

I catch myself slipping. I should just hang up, let Alexei deal with him, but something about the man's voice nips at me. He makes me want to tussle.

"*Hein? Monsieur Jérôme Michel de Villiers!*" I say in my mother's perfect French. He isn't the only one with an immaculate Parisian accent around here. I take a breath to collect myself. "I assure you, I am my father's daughter."

"Impossible! I would have heard about it—about you—in my own newspapers, at the very least."

My newspapers. His egotism is stupendous. "I'm sorry to disagree with you, but he was my father. My parents never married, and—not that it is any of your business—my father felt it was best to keep my paternity private."

Even the imperturbable *Rome*—as he is known in the tabloids to his million or so closest friends—probably hears the slight undercurrent of deep emotion that I'm trying to conceal.

"Look. Sorry to get off to a bad start," he says. His voice is suddenly soothing in a way that I find even more disconcerting than his arrogance. "I am very sorry for your loss." He pauses. "But I was just handed this ludicrous contract and thought I was calling to discuss terms with Alexei. To negotiate. I'm really sorry about your . . . father." There's something bordering on tender in that sexy-as-hell frog voice of his.

"We don't need to get into all that," I reply with dismissive ease. I shuffle a few papers into a neater pile on the already-neat desk. "Let's discuss the contract."

What the hell am I thinking? I don't know the first thing about how to negotiate this deal. *In theory*, I know everything about how to negotiate it. I teach lecture halls full of students exactly how to do it. How to analyze the information, how to effect change, what not to give. I write papers and publish them in highly respected academic journals. But this is real.

And it's thrilling.

. "Very well," he says slowly. *"Allons-y."*

Good. The last thing I need from him—or anyone else—is sympathy.

We go back and forth for a few minutes. Jérôme de Villiers keeps raising his offer but comes nowhere near the shocking amount I suggested. I finally feel like I need to put him out of his misery. Plus, his velvety French voice is starting to unnerve me, and I want the conversation to end altogether. The way he says *exit strategy* and *alpha* makes me feel like he's trailing his finger down my spine.

"Look, Monsieur de Villiers, there's really no point in going on if you're not able to match the German offer. They're a premium company, and we have no reason to go with you instead." We have lots of reasons, and he knows it, but I am sticking to my guns.

And he is justifiably insulted.

For a few seconds, I think he's ripped the phone out of the wall and thrown the whole mess out onto the Avenue Montaigne. I pulled up his website as we were speaking, and it shows the Beaux-Arts mansion where his offices are headquartered, in the eighth arrondissement in Paris. The place is stunning—over the top and showy—just like the man himself, probably. I am tempted to let him know his building is supposed to reflect the professionalism of a media conglomerate, not a brothel, for goodness' sake. I hold my tongue.

"Allow me to . . . enlighten you . . . *whoever you are*. Clairebeau has epitomized *premium* since *my* great-great-grandfather Ferchault de Réaumur invented the wood-pulp process. I am not going to be drawn into an argument about the comparative quality"—he nearly spits the words—"of some German parvenu like Kriegsbeil. Just tell me your best terms, and I will give it some thought."

"Very well, but I was merely trying to save you the worry." I look at my father's notes one last time, inhale, pause, then give him a slightly lower but equally offensive figure.

"Miss Voyanovski," he says slowly, but with clipped formality, "I congratulate you."

"Why, thank you." I feel kind of proud of myself, actually.

"Your shortsightedness is to be commended!"

"What the—"

"You go on and take that obscene German offer, you greedy little—"

"How dare you!" My voice is starting to sound shrill.

"You go roll around in one year's worth of overflowing profits—"

"Monsieur de Villiers!"

"And then, as the song goes, I want to be around. Because that's when the gentle folk at Kriegsbeil will devalue the factory and offer you half that amount next year or the year after . . . and you will call me with your swishing, predatory tail tucked firmly between your"—he pauses to contain himself—"legs."

And then he simply hangs up on me. I set the phone down slowly. I am so hot in the face, I bring both my palms to my cheeks to cool the rage. How dare he? What a self-satisfied, arrogant, pompous . . .

I am still fashioning insults when I look up across the room and see Alexei standing there.

"So, how did it go with Clairebeau?" Alexei asks carefully, staying near the door. Wise man.

"How did you know I was on with Clairebeau?"

He shrugs. "I heard you yelling '*de Villiers*' down the corridor."

I smile despite myself.

"You liked it, didn't you? The conflict?"

I frown. "No. It was horrible." But my face is still flushed from the interaction, a potent combination of intellectual excitement and something else that I am not about to reveal to Uncle Alexei.

"Do you want me to call him to follow up," he offers, "so you don't have to speak to him again?"

"No," I answer, too quickly. "I mean, no. At this point it's a matter of pride. I don't want de Villiers to think I'm too much of a lightweight to pick up the phone and call him myself. I'll renegotiate. He's probably right in the end. We should have multiple investors on this project anyway."

"Yes!"

"Did you just do a fist pump?"

"Yes," Alexei crows, proud of knowing what a fist pump is. "I'll leave you to it, then." He clasps his hands in front of him. "Call me at home if you need anything else, and I'll call Kriegsbeil tomorrow to let them know they are not going to be the sole investors. The bastards. After that, we should be pretty much set for the board meeting on Friday."

"Board meeting?"

"Yes, just a formality."

"What kind of formality, Alexei?"

"The kind that makes you the interim CEO until we find someone else?" At least he has the good sense to sound timid.

"Seriously. You need to leave this office right now, before I throw this enormous ashtray at your head."

"Fine. We'll talk more about it later." He ducks out quickly as he sees me reach for the hunk of crystal on the far side of my father's desk.

My cell phone starts ringing a few minutes later, and I answer it with a deep sigh when I see the contact info.

My mother.

"*Darling*! Are you sure you're okay? I am so sorry I can't leave the set to be with you. It must be dreadful. All those horrible *Russians* everywhere."

"Hi, Mom." I exhale. It never seems to dawn on her that I am half horrible Russian.

"How is Alexei holding up? He's so dear, but don't let him make you all soft with his talk of passion and commitment and family. Those are myths, darling. He's going to try to get you to stay in Russia." She makes a dramatic shuddering sound, which I choose to ignore.

"Where are you? What time is it?" I ask, trying to turn the focus of the conversation back to her. Which always works.

"Oh, I don't know, about three in the afternoon. We're having piña coladas. I'm in Acapulco. I told you, remember? We're doing that small independent film Jamie wanted me to do."

"Who's Jamie again?"

"Stop that."

"It's just a joke. But what's his last name?"

"Miki!"

Jamie Robinson has been dating—or sleeping with, or using, or what have you—my mother for the past two years, and he has yet to remember I even exist. Not that my ego relies on the attention of my mother's too-young boy toys, but it would help at family functions if the parasites could remember my first name when they want me to pass the salt.

I sigh into the silence.

"Are you really okay?" Her voice sounds weird, like she is actually concerned about someone other than herself.

"I'm fine, I guess. It's not like Mikhail was some huge part of my life." If I didn't know she hated the guy, I might mistake that weird hiss for weeping. Instead of pursuing that awkwardness, I remember to tell her my other news. "Oh my god, Mom, I forgot to tell you. Landon asked me to move in with him."

"What?" She blows her nose. "Sorry. Allergies."

"Are you okay?"

"I'm fine. Go on."

"Anyway. It's a little soon with Landon, I mean. But I said yes."

"Well, of course you said yes. That's the sort of life you say you want."

Whatever the hell that means. I don't say anything for a few seconds, so she plows ahead. "Which is good, I suppose. At least now there's no chance of your moving to Russia to run some horrible paper company. It's just too awful. Get out of there as quickly as possible, darling."

I do not like when I agree with my mother. It never feels quite right, because she is so wrong so much of the time.

"Well, it's not a *horrible* paper company. It's just not what I signed up for. I have my job at USC—"

"And your life with Landon. I know, I know. And he'll want you to have babies and look fabulous at charity events with your two high-powered jobs. That's what you've always wanted, isn't it?" The way she says "*I know, I know*" makes it sound like *blah blah*.

Is it what I want? Sort of? The truth is, I have no clue what I *really* want. I remain silent.

"I don't understand you at all, Miki."

Well, that's a relief. I always feel better when my mother doesn't understand me *at all*. That usually means I'm doing something most people would consider rational. "Don't worry about me. I'm fine. I'll be back home on Sunday."

"All right. Call me if you need me. My phone is a bit spotty here, but you can always leave a message with Tori if it's an emergency."

"Okay. Thanks for checking in. Bye, Mom."

I stare at the phone and try to let all the weirdness dissipate. Ever since I was a little girl, I've played this internal game, especially when my mother is being particularly *outré*. I close my eyes and pretend I'm a normal girl from Southern California, born to normal parents. When I was young, *normal* meant my parents were married, of course, and my dad worked at one of those jobs I always saw in my first-grade social studies book: teacher, postman, carpenter. One of those tangible occupations. And my imaginary mom cooked and cleaned and sewed my clothes. Or maybe she had a job, too, but in my imaginary world, she was always physically there for me. And she loved my imaginary dad.

But somehow I got switched at birth and hurled into the life of this *other* girl, the one who happens to be the secret, illegitimate hate child of an Academy Award–winning French actress and a Russian paper tycoon of dubious repute.

So, instead of going to swimming camp at the local YMCA—like a normal kid, I used to whine—I spent my childhood summers in Sardinia. Surprisingly, that part seemed really normal. Uncle Alexei was always there with his lovely wife. And my Russian second cousins always seemed to materialize from every corner of the globe: Olga from Mexico City; Maria Teresa and Joaquin from Bogotá.

But in the background lurked my father, Mikhail Voyanovski. My namesake. I always called him Mikhail; the idea of calling him Dad or Papa never made sense. He was more like a high-end travel agent crossed with Albert Einstein. We had entire phone conversations that sounded like this: "You will meet me in Corfu. I have to go now."

Totally unreachable. Totally brilliant. Totally gone.

Ugh. I shake my head free of the fresh sadness and return my attention to reworking the Clairebeau bid/offer analysis.

CHAPTER FOUR

Many hours—and four strong coffees—later, I pick up the phone and call de Villiers. He must be sitting at his desk with his hand hovering over the receiver, because he answers before I hear a single ring.

"*Allô*!" he barks.

"Hello."

"Yes?" he asks. It sounds like he is unaccustomed to answering his own phone. "May I help you?"

"Yes. This is . . . Mikhaila Voya—"

"I know who it is."

"Oh. Okay. Well, I wanted to see if we could start over."

I try not to sound too contrite. Yes, the shark in me wants to leverage a little sympathy, but I don't want him to think he actually affects me. Maybe he'll give me some slack because my father just died. Or not.

"Who are you, anyway?" he asks coldly.

"You know what, de Villiers?" I start, guns blazing.

"No, no!" he protests. "I'm sorry. I didn't mean it like, 'Who do you think you are?' I'm sorry. I meant . . . is Mikhaila Voyanovski your real name? Because I asked my assistant to do a search on you, and she came up with nothing. I mean, it's odd for anyone these days not to have a single reference on the Internet. Don't you agree?"

I sigh. "Yes. It's unusual."

"So. Why?"

He's too direct. His French accent is molesting me again. "It's my middle name—I mean, it's my father's last name—but I was raised in the United States, by my mother."

"Are you going to tell me your surname?"

"Does it matter?"

"I suppose not. But yes. It seems to matter to me to know with whom I'm dealing. Are you a senior consultant from McKinsey who just acquired your father's business? A stay-at-home mother of seven who enjoys balancing the family checkbook in your spare time?"

I repress a laugh at the wandering nature of his thoughts, then try to make it sound like a small cough. *I might like him to make me laugh all the way.* Then I scowl at myself for thinking such an unprofessional, stupid thing.

I hesitate. "My birth certificate reads Mikhaila V Durand."

I say my last name—my famous mother's last name—in the French way, and his quick intake of breath lets me know he recognizes it immediately, but I continue as if it's not a big deal.

"My mother left the space marked FATHER blank. I guess writing that simple *V* was her small concession to acknowledging my father's existence. Not that she ever kept it from him, or from me, but she certainly didn't want the rest of the world having a hand in any of her private affairs . . . affair."

I can practically hear the wheels of his mind clicking and spinning across the time zones as he processes the pieces of the puzzle in the order in which I relay them. A love child. Now it makes sense to him. He must know that Mikhail always set aside time, inviolate time, for summer vacations and winter holidays with Alexei and all the cousins. And me.

"So . . . Mikhail and Simone . . . Interesting . . ." de Villiers says in a low voice.

"Not really. Trust me, it was too brief to be interesting."

"Fair enough." His words sound satisfied, but I can hear him typing away in the background, probably running an Interpol search on my entire extended family.

"So, I've taken another look at the Segezha deal, if you're still interested," I say.

"Very well." He sounds like he wants to rub my nose in it but refrains. "Now that you've had time to . . . reconsider. Where would you like to begin?"

We spend the next two hours hammering out a three-year deal that ensures both Clairebeau and Voyanovski Industries will be reasonably compensated at the end of it. In the midst of the negotiations, I Google him and then myself to see what he is seeing. There is my dour headshot on the USC website. Glasses, floppy tie. I'm a caricature of what a female management professor should look like. It isn't too much of a stretch to remove the glasses and see the resemblance to my mother's famous beauty, but I still think of myself as a bit coarse compared with her gamine style. More solid, like my father.

"Rome?" I prompt a second time. We are long past all that de Villiers-Voyanovski nonsense.

"Yes, sorry, Miki . . ." he says slowly, distracted. "It's getting late."

I am exhausted and losing patience. "Not that I'm trying to one-up you, but it's two hours later here. Almost midnight, actually." I want to tie this up and move on. Sort of. It's not every day I get to talk to someone for that long about business, to hear how his mind gets around ideas, how he works through the numbers the same way I do. I feel like we would get along in real life. Which is a really stupid thing to feel.

Since I am moving in with Landon.

The thought drags itself to the front of my mind like a disgruntled teenager.

"You're right," he says kindly. "I'm so sorry to have gone on so long, but you are very enjoyable."

My stomach plummets. It is a silly trick of his English, I tell myself, how he infuses the word *enjoyable* with something akin to an orgasm. Then again, he is too smart to say it that way by accident. "Rome."

"Miki."

And just like that, my heart is off at a very steady gallop. There is no longer talk of corporate finance or management structures. There is the raw scrape of a man's voice—two syllables—strumming every chord in my body. I stay quiet, not knowing what else to do.

"So . . . what are you going to do about USC? Do they know you're leaving?"

I am dead quiet; then: "Have you been Googling me while we've been talking?"

"Obviously. And you should definitely rethink the glasses."

This is so far from a business conversation. I feel heat fly up my neck to my cheeks. His voice is way too intimate. Knowing.

"I got contacts last year." I try to sound practical. "That picture's from a couple of years ago. Not that it's any of your business." I clear my throat. It is sounding way too . . . throaty. "As for USC . . ."

He lets me lean into the silence, which is pretty exciting all by itself, since Landon typically jumps to finish my thoughts for me. In a helpful way, but still.

How much do I want to tell this guy? And why am I comparing him to Landon?

I decide I might as well confide in him, since I am never going to see him in real life. "If you must know, USC is about to offer me a full-time, tenure-track position at Marshall. I came here on my vacation to tell Alexei and Mikhail in person that I am taking that job. Paper-and-pulp factories are not in my plan."

"Yet there you sit."

"Alas. Here I sit."

"We should meet."

The heat that started to recede with our transition into a more normal conversation flies back up my face like a flare off the sun. "Why?"

"Because I want to."

"Does that line usually work for you?"

"Quite often. Yes, now that I think about it. Yes. I think people appreciate honesty."

"Honesty?"

"You know what I mean. I could pretend we need to sign the documents in person or I want to shake on it or whatever. But I like talking to you; there's something about the sound of your voice. And so, yes, I want to meet you. Very simple, really."

"Do you have plans to visit Saint Petersburg?"

"Is that an invitation?"

I am so grateful the scalding heat on my cheeks is not visible through the phone. Even so, I feel like I might as well be naked in the same room with him, given how it makes me feel, the way he talks to me—as if he is unwrapping me.

"I'll have to think about that," I hedge. "Probably unwise. You know what they say about business and pleasure. *Bonsoir.*"

I hang up quickly, not wanting to hear some velvety parting shot laden with innuendo. And then I resume breathing.

I fall asleep at my father's desk, my face pressed against the back of one hand. The morning sky is just beginning to lighten outside the window when I look up and hear the murmur of voices in the corridor behind the closed door to the office. I let my head fall back down when I realize it must be the two security guards making the rounds. A few seconds later, the door swings partially open.

I jump up so quickly that my modern, black mesh desk chair flies behind me and then spins around like a top.

"May I help you?" I ask the guard who is poking his head in, as I try to rub the sleep out of my eyes. Highly professional, I know.

"Thanks, Georgi." *Smooth. French. Voice.*

Oh. No.

There is no mistaking that damnable accent.

I look from the wrinkled, leathery face of the ex-KGB henchman who protected my father through all those strange, violent years to the man who emerges from the hallway behind him.

Men are not supposed to look like that in real life. All the pictures online made him look hot and sexy, but I assumed it was a trick of the lens. At thirty-three, he should've looked sallow or washed out in real life. Fatter. Hungover. *Something.*

As it turns out, real life makes him even hotter, because he emanates a physical energy that's impossible to convey in any photograph. He crackles.

And obviously he is an old acquaintance of Georgi's, the guard who worked for my father since forever. Since my father sat behind this big desk at the Kremlin.

"I'm sorry, Miki," Georgi explains in Russian. "Mister de Villiers is such an old friend of your father's, and he says he flew in just now on his private plane especially to see you and to pay his respects, so . . ." He shrugs, hoping I won't be mad, I guess.

"That's fine." I turn my attention from the apologetic guard back to de Villiers. His clothes look like they were created to hug his body. Speaking of which, how dare he look so perfectly turned out, when I spent the night slumped over a desk? His white collared shirt is neatly pressed and open at the neck. The skin there looks really . . . good. Groggy thoughts. Groggy, half-asleep thoughts. I shake my head to wake up and force myself to quit looking at that patch of skin.

My eyes skim lower. He probably hires someone to wear his blue jeans until they achieve that ideally worn-in look. Do the faded creases have to make him look so good?

To be honest, I am not the type of woman who falls flat on her face for a good-looking guy. My mother's been doing it for so many years—yes, sure, she's all feministy and sex-positive and all that crap—but the bottom line is, I can't look at her endless sexploits as anything but an uninspired attempt to relieve her boredom. So she likes to screw around? Fine. I'm not judging her moral code. It's just that when *I'm* bored, I go to the Getty Museum or go surfing. I don't go seduce a stranger.

But, damn. This guy. He is the gold standard of stranger seduction.

I reach up to touch the necklace Landon gave me for my birthday a few months ago and try to stay grounded in some version of reality. And anyway, there is no way Rome de Villiers just flew to Russia to see me. *Wake up, Miki!*

I finally look away from him and answer Georgi in Russian. "Thank you for showing him in. Of course I'll meet with him." I walk to the door and shut it after I see the older man's wide, strong back recede down the hallway. As the door closes and I turn slowly to face Jérôme Michel de Villiers, I have the strange sensation there is no longer enough air or space in the large office.

He hands me a huge, hot coffee. "I thought you would be the type to work all night and might be in need of a little pick-me-up." He speaks in a slangy French, and it sounds delectable.

"You just flew here from Paris to bring me a coffee?" I ask in the same language. I bring the hot container to my lips and let my eyes drift nearly closed when the smell reaches me.

"What can I say?" He shrugs with a guilty smile. "I am impatient and spoiled. What's the point of having my own plane if I can't get on it in the middle of the night to bring you coffee?"

Of course—that makes perfect sense, the not-awake, coffee-loving part of my psyche nods enthusiastically. *He wanted to bring you coffee.*

Rome takes the liberty of sitting in one of the comfortable chairs across from my father's desk. I hesitate for a minute, not knowing whether I want the desk as a barrier between us or if I want to sit in the matching chair a few inches from his.

He pats that chair. "Just sit here. You must be exhausted from working straight through since our phone call."

I move very carefully from the door to the chair by him. I am not going to let him think I am afraid of him, or intimidated by that predatory kindness of his.

"I fell asleep for most of it, actually." Before I sit down, I realize my shirt has come untucked from my skirt in the back, and I make a halfhearted effort to reach one hand around to tuck it in. I am torn between wanting to appear professional and not wanting him to think I give a damn about what he thinks of my appearance. Because I don't give a damn. Except I totally do. And I probably look like a wreck.

Oh, well. He can't expect perfection when he barges in on someone at six in the morning after an all-nighter.

I sigh when I sit down, then stare at him for as long as I can. His eyes are dark blue around the edges, until they turn into these gorgeous Mediterranean turquoise things with tiny spindles of yellow shooting around the pupils. Almost painfully beautiful. And then the bastard has the audacity to smile the most insanely sexy, suggestive smile I've ever seen.

"Does that usually work for you, too?" I ask.

"What? The smile?"

I have to give him credit. Even as he is making fun of himself and his sexy-as-all-hell pirate smile, he keeps smiling.

I wave a hand in his general direction. "Yeah, the smile."

"Pretty good odds, to tell you the truth." He looks down at his lap for a second, and when he looks back up, he is still smiling but with complicity this time, as if I am now in on the secret, because I am so much smarter than all the other women who fall for the first smile.

"And that?" I point. "The second-round complicit smile? Does that work with the women who question the first?"

"Definitely. I have a more pensive look that I reserve for the really serious women. But that might be too powerful for you."

"I think I can take it. Try me."

He contorts his face into some weird approximation of a deranged male model's, and I burst out laughing.

Because he is hilarious. And ridiculous. And I have to stick with ridiculous, because he is so damned attractive that if I consider him for even a nanosecond as a smoldering, real man alone in the same office with me, half a world away from my dependable boyfriend, I just might do something really insane and make a pass at him.

And then the damnedest thing happens. Instead of being put off by the full, snorting Miki laugh and the puffy eyes and the untucked shirt and the general mess of me at the moment, he smiles in a way that appears to be entirely unrehearsed and shows his gorgeous white teeth and crinkles the skin around his eyes and makes him look boyish and delighted and makes my heart pretty much . . . stop.

I stop laughing. I try to make it a gradual wearing-down of my mirth, but really it is more of a terrified halt. But he keeps smiling. The real one.

CHAPTER FIVE

S o," I say in English. For some reason, English feels safer. It creates a barrier with him. I pick at something invisible on my beige pencil skirt. Unfortunately, the fabric has scooted up just enough to show the top of my lacy thigh-high. I quickly tug it down, and just like that we've left ridiculous and headed back into smolder territory. I've dealt with men staring at my legs before, and I'm reluctant to admit the truth: his eyes on me feel far more welcome than some leer from one of my pervy colleagues.

He keeps staring at that part of my leg, even after the lacy bit is covered.

"So?" he asks, looking up at me finally.

"So, what the heck are you doing here?"

"To be with you, of course. To ask you out to lunch or dinner." He pulls out a cigarette pack and holds it aloft to see if I mind if he smokes in my father's office. "Do you mind?" The ten-pound crystal ashtray sits empty on the desk in front of us. My father smoked without ceasing from the time he was a twelve-year-old boy. I can't very well pretend smoking isn't allowed in the office.

"You still smoke?" I ask.

"You say it like . . ." His voice peters out.

"Like someone from California?" I fill in.

"*Exactement!*" he exclaims, then raises the pack a little higher. "*Oui ou non?*"

"Oh, fine," I wave my hand in front of my face. We are back to sexy French. "It just seems so antiquated. I mean, look at the pack. You can barely see the brand because the warning label is so huge. *Fumer tue.* It doesn't really get any clearer than that, does it?"

As soon as he lights the rich tobacco of the Gitanes, I drop the antismoking tirade. I hate to admit it, but I still love the smell of cigarette smoke. Like everything about this guy, I know it is wrong wrong wrong, but knowing that only makes everything feel forbidden and sexy.

"You want one?" he asks, shaking out the pack to extend one cigarette a bit longer than the rest. He's quite accustomed to offering a lady a smoke.

"No. I really shouldn't."

"Of course there are many things you *shouldn't* do, but that's part of the fun, isn't it?"

I am looking at the strong turn of his fingers around the pack, but when he asks that tempting rhetorical question, I look up to see his gaze boring into mine.

"Is it?" I ask. I am genuinely curious. "I'm not really the type of person who takes pleasure in doing things I know I'll regret later."

"Who said anything about regret?"

"The way I see it, I have lots of outrageous friends who let me live vicariously. Friends who get arrested for having sex in a movie theater or who try creative bondage. I even have one girlfriend from high school who lives with a guy and a girl. You know, *lives with.*" I widen my eyes for effect, and he smiles, as if I'm some poor little match girl who doesn't have tons of polyamorous friends. I shrug. "Don't get me wrong, I love the sound of it all, but really, it's just too complicated."

He smiles his encouragement. "Vicariously, eh?"

"Look. I know what you're offering. Your reputation precedes you, all right? International playboy. All that . . ." I gesture at his face.

"So far I've only offered you a cigarette. Did you have something else in mind?"

Bastard. I turn bright red.

He taps the pack against his thigh to retract the offered cigarette, then slips it back into the breast pocket of his shirt.

"Not for everyone. Apparently." He lights a cigarette for himself and inhales a deep draw.

He smokes. I drink coffee. Once my face cools off, it is surprisingly comfortable to simply be in the same room with him. After a few minutes, he puts the cigarette out in Mikhail's big ashtray. "I gave him that," he says, lifting his chin slightly.

"What? The ashtray?"

"Yeah. It was my grandfather's, and Mikhail always admired it when he visited my office in Paris. He said it was *unapologetic.*"

I smile. "That sounds just like him." My smile fades, and I feel the slash of misery like a sword across my chest. I exhale slowly to let the emotion flow around and out of me. Rome reaches over, to offer some sympathy, and I recoil. I draw the cardboard cup closer into my chest, both hands tight around the cuff, and pull my shoulder away from him. "Don't do that." I sound mean, even to my own ears.

He pulls his hand back slowly. "Got it. No sympathy."

I stare at his profile while he stares out at the rooftops of Saint Petersburg. The sunrise colors everything peach and purple and golden caramel.

We sit quietly for a while longer. My shoulders relax finally, and I sigh again. "Sorry about that. I'm not particularly . . . warm."

He turns and raises his eyebrow, then smiles.

I smile, too. "All right, I'll grant you maybe sometimes I do get a bit . . . exercised, but I don't like to get all emotional and mushy, okay?"

He makes that quintessentially Gallic expression, pursing his lips almost into a kiss and narrowing his eyes. He is weighing whether or not I am telling the truth. "Good," he says at last, relieved. "I hate all that sentimental mumbo jumbo."

He totally mispronounces the phrase—*moomboh joomboh*—and I laugh under my breath. He smiles again, the big one.

"I like when you're happy," he says. As if he knows me. It feels like he does, like we are old friends already. I kind of want to punch his upper arm to let him know I like him.

He takes out his cigarettes again and eyes me for permission.

"Oh, stop asking if it's okay and just smoke, already. It's gross, but you know I don't mind."

"I know you like it."

The voice. The voice is the problem. He works it like an instrument. "Okay, see that right there? All the suggestive sexiness and double-entendre-ing? Enough with that." I try to sound full of conviction.

"Why? It's fun. And I knew it would be even more fun in person."

"Fun?"

"Yeah. Fun. Remember your long-lost friend *Fun*?"

He kind of has a point. Fun and I haven't been spending a lot of time together lately. Ambition and Responsibility do visit, though, and I have also been hanging out a lot with the resolute spinster Ms. Long-Term Planning.

"Perhaps you might reintroduce us?" I suggest, barely recognizing myself. Miki the Flirt is new to me. Growing up, I was much more the math-geek, late-bloomer type.

"That's better."

Can I do this? Can I just flirt with this ridiculously handsome man? Why not? I'm a big girl. It's only flirting.

"I have a boyfriend," I blurt. Apparently, I am not the flirting kind.

He blows out a narrow stream of smoke, assessing me. "Do you live together?"

"No, but—"

"Was he here for your father's funeral?"

"No. But I told him not to—"

"So you're pretty much single?" he presses.

"No. I have a boyfriend. Look, I hardly know you."

But he smiles and shakes his head like I have much to learn. "I'm doing my best to remedy that."

"All right. Maybe we could just hang out." My heart is pounding, but I try to act like this could be normal. "Like you said, lunch or dinner or something. I could use some company for the next few days."

"Sounds perfect."

I have a momentary vision of riding on the back of his scooter à la *Roman Holiday*. Unfortunately, within about a nanosecond, my traitorous imagination turns the innocent scooter down a quiet sun-dappled lane, and—in that only-in-the-movies way—Rome throws me to the ground in some frenzied passion (without sticks and rocks in my back).

Of course, when I look up I feel like he knows exactly what I am thinking. I look back down at my wrinkled skirt. "So. What kind of fun do you have in mind?"

"Mmmmm."

Oh, god. That *mmmmm* is sort of a growl and a promise all rolled into one. He is insanely alluring, no way around it. The guy exudes sex. And he probably does it in lots of nonbed locations without thinking twice about it.

Stop comparing him with Landon! my rational self pleads.

"You know what? You should probably go." The sensible part of me is finally coming up for air. I stand up and throw away my empty coffee cup.

"What? I just got here." He sounds strangely crestfallen.

"I know, but . . ." I rest one hand on my hip and the other on the edge of the desk. His gaze is all over my body. I try to breathe normally. "You're not just here to take me out to lunch. Seriously. I'm not a player or whatever you call yourself."

He laughs at that. "I call myself Rome. That is all."

"Quit being coy. You're totally coming on to me, and you know it."

"Guilty."

"That's it? Guilty?"

He shrugs but says nothing.

"Anything more specific?"

"I just want to get to know you. Honestly."

I try not to smile.

"Okay, of course I want more. Look at you . . ." He shakes his head with blatant admiration, and I feel it like a kick in the head. "You're phenomenal."

"Stop it."

"Fine. You're mediocre at best."

I give him a smile.

"Look." He shrugs again, all innocence. "Let's just go for lunch, go to the museums, have a few drinks. No big deal. I won't push. I promise."

The silence settles between us again. As electrifying and tempting as he is, there is something profoundly comforting about him, too. He knew my father. Maybe that's it. He's already gone through a lengthy business negotiation with me, brutally and honestly, so he knows how my mind works—my mathematical mind.

But there is this other thing that scares me. Standing there, looking at him, I feel the thing I've always dismissed as absurd: he feels like fate, like the ace to my queen has just been snapped onto the green baize table.

Everything about him screams risk. High risk. I am not a risk-taker. I abhor games of chance. The fact that my parents met over a roulette table in Monte Carlo pretty much says it all.

"What are you thinking?" he finally asks.

"Stupid thoughts about my parents." I cross my arms and lean my hip against the desk.

He takes a deeper drag off his cigarette and contemplates a response.

"Well?" I prompt, feeling like I gave a small truth and now it's his turn.

"Well what? Do I have stupid thoughts about my parents? *Bien sûr.* Because they were careless, stupid people, and that is the honest truth."

Wow. Maybe I'm not prepared for that much truth. He looks at me to see if I'm going to scurry.

"And?" I ask.

He smiles again. He has so many smiles, it makes me feel a bit parsimonious with mine. I smile back.

"That's better," he whispers.

Oh, god. No smiling back, then. Too dangerous. I widen my eyes to get him to talk more about his stupid parents. Alexei hinted that Rome's father was a degenerate scoundrel, but for some reason I want to hear it straight from Rome.

"So tell me about your parents," I push.

"Is this a shrink appointment?"

"No." I keep staring at him, not letting him off the hook.

When he finally starts talking, I am barely able to process the words because there's something sort of mesmerizing about how he looks at me while he speaks. "My mother was the eldest daughter from a prominent family . . ." It's like sitting around the fire with Isak Dinesen—if Isak Dinesen were French and hot and beddable. And a dude.

I already know his mom is a Rothschild, from what I've culled on Google (along with the girlfriends of the week and the jet and the apartments in Paris and New York and the incessant partying).

"Don't talk about it if you don't want to," I offer, suddenly feeling like I'm somewhere I don't belong, prying into his feelings about his parents. Silly celebrity gossip is one thing; parents are another. "I was just continuing the conversation. I have plenty of stupid-parent anecdotes; I certainly don't need yours to build up my repertoire."

"My father sent me to boarding school in Switzerland when I was eight." He throws it down like a challenge.

"Poor baby," I tease. "My father didn't *meet* me until I was seven."

"The few times I was home from school, my mother left every night after dinner to sleep at her lover's house." The words are like notches on the bedpost of a miserable childhood.

"My mother brings her lovers to dinner. Occasionally to the same dinner."

"My father married my mother for her money."

"My father never bothered to marry my mother." I give him a smirk. "I could do this all day. It's kind of therapeutic."

He keeps staring out at the rooftops. "Can we go have some fun now?" He sounds tired for the first time. "Have I paid my toll?"

I feel that keenly. Damn him. I suppose I am trying to taunt him, or wring something out of him, and now I regret it. "I'm sorry, Rome."

"No worries. Deep down, everyone wants to pry. My best-performing newspapers are the most salacious." He raises one shoulder like nothing really bothers him anymore.

"Oh, I don't mean it like that. I meant . . . I'm really sorry for all your stupid-parent stories. I'm sorry for mine, too." When he turns to face me, I see the briefest flash of sadness in those magnetic blue eyes.

"So am I. For both of us," he adds. When he speaks like that, without any undertone of pleasure or mischief, he cuts so deep into me I can't really breathe.

"I think that might be the truth after all," I whisper.

"Might be." He smiles again, running fast from the depth of the conversation. "So, do you need to work?" He gestures with his coffee cup toward the huge desk. "I'm at your disposal. I can tell you all the terrible stories about my competitors and help you run the numbers on the bastards."

"I bet you can." I look out the window, away from his too-knowing gaze. It is a gorgeous spring morning in Saint Petersburg. Suddenly, I don't want to squander it indoors.

It's not like this one day is going to make a difference to any-one. And I am in Saint Petersburg, and nothing I do here really matters back in my real life. And even if Landon ever gets wind of my gallivanting around Palace Square with Jérôme de Villiers, it is all business anyway. Colleague of my father and all that.

Work, work, work. That's me. The worker bee.

I shake my head.

Damn my mother. This is all her fault. I always secretly sus-pected I was going to be struck down one day by her congenital lust. On the bright side, as lightning strikes go, I'm sure I can contain this.

"You know what?"

"What?" He is smiling again, liking the hint of optimism in my voice.

"Let's forget about work. What's one day?"

"Only one day?" he asks with a goofy puppy-dog look of supplication.

"How many days of *fun* did you have in mind?" I ask.

"*Alors*, when you say it like that, I might like many, many days."

I open my mouth to protest, but he speaks quickly to stay my retort.

"*Mais* I will settle for one day . . . and one night. A day and a night in Saint Petersburg to get to know each other. Then"—he snaps his fingers—"*poof.* Back to floppy ties . . . and cardiologists."

My heart starts pounding again. "What do you know about cardiologists?"

"I have Google, too, remember? I wouldn't be a very good snoop if I stopped at your teacher page on the USC website, now, would I? And I saw he has a very successful career ahead of him."

I look away. "He does. But—"

"But?" Rome isn't leading me on, exactly, but for some reason I feel like he strips away all my bullshit. When I look at him, I want to say everything that I really feel. Rome makes me honest. I certainly don't feel coerced into bad-mouthing Landon. I want to.

"But he's not all that *fun.*" I smile at our overuse of the word. "He's a really good, solid man, and good relationships are supposed to be solid, right?" I look to Rome to weigh in.

"Don't look at me! I know nothing about what the words *good* and *relationship* mean in the same sentence."

I shake my head to clear my thoughts. "It's probably wrong to talk about him to you anyway."

"No, it's not. You can talk to me about anything."

And the strangest part is, I totally believe him. He reminds me of my friend Margot Montespan from MIT. We met on the first day of classes and were pretty much inseparable from then on. We clicked. Whenever I try to hedge around my feelings, she always calls me on it. I feel more honest when I am with her than I do when I am by myself.

It dawns on me that *she* would never move in with Landon just for a white fence and an imaginary dog. Margot might be as cautious as I am in certain ways, but she would never spend the rest of her life in a relationship just because it was safe. Now that I think about it, that is probably why the two of us have lost touch over the past year. Deep down, I know she'd ask me all the hard questions about what I *really* want to be doing with my life . . . and with whom.

"You remind me of my friend Margot."

"Is she handsome and charming?"

I smile. "She's quite beautiful, actually. In that dark hair–fair skin way."

"Sounds lovely. Go on."

"She always makes me feel like I have nothing to do but tell the whole truth. You kind of make me feel like that."

"You make me feel like that, too," he adds softly.

I take a deep breath and feel like I am blindfolded and stepping off a cliff. "Okay." I look at the neat desk and realize there isn't really anything else I need to do until Friday afternoon, when Alexei wants me to meet with the board. "This can all wait. Let's go have some fun."

"Excellent."

"First off, I need to get cleaned up." I glance down at my wrinkled blouse and skirt, then catch his eyes on me.

"Debatable." He looks up with something in his expression that I can describe only as raw desire. I lose my breath for a few seconds.

"Trust me. You want me to take a shower." My voice is all scratchy.

He stands up slowly, his body trailing up mine in the narrow triangle of space created by the two chairs where we were sitting on one side and the large desk on the other. "Oh, I trust you."

I watch with a strange detachment as his right hand reaches up to my face and traces the line of my jaw. I hold my breath. That touch sends a wave of heat right through me. My chest tightens; my lips gape slightly.

"Where should I get you?" he whispers as his finger trails down my neck, so slowly.

"Uh . . ." I pretty much lose the power of speech. "Uh . . ." My reptile brain is screaming, *There! You should get me right there! Where your finger is! And lower!*

"Where are you sleeping?" he asks. The low roll of his voice coats every word with sexual tension.

Of course he doesn't say, "*What hotel are you staying at?*" No, he says, "*Where are you sleeping?*" I am lost.

"A-at the Astoria," I manage. It is so difficult to concentrate when I want to lean into him and inhale him. The grief. The sleep deprivation. I don't know what it is, exactly, but the ever-practical Miki Durand has obviously left the building.

"Me, too. Let's go." He reaches his strong fingers around to the back of my neck and rubs at the tension there. The stiffness in my muscles from my night at the desk begins to ebb.

"God, that feels great." I lean back into the strength of his hand at my neck and let my eyes slide shut, which is a pity because I was enjoying the view of his lips a few inches away.

"Let's get your things and get out of here." He finishes rubbing my neck, then puts both of his hands on my upper arms. "You okay?"

I open my eyes slowly. "I'm good." I shiver. "Let me just grab my computer, and we can go to the hotel together. I mean—"

"I know what you mean." He steps away from the narrow space where we were standing to let me pass.

I put a Post-it note on the Segezha file for Alexei. My hands are shaking, and I feel like my fingers are swollen and inept. I power down my laptop.

Rome is standing by the door with his arms folded across his broad chest.

I take a deep breath. *What the hell am I doing? A last hurrah? A little fling before settling down with one of LA's most eligible bachelors?* It doesn't have to be anything destructive, I keep telling myself. I can just be Audrey Hepburn on the back of Gregory Peck's scooter, I keep telling myself. I exhale slowly, then slip my laptop into my bag and sling it over my shoulder. I look around one last time. "Okay. I guess all of this will keep for . . . one day."

"And one night." He smiles and opens the door.

CHAPTER SIX

I let the hot water of the shower wash away my insanity. What in the world am I doing? Or thinking of doing? Maybe I'm going through some sort of post-traumatic stress, doing something crazy and irresponsible so soon after my father's death. Or maybe I just want to have sex with Rome de Villiers.

I convince myself that it can be that simple, an isolated incident, nothing to do with my real life. An interlude.

I turn off the shower and scrub myself with one of the enormous white towels. I am trying to apply all sorts of statistical analyses to the facts, but the bottom line is, I want to get into bed with that man, and that fact pretty much trumps any other variables for or against. I brush my long blond hair with firm strokes, then weave it into a thick braid down my back. I look at my face in the mirror to make sure I got rid of any residual mascara, then brush my teeth and put on a bit of lip gloss. I rarely wear makeup during the day, and I am not about to start now. If my messy appearance earlier didn't scare him off, maybe the circles under my eyes will.

I put on a pair of jeans and a gray cashmere sweater, then slip into a pair of heeled boots. I pull my laptop out of my bag and store it in the safe in the closet. I grab my leather jacket and head to the lobby.

When the elevator doors open, I see Rome talking to a beautiful young Russian woman who works at the hotel. She is blond and ultra-skinny, and—like so many of the model-thin women in Saint Petersburg—she makes me feel clunky. I am in good shape, but I'm definitely not skinny. I surf and run and like to hit a punching bag a couple of times a week. I inherited my father's shoulders. I like feeling strong. The only downside—if you could even call it a downside—is the rare occasion when I allow myself to buy into the stupid cultural stereotype that every man really wants a woman with a little-girl body. I am never going to be a waif.

When Rome sees me over the woman's shoulder, I am instantly and firmly recommitted to strength over waifdom. His face lights up at the sight of me, and he quickly says good-bye to the skeletal thing and crosses the lobby in a few powerful strides to meet me.

He went to his room while I got changed, and he's put on a light jacket of buttery brown suede. He leans in and kisses me lightly on the lips, as if we are the oldest and closest friends meeting for breakfast in Saint Petersburg. He slides his arm around my waist and starts leading me out of the hotel.

"I love a woman who can look like that after a fifteen-minute shower and wardrobe change, by the way."

I lean into his strength, enjoying the way my shoulder fits neatly into the space beneath his arm. I reached around his lower back so we can walk in tandem more easily. It feels good. He's so casual about everything. So easy. It is going to be a fun day. And don't I deserve this after my father's death?

We walk everywhere. Miles and miles through the Hermitage, the two of us stopping and gaping and sighing over the same Rembrandts and Titians and Matisses. We spend nearly an hour staring at *The Red Room* by Matisse.

When I was a girl, I always wanted to be an art history major, or even a painter, but it all seemed too ridiculous. Too artsy. Too dependent on the whims of others. Too much like my mother. I always tested strongly in math, and that seemed to make my mother roll her eyes, so I figured it was a good way to go.

But staring at that Matisse, so deceptively primitive and so glorious, brings all of that visceral adolescent joy surging back, all of the ecstatic freedom I used to allow myself when I would spend long afternoons alone at the Getty Museum. That joy doesn't feel adolescent anymore; it feels all grown-up and subtle, because now that ephemeral feeling is being buoyed by this laughing, strong man next to me, subtly seducing me with his murmured French suggestions and his stray caresses along my forearm or lower back or cheek. I feel like my younger self is bubbling to the surface, but with adult desires and a man who can fulfill them.

All the while, Rome is looking at the painting and then looking at me. He murmurs something academic about the composition of the chair, and then he dips his face into the curve of my neck and kisses me there. I sigh like a schoolgirl.

How is it that at USC or when I'm out with Landon, I always feel rushed and pressed for time, yet I haven't spent even one whole day with Rome and he makes me feel as if this single day could go on forever if we wanted it to?

Again, I return my attention to the image and my imaginings. Is she a maid? Is she the mistress of the house? Does her arrangement of the fruit and flowers give her pleasure, or is it drudgery? Is she in the room, in that space and time, because she wants to be there or because she has to be there? Is she so happily focused on her tasks that none of those other worlds even matters?

Have I created that kind of interior world in my own life? I wonder.

I don't realize that I've asked the question aloud.

"We all do. That's why it's such a powerful painting," Rome says. He touches my wrist gently while he speaks.

I turn to look at him. He is just as powerful as the painting but much harder to read. Does he know he is helping me disassemble my life, one light caress at a time? He is joyful and boyish, and, as he stated the moment he walked into my father's office, spoiled and impatient. Every touch and gesture is part of his wanting me. Winning me. He's already won, on some level, but his eagerness is delicious. In a moment of candor, I tell him about my vision of the two of us on the innocent scooter, and he laughs so hard he almost chokes. I don't bother mentioning the whole throw-me-to-the-ground part of my imaginary scenario, because the last thing Rome needs is to be encouraged in that department.

We finally leave the museum in the late afternoon, and Rome suggests we make our way to a teahouse on Vasilyevsky Island, near the university. The late afternoon sun is bright and the wind is cool off the Neva as we cross the Palace Bridge. He is holding me in that possessive way again, folded into him somehow, and when we are about three-quarters of the way across the bridge, he turns me so my back presses against the stone balustrade and his big arms wrap me into a cocoon. He leans in and kisses me.

Properly.

If I was having any residual guilt or doubt, the kiss puts a stop to all that. There is nothing in the world at this moment except the two of us.

Rome is glorious. Not just his mouth and the smell of him, but the way he pulls me into him, against him, with a firm hand at the small of my back so I can feel the strength and pleasure we are giving and taking all at once.

His other hand slides tenderly around my neck while our lips explore and we begin to open up to each other—at first tentatively and then with a sort of wild abandon. My hands slip eagerly into the warm space between his suede jacket and crisp white shirt, palms stroking along his hard abdomen and broad chest. When this powerful man suddenly melts under my touch, it's fabulously exhilarating. My hands are all over him, and his answering groans are intoxicating as I tease and explore.

When my hands start to roam lower, he gasps slightly and pulls his lips away from mine. He looks into my eyes with an intensity I can't really process and then turns to look back toward the Hermitage. The afternoon sun gives everything a golden edge, including the angles of his face. I lean my forehead against his chest and take a deep breath. I keep thinking—not thoughts, really; I can barely think at all—but what goes through me when I inhale and feel him all around me is a deep and promising freedom.

I chastise myself for my romantic silliness—what the hell are face angles and the smell of freedom, anyway? Just bone and muscle and sinew! I suddenly picture one of Landon's anatomy books with the intricate paintings of tendons and joints. I scowl.

Rome brings his hand under my chin, and I lift my eyes to his. "Fun, remember?"

I smile and turn my lips into the palm of his hand, then catch his gaze again. "Bring it on."

We wander around Pushkin House, then have drinks at a university bar that makes me feel a bit old and stodgy—because it reminds me I'm a teacher at USC and I wouldn't be socializing with my students if I were back in University Park, even though I am only a few years older than most of the kids here. All these students are smoking and drinking and looking entirely carefree. Rome has this way of engaging people right at their level. When some rough-and-tumble college kid asks him a question while they are jostling at the bar, he makes a comment about some hip French rap band that I've never heard of. When the Pushkin House attendant asks him something in French, he replies immediately, interested and attentive.

We go to a tiny restaurant with about four tables, and an older woman comes out from the back and embraces Rome like a long-lost son. He kisses both her cheeks, and she actually blushes. He is a disgusting flirt, and I am disgusting for wanting to remind the old woman that he's with me. She serves us a wonderful mix of homemade food that her husband makes in the tiny kitchen at the back—traditional *shashlik* and *khachapuri* on mismatched plates with banged-up cutlery—and it is really . . . fun.

We finish the simple meal with strong coffee and a plate of powdered rosewater sweets. For all his supposed eagerness, I am starting to feel like Rome has decided he wants to make me wait—or lead, or something—before we go to the next level.

I take another sip from the tiny demitasse cup. The saucer is delicate Russian porcelain, edged in a swirl of pink, chipped at one side. Like so much in Russia, I think, delicate and slightly damaged, but enduring nonetheless. I look up to see Rome has finished paying the older woman and is staring at me. He reaches across the small, rough wood table and tucks a strand of my hair behind my ear. His touch sends a thrill down my spine.

"Ready?" he asks softly.

"I was." I tilt my head. "But now I'm not so sure."

He smiles sweetly and raises his palms. "I am at your command. Take as long as you like." He glances at the dregs of my espresso and the half-a-sweet that's sitting on the mismatched porcelain plate between us, even though we both know we are no longer talking about whether or not to leave the restaurant.

He pulls out a cigarette and lights it. I watch as his cheeks pull in on the drag and his eyes crease and narrow. I watch the way his finger lightly touches his bottom lip as he pulls the cigarette away from his mouth. I am so turned on by his mouth.

"I can't believe you are still allowed to smoke in restaurants here," I say, trying to change the subject. As if that's the reason I'm staring at his lips.

"Funny ideas of freedom, eh? In your land of the free?"

I look away from him. Why must he talk about freedom? It crashes my mood right down to the cracked and patched linoleum floor beneath my feet.

When I finally meet his eyes again, he pauses to see if I want to answer, then flicks the ash of his cigarette into the ashtray and shrugs. "Sorry. I guess talk of freedom is not fun."

"You're right. It's not." I sound moody, and I don't like it. "Let me have a cigarette."

He smiles like the devil he is. Corrupting the youth. He tips the cigarette out of the pack, and I feel like a million girls have had the same hand make the same offering gesture. And then I look into his eyes and feel like the only woman in the world. I put the cigarette to my lips, and he snaps the gold lighter open and strikes the flint.

I inhale and try to look seductive . . . then cough horribly, eyes watering, chest burning. That smoke is the most disgusting thing I've ever experienced. "Ewww!" I gasp between inhalations of clean air and sips of water. "That is so revolting. What the hell are you thinking?" I drink more water.

He takes the cigarette out of my hand and slowly stamps it out in the brown glass ashtray on the table. I wipe at my eyes with my napkin.

"Honestly, I think I might throw up," I wheeze.

"Maybe the French ones are too strong for you."

I know what he's saying: maybe *he* is too strong for me. I have

to give him credit—in a backward way, he's trying to be a gentleman, to give me a last opportunity to scuttle away from my immi-
nent indiscretion.

"They're not for everyone," he adds.

I burst out laughing at that, because the truth is, he probably
sleeps with *nearly* everyone. I wipe at my eyes one last time, then
put my napkin on the table.

"The French cigarettes might be too strong for me, but I don't
think you are." I feel bold and empowered. I reach across the table
and take his hand in mine. "Let's go."

We stand up at the same time, and I nearly stumble when he
pulls me into a rough embrace. I think I hear the older woman
give a low whistle as she retreats back toward the kitchen. When he
finishes kissing me—because that's what is happening: I am *being*
kissed as I half stand, half cave in to him—he gives a tug on my
braid and asks, in a sinister, deep growl, "Was that too strong?"

"No." I breathe the word more than I say it. It escapes from my
lungs like a sigh of relief. "I can totally handle you."

That intense look flashes in his eyes again, but it's gone just as
quickly, and then he's smiling and we're saying good-bye to the lady
at the back and leaving.

And then we are suddenly back at the brightly lit hotel, in the
shiny lobby with all of its sparkling chandeliers and brass accents,
and I barely remember walking from the restaurant on that narrow
street near the university and hustling back across the bridge.

Then we are in his room, and, well, I don't really know how to
describe what is happening, because it is fast and bewildering. As
soon as the door to the room closes behind us, Rome whips off his
suede jacket, and then his white button-down shirt is gone a second
later. I am walking backward, not really knowing what to do with
my hands. I drop my bag on the floor near the coffee table in the

seating area of the suite and look around for the bed. His room is huge, much bigger than mine, and I feel disoriented. The bed must be in another room.

He kicks off his shoes and bends down to pull off first one sock and then the other, sort of hopping as he does, to keep his balance. And then he walks toward me—in nothing but those damnably perfect blue jeans—and he starts to unbutton his fly, and I whimper or make some desperate sound that throws him off, and he freezes.

"What?" I cry. "Don't stop now!"

He closes the distance between us and starts to undress me. He pulls the rubber band from the end of my braid and rakes his eager fingers through my hair. He is touching me everywhere, helping me get my jacket off, and then my gray sweater is up and off, then I am bending over to take off my boots and kissing his hard stomach on my way down, and he's stroking my bare back and the bumps of my spine as I stretch to get the other boot off. Then I shimmy out of my jeans, and all of a sudden I am standing there in a silvery-gray lace bra and panties and nothing else.

I feel like I've run a marathon, and all we've done is get undressed. Nearly.

"Oh, Jesus, Miki, you're so gorgeous." He rakes both of his hands through his hair and looks almost angry.

"You say it like it's a problem," I quip, but I feel all sultry and tempting when he looks at me like that, so I just go with my instincts, reach for his jeans, and finish unbuttoning his fly. Bless the man for not wearing anything underneath.

I kneel down to get his jeans off faster. And then slow. Way. Down.

Holy hell.

He steps out of his jeans, then stands perfectly still. I am on my knees and then lean back onto my heels. Pretty much stunned.

"You're gorgeous," I whisper.

Here's the thing I failed to mention when I was spewing all that talk about living vicariously through my sexually ambitious friends: I love cock. I think I love going down on a guy because it's one of the few times—maybe the only time—that I don't think about anything else. When I am totally in the zone, my brain kind of flies off, free.

I get a little shiver just thinking about it. Well, thinking about it and having my face about six inches from the best view imaginable.

"You're killing me," he says, his French accent thick.

"Just let me admire it for a few seconds more," I say, keeping my chin low but lifting my gaze slightly to see into his smoky blue-gray-yellow eyes from my perch, right where I want to be, on my knees, about to devour him.

His hand reaches around to the scruff of my neck and yanks hard, pulling my neck taut so I am forced to look up at him full in the face. I lick my lips and stare into his eyes, the tension in my neck causing a straining, laughing moan of pleasure to escape my throat.

The moment cracks like a whip between us. It's incredibly intense, but I chalk it up to something primitive—like grade-A prime lust. I lean forward slightly and caress his silky skin against my cheek. I reach my hands up his legs, rubbing his strong thighs. Up and down, relishing the brush of fine hair that traces over his tensed muscles. He has incredible legs: stable, hard. But I can also feel the pulse and zing of pleasure making him quiver. I breathe in and shut my eyes, then find him with my mouth and lose myself in pleasure.

I reach my hands around to his ass and pull him deeper into me, loving the feel of his hand in my hair, that possessive, thrilling grab. Every motion is a pure expression of this animal give-and-take; the more I give, the more I get. I let my tongue explore every ridge and curve, let my jaw and cheeks burn with the tension of holding him inside my mouth. And every time I take him as deep as I can, I feel the concurrent pulse of anticipatory pleasure between my legs. The heat is pinging through me like a call-and-response, rising and building, my orgasm feeling closer and closer every time that incredibly silky flesh fills my mouth.

I'd probably never have the guts to do it in real life, but this is right about the time when I consider the remote possibility of another man, another Rome, really, who could take care of me—fuck me—so I could be fucking and sucking at the same time.

I must be groaning at the lascivious possibilities of cloning Rome de Villiers, because he shoves me away and says, "The groaning will put me over the edge. No." His voice is so rough with his French accent, I feel like I've really accomplished what I set out to do—namely, to blow his mind.

My mouth is wet and slack as I smile up at him, my eyes moist. He reaches down and grabs me up into his arms and carries me into the other room. We collapse onto the enormous hotel bed, and he has my underwear and bra off before I know which way is up. The light from the living room is just enough to cast him in a particularly flattering light. Not that he needs flattery. His body is insane. The strong upper arms. The hard, ridged stomach. The thighs. Those goddamned thighs. I reach out one hand to drag my fingernails lightly down his left thigh. He is trying to put the condom on and swats my curious hand away. "Arrête!" he chides.

I squirm and stretch for a few seconds; then he's finished messing with the condom and he cages me with his body and the hard sinew of his tensed arms. I reach my hands around to his lower back and pull him into me. My last conscious thought is, *One night, here I come.*

CHAPTER SEVEN

The next morning, we are both surprisingly awake at dawn. My internal clock has been haywire for days. He is just tireless by nature.

"Are you awake?" He is on his side, resting his head on his palm and looking down at me.

"Awake enough. What did you have in mind?" I mumble.

He burrows his head under the sheets and roots around, kissing my hip and tickling the soft skin. I am facedown, and he starts to massage my lower back. I think he's gearing up for round . . . five, is it? . . . when I shriek.

"Oh my god! Did you just bite my ass?"

He slides out from under the sheets at the foot of the bed and stretches to his full height, extending his arms nearly to the ceiling, an idiotically self-satisfied grin plastered across his face. "*Bonjour.* I'm glad you're awake. Now, let's jump in the shower and go for breakfast."

"You're unbelievable."

He's already crossed to the bathroom door when I reply. He turns slowly back to face me. "It is better in French. And you're the one who's *incroyable.*" He pauses, then gestures toward his mouth. "You have the lips of a goddess."

He turns into the bathroom without looking back and calls, "Now get in here."

I swoon a little at his insane bossiness, then smile, because French people are the most beautiful bullshitters in the known universe. I should know. I learned at the foot of a master (mistress?): my mother is a seducer by trade. And not just sexual seduction, either—the woman nearly makes love to a croissant. I don't even resent it anymore; it's just the way she is. So if Rome wants to play it all goddess-lips for a few more hours, that's fine with me. Compliment away.

I stretch out in every direction in the now-free bed and take a deep hit off the pillow where he slept. It's a mix of earthy, exotic French cologne and Rome's own smoky, masculine scent. I try to capture it like an image. I read somewhere that olfactory memories can be really powerful. I want to be reminded of how I feel just now, physical and alive, with my body humming in the perfect balance between what happened throughout the night and what is about to happen in the shower. I want to keep this as a private hidden memory just for me, something separate from my regular life back home in the States.

"Now!" he calls from the shower, and I bound out of bed and into his slippery, welcoming arms.

An hour later we are driving back to my office in silence and it's like a curtain is coming down on our little one-act play. We're in the back of his hired limo, and it no longer feels like the languid silence of the hotel room while we were getting dressed and still giving each other all those flirty once-overs. I start to check emails, when my cellular signal perks up and then my phone rings. My thumb is already hovering over the screen, so I accidentally answer the call.

Landon.

"Hey, beautiful! Where've you been?" He sounds like he is walking and talking. I can hear the hospital loudspeaker in the background. In the quietness of the backseat, Rome probably can hear it, too.

"Hey," I answer. "Sorry, I was out of range for a while. I ended up going out—"

"No worries. I won't keep you. We've been invited to the Pearsons' for dinner Sunday night. Do you want to go? Think you'll be back in time? Up for it?" He answers a nurse or someone who is asking him to confirm a dosage for a patient, saying something about micrograms.

"I should be back," I say. "Do you want me to call Stephanie, or will you?"

"I'm playing tennis with George today, so I'll tell him we'll be there. Have a safe flight back. I'll talk to you soon. Have to hop."

The line goes dead, and I look up to see Rome staring out the other window. Smoking.

"Sorry about that," I say.

He turns to look at me. His game face is back. The half grin, the slightly raised eyebrow. "Don't be silly. No need to apologize. Real life returns, eh?"

He doesn't sound particularly disappointed . . . Oh, but his eyes.

I can see that his phone is also lighting up to indicate an incoming call, but instead of taking it, he slides his thumb across the DECLINE tab and slips it back into his pocket. I feel like I was the one who put an abrupt end to the end.

He starts to speak, then stops.

"Just say it," I mumble to my lap.

"Do you love him, Miki?"

It's my turn to look out the window. How the hell should I know if I *love* Landon? I'm just trying to do the next right thing.

Landon is definitely the next right thing. Deep down, I think love is a bit of a racket. I guess I'm a cynic.

"Rome . . ."

"Forget I asked. It's none of my business."

Damn it. I suddenly want it to be his business. I want him to *want* it to be his business. I know he is trying to respect that I had a life before he showed up—*have* a life. Even so, for a split second, I wish he'd be a tad less respectful and just demand things of me and tell me how he is going to rip me out of the life I had before he showed up.

I guess he is the grown-up after all, because the fact that I think I need to be rescued is seriously messed up. Plus, even if I were to go out on a limb and pursue it, what sort of long-term relationship could ever live up to this spectacular day and night of bliss?

That sort of thing just can't be maintained over the long term. I think of my parents. All that roiling passion one minute, and then . . . kaput. Nothing. Or worse than nothing. I suspect they'd actually come to hate each other and how badly they screwed up. How badly having me screwed up their wild, crazy love affair.

In this moment, I convince myself that a perfect day and night is a million times better than a long, drawn-out two years—or even two decades—of trying to recapture some magical moment on a bridge.

"Rome?"

He turns back to face me, but he doesn't say anything. I stare into his eyes, and he waits for me to say whatever it is I'm trying to say, which is impossible, because I certainly don't want to say any of that craziness about ripping me out of my life. A sexy night is one thing. Changing my entire future is something else entirely.

I take a deep breath. "It's taken a long time for me to build my life the way I want it. I don't want to do anything to ruin that. It may not be perfect—"

"You deserve perfect, Miki." The way he looks at me, like he believes such a thing is even possible . . . it's too much. I can take all the crazy-parent stories he can throw at me: water off a duck's back. But a look like that? That asks me to believe I deserve perfect? I can't do it.

"I . . . I don't know what to say, Rome. I guess I'm a realist at heart. Landon is real."

He pulls his lips into a tight line. "Well. I won't interfere. If you want to talk . . ." He takes my cell phone out of my hand and punches in his number. "That's my private line. Call anytime. For any reason."

I get the feeling when he says "private line," it means really super-duper private. Like maybe I'm the only person—other than his assistant—who has the number.

When we pull up in front of the office building, the driver hops out and opens my door for me.

I turn to say good-bye to Rome one last time, and he leans across the backseat and kisses me quickly on each cheek. Very French. Very nothing.

"Au revoir, Mikhaila. It was a wonderful night." His eyes shimmer, or maybe they don't, but for that brief second I think he is about to tell me he loves me. That I should run away with him. But he doesn't.

God, of course he doesn't. It was a one-night stand with a playboy, Miki. Get ahold of yourself.

Still, my heart breaks a little for our tiny, isolated romance, and then I take a deep breath and reach out my hand to shake his.

He smiles and takes it, respecting my need to call it over.

"It was wonderful to meet you, Rome," I say as I shake his hand. I might sound overly formal, but I am being completely honest. It *is* wonderful to have met him. I am very much in a state of wonder.

"You, too," he whispers. Then he releases my hand and I slip out of the car. I watch as the limo pulls away, until I can no longer spot it in the sea of traffic, and I make absolutely sure he never looks back.

I take a deep breath—at this rate of constant deep breathing, I am going to start hyperventilating—and walk slowly across Nevsky Prospect to the new Starbucks. I need a taste of home.

For the next few days, I reluctantly bond with the management team at Voyanovski Industries. At the board meeting on Friday afternoon, my last work day in Russia, I agree to be named temporary CEO, only after assuring them that it will be in name only, to keep things running smoothly until they find a proper replacement. My resistance is starting to sound hollow even to my own ears, but I hope that once I get back to USC, this burgeoning tug of filial allegiance will evaporate.

I spend Saturday going through all the leftover paperwork in my father's office. Uncle Alexei and I spend hours shredding everything from old passports to faded ticket stubs. It feels so final, but Alexei and I both agree it's better to clear everything out than to leave it for another time. He goes through the old business documents, setting a few aside to make sure he also has copies, and I go through most of the personal files, keeping a few things for sentimental reasons.

There are some old clippings I decide to save, especially of Mikhail with my mother. One in particular, from *Paris Match*, shows them in some café in 1984. I count back from my birthday to the date in the magazine and realize Simone must have been pregnant with me when it was taken, but she's not showing. They both look bored. Simone is all blond and leggy, with huge shoulder pads and a miniskirt, and Mikhail is looking all Russian Mafia as he reads a newspaper. I shake my head while I look at it.

"They really should have stayed together," Uncle Alexei laments.

"Oh, please." I snort. "They would have killed each other. She was probably already looking at another man behind those enormous Chanel sunglasses."

Alexei laughs. "You're probably right. But they were happy with each other in a way that neither one ever was after they parted. Or maybe your mother is now; I don't know." He shrugs.

"She's not, not really. But maybe that's why it would never have worked, eh?" I pat Alexei's shoulder. "Maybe we're not really meant to be that happy every minute of the day." I think briefly of Rome, of pursuing him, of how happy I felt when I was with him. It would probably end horribly, like it did for my mother and father, bored with each other after a fortnight. I turn my attention quickly back to the busywork in front of me to chase away the thought.

Early Saturday evening, after Alexei and I finish clearing out my father's office, we say our good-byes and I decide to wander through the city. I know something is changing—or has changed— in me. I try to parse whether it's just a matter of being carried along by circumstance: the excitement of what I discovered by doing *real* work for a change, the raw sensuality of Rome, the death of my father. Or am I really evolving in some way instigated by—but ultimately unrelated to—what is happening around me?

Without realizing where I am going, I end up back at my father's apartment. I walk up the sweeping spiral staircase, which must have been so grand when the building was originally constructed in the 1920s, before these beautiful buildings were carved up into small warrens to house The People. Despite my father's wealth, I think he actually believed in those principles on some deep level. Of course, he had his beautiful house in Sardinia, but he always lived in this same modest apartment.

After I unlock the front door, the first thing I notice is that the hall clock is silent, no longer ticking without my father there to wind it. I set down my purse and stare around the darkening living room, then turn toward his bedroom.

I hesitate before sitting on the edge of the bed, and then I set both feet onto those worn spots on the carpet. My legs are long enough that my feet rest flat on the floor. My father and I were about the same height, nearly six feet. He was even taller when he was young and powerful and seducing my mother, but age shrank him in the usual way. I glance at his bedside table. It is more of a small chest, with five drawers. I open the top one.

It feels like snooping, until I remember he isn't around anymore to catch me. It still feels like snooping. He was so private, so old-fashioned. His ideas of propriety and rules of behavior were from another era. The top drawer has a comb, and a shoehorn with a well-worn antler handle, and a recent ticket stub from the opera. An extra pair of reading glasses. A nail file. Blood-pressure pills. Aspirin. All neatly lined up in a drawer organizer with little areas for each thing.

The next drawer down has small containers holding a few pieces of jewelry . . . if you can even call it jewelry. Man jewelry? Some are pins from different organizations, then a couple of enamel flags, other shiny bits he used to wear on the lapel of his jacket. And then a few medals or something. Uncle Alexei will need to take those and decide what to do with them. Weird communist stuff.

The third drawer: three handguns. And boxes of bullets. I shut it quickly.

The fourth drawer has stacks of neatly folded handkerchiefs and knotted silk cuff links in small boxes lined up on either side.

The bottom drawer is the memory drawer. Pictures and a few yellowed newspaper articles. Receipts. Mementos. A few packs of matches. Random, or seemingly random, bits of his past. And it is all thrown in together. A French postcard. A theater ticket.

I pull the whole drawer out and put it on the nubby off-white bedspread next to my thigh. My fingers touch things: a piece of red ribbon, a chip from a casino in Monte Carlo. That casino. At the back and beneath the rest, I find a red leather billfold that turns out to be a case for two photographs, like something you'd carry while you travel on business.

I look up and around the room before I open it. Maybe I'm about to discover Mikhail has another family somewhere. It seems highly unlikely he fooled around with my mother in the South of France one night in the 1980s and then never had sex again. Highly unlikely.

I open the smooth, aged leather.

And stare at my gorgeous mother.

So, yeah. Right up there with my daddy issues, I am also a bundle of clichés when it comes to my mother. *The Movie Star.* I don't think I've ever seen her look as beautiful as she does in this old Kodachrome snapshot that this supposedly disinterested Russian man kept in his bedside table. For his whole life. She is in a fabulous string bikini, white triangles against her tan young body. She is looking up—at him, obviously—and her smile is completely unfamiliar to me because it looks so . . . genuine.

In the facing picture, she is in some glamorous, tiny, strapless beach cover-up, and my father has her tucked into his strong, tanned arms. She has that glorious smile again, and he is gazing down at her, looking as if he's just received the best news of his entire life.

I put everything back where I found it, except the red leather photo case, which I slip into my handbag. After a few awkward attempts, I am able to get the drawer back into the opening at the bottom of the small chest. I get up and smooth the bedspread where I wrinkled it and take one last look around my father's bedroom.

An unexpected crack of emotion, like a single fist, pounds once against my chest. It washes through me while I stand in the doorway and stare at everything. I don't cry or gasp; I just feel like this is the beginning of something, like I am getting my very first glimpse of my father, rather than my last.

I turn back down the hall, pick up my purse where I left it by the front door, and return to my hotel room in the nicer part of Saint Petersburg.

Sunday morning, I leave the hotel and head to the airport. It seems strange I didn't even have to change my original flight plans. My spring holiday has run its course, and my father happened to die while I was visiting. Quite practical of him, really.

Oh, and I had hot sex with some guy I will never see again. I can check that off my bucket list. And I became the CEO of a flourishing manufacturing company. Check.

The morning flight leaves Saint Petersburg right on time. I change planes in Moscow and am back in LA by midafternoon, with plenty of time to make the dinner party at the Pearsons'. I get home, shower and change, throw in a load of laundry, and meet Landon there. It feels good to be with my friends, to put all of the craziness of the two weeks in Russia behind me. Landon gives me a firm hug when he sees me. He tells me he's sorry about my dad and gives me an extra squeeze, but I can tell he doesn't want me to make a big, emotional mess in our friends' living room.

With a quick nod, I assure him there will be no hysterics, and he goes off to get me a glass of wine. My best friend, Vivian Steingarten, is also at the small party, and I fill her in on everything—well, almost everything. I leave out any talk of French billionaires.

"You're going to what?" she asks in a stage whisper. We are standing out on the back terrace after dinner. No one else can hear us. Vivian is what is commonly known as a powerhouse. Our mothers were very close when we were growing up—both of them really successful actresses who were far less successful mothers. Vivian and I were thrown together as far back as I can remember, while our wayward guardians gallivanted. She's a great role model: tough, confident, and, most of all, kind. Well, kind in her way—tough kind.

"I'm going to be the temporary CEO of my dad's company."

"What about Landon? Have you run it past him?" She's never been a huge fan of my whole "Mrs. Doctor Clark" life plan, so I'm not sure why she's suddenly acting concerned about his part in all this.

"It's my life. Why do I need to run it past him?"

She raises an eyebrow and takes another sip of her wine. "No reason."

"Of course I'll tell Landon eventually, but it's only temporary, and you know how he is. He'll see this as a threat to our plan or something." I wave my hand as if anyone can run a company on the side.

She nods and gives me another half smile. "If anyone can do it, you can."

"It's just temporary," I repeat lamely.

Landon comes out of the house and cuts our conversation short, letting us know the party's winding down and it's time to head out.

"Lunch next week," Vivian whispers. "There's something you're not telling me."

Landon and I kiss good-bye in the Pearsons' driveway, and I feel like I'm back on track. Nosy best friend. Self-assured boyfriend. Real life resumes.

CHAPTER EIGHT

That first week, I do my level best to dive into my routine. I surf and work out hard every day. Almost too hard, actually. I start taking some rougher waves and going farther out than I usually do. For most of my life, I've been a longboard surfer, more of an easy rider, I guess. But since I got back from Russia, since the rush of being with Rome, I feel like a bit of an addict who's clamoring for a better buzz, picking the riskier waves and cutting in more aggressively with my shorter board. I try not to read too much into it and just enjoy the thrills where I find them, rather than pining for French pirates.

Landon and I seem good. We talk and text every day, even though we never end up getting together. All of which is totally normal for us. He's busy. I'm busy. And we have plans to go away together for the weekend, so I'm not really worried about it. I show up on time for work; my research grant application is under review and seems to be moving forward. Even so, Alexei's words keep echoing in my mind—about how teaching is an approximation of *real* work—and I can't quite shake it. Well, I probably can't shake it because his words are not just echoing but actually in my ear.

In addition to all my usual responsibilities at USC, Alexei keeps right on treating me like the CEO of Voyanovski Industries. I get about fifty emails throughout the day, and nearly that many phone calls, that either bring me in on various deals that he has going or ask a quick question about how I'd handle a certain labor dispute.

He's a sly bastard, because of course I have opinions! And he knows that if he frames it as a *"quick question"* or *"just a little something"* he's been meaning to ask me, of course I answer. (Under no circumstances should the foreman be given the authority to negotiate!) We also talk every night. Around ten o'clock my time, the phone rings, and even though I know I could simply let it go to voice mail, I'm getting sort of addicted to the conversations: speaking Russian, making decisions that affect hundreds of people's lives for the better, and, I'm not ashamed to admit, making a boatload of my own money. I am reluctantly coming to realize that Alexei is a spectacular mentor.

The idea that I'm pinch-hitting for Voyanovski Industries is one that I'm holding on to by a very thin thread. Landon senses that I'm exhausted and tries to be sympathetic, but I can tell he's not happy about all the new responsibilities I'm taking on. I keep telling myself it's all fine. We have plans to drive up the coast on Saturday, so I tell him we'll get to catch up properly then.

I also try to remain hopeful that sparks will fly after we've been apart for three weeks and I'll simply forget about a certain sexy Frenchman. On a practical level, forgetting is becoming easier by the day; Rome hasn't sent me a single text or left one phone message.

The realistic part of me knows he is being a normal, respectful man of the world who probably wrote the rules for this sort of thing. One night of sex in a foreign hotel room is likely in the *Dictionary of Meaningless Flings*. I try to remind myself of this on a regular basis. I make up little jokes, like:

What happens in Saint Petersburg . . .

An affair *not* to remember . . .

From Rome with love . . .

Yeah. No. That last one is *not* good, because the mention of *love* and *Rome* in the same sentence puts me right back in that limo in Nevsky Prospect, with him looking at me like he truly, deeply, et cetera, believes that I deserve the best damn life and that he somehow knows how to make that happen.

In my initial contain-the-lust plan, I didn't expect to actually miss him so much. Not just the sex. I keep trying to *tell* myself it was just sex—to diminish it somehow—but that isn't working, either. I have the terrible feeling, a real self-loathing doozy, that if Rome were to call, I would drop everything and . . .

So. Right. Thankfully, he never calls. After ten days of silence, I come to accept that our fling in Saint Petersburg was just that. A fling. Nothing worth wrecking my life over.

By Friday afternoon, I'm caught up on all my correspondence at USC, I've told Alexei I will not—under any circumstances—answer any of his emails or calls for the next forty-eight hours, and Rome is starting to seem like a vague, surreal memory. When Saturday morning rolls around and Landon pulls up in front of my place, Rome has become a dream—a sweet dream, but a dream nonetheless. Something I can shake off in the light of day, even if some pieces stay with me.

Landon picks me up in his very practical Saab convertible around nine on Saturday morning. I throw my bag in the backseat and get in the front. I lean over and kiss his cheek. I'm so hopeful, so eager for him to show me he's the right guy for me after all. To prove that I've missed some critical part of him that is really spontaneous and joyful.

But he isn't making it easy.

"You're wearing that?"

I have on an old pair of cutoff jeans and a fitted tank top. I was cleaning up my house for a while before he arrived, and I thought we might go for a hike when we checked into our hotel in Ojai, so I didn't bother changing. I also think I look kind of sexy in a biker-babe sort of way, with my strong, tan arms and the small tattoo behind my left shoulder showing, and my long legs all exposed for his delectation.

"As you can see." I settle back into my seat and pull the seat belt across my chest—which is also looking pretty hot, if you ask me—slip my sunglasses down over my eyes, and look determinedly straight out the windshield.

He is wearing khaki shorts and a green polo shirt and a pair of Top-Siders. I may be slightly underdressed, but who cares? He is always so pristine.

He exhales slowly and says, "Fine." He depresses the clutch, and I put my hand over his on the gearshift to stop him from moving the car.

"I'm sorry. Did you want to stop for lunch someplace nice or something on the way? I can change. I just thought we might get there in time for a quick hike, and I was grubby from cleaning up anyway."

He smiles and kisses my bare shoulder. "I love you like this." He even glances at my breasts for good measure. "Maybe I'm jealous that you can just throw on something and look like that"—his eyes slide down to my bare legs and then back to my face—"while the rest of us have to actually go to a bit of effort."

I pat his hand and pull mine back into my lap. "You don't need to try very hard, honey." Landon is quintessentially handsome. Thick, light-brown hair with those sun-kissed California highlights. He's thirty-five and looks twenty-five. Whenever someone compliments him on his youthfulness, he never disagrees; he merely replies, "Clean livin'."

As we drive out of town, I steal the occasional glance at his handsome profile. Landon grew up in a really solid American family. His childhood feels almost magical to me. An Ohio suburb. Committed, loving parents. Two younger sisters who adore him. Ohio State. Johns Hopkins medical school. Residency at UCLA with the top cardiologists in the country. He is the genuine article. Athletic. Healthy because he loves the way it makes him feel to be healthy. He rarely drinks, never smokes, and loves running.

Why do I feel like enumerating his many assets is an exercise in trying to convince myself of something? He is everything I've always dreamed of: The Right Man. The one who would be a permanent remedy to the escapades and frivolity of my unstable upbringing.

Is it so wrong that I want some *tiny* thing more? Some bit of playfulness without upsetting the whole apple cart? A spark?

We are about an hour outside LA, past Oxnard, when I make my foolish suggestion. "Why don't we pull off the road and I'll give you a blow job?"

He swerves the car a bit, then laughs. "Very funny. We'll be in Ojai in about an hour. Why would you suffer across the gearshift when we have an excellent bed with our name on it only a few miles up the road?" He turns to look at me to make sure I'm not crazy, then shakes his head and returns his attention to the road with a patronizing, *you're adorable* half smile.

And then I have a horrible thought—a treacherous, evil, serpentine thought: Rome would pull off the highway right away, no hesitation. And he would turn off the engine and unbuckle his seat belt and lean across the armrest and grip the back of my neck with his hand and pull my face . . .

I get sort of hot and squirmy in my seat just thinking about it. *Damn it.* "You're right—silly idea."

I look out the window for a few seconds, then sense that the rusty wheels of adolescent lust must have started cranking in Landon's brain. He seems to slowly grasp that it might have been rash to turn me down.

"I mean, we could stop if you want," he offers.

Even the most obtuse man seems to sit up straighter when the idea of a blow job is hurled in his direction.

I turn to face him and wave him off casually. "Never mind. You were right. We'll be in Ojai soon."

He smiles and puts his hand on my thigh and gives it a quick squeeze. I suppose that's a display of passion, as far as he is concerned, and I need to step up to the truth and admit that responsible, intelligent, reliable people do not pull off roads to engage in activities that are still illegal in some third-world countries.

I don't push my luck after that. It is a fun weekend.

God, how I hate the word fun *lately.*

We have a couple of great meals at two of our favorite restaurants in town: delicious organic vegetables and fresh farm-raised chicken and sparkly white wines. The weather is spectacular, and we hike out into the mountains for hours each day and talk about our plans for the summer.

Margot, my roommate from MIT, called me earlier in the week to invite us to her last-minute wedding in June. In France, of all places. Landon and I both agree we are too busy. No crazy weekends in Europe, thank you very much. Everything back to normal. Sort of.

Until I overhear him talking to the concierge of the hotel on Sunday morning and asking questions about whether or not they host weddings and how far in advance they get booked. While we are walking after breakfast, I bring it up. "Hey, I meant to ask you, did you tell everyone at the Pearsons' dinner party that we're moving in together?"

Landon is walking ahead of me on the path, and he turns back to look at me over his shoulder, then looks ahead again without changing pace. "I guess I mentioned it. I thought since we were talking about it, you know, before you left. Was I wrong?"

Ouch. *Was* he wrong? Sort of. Maybe not. Everyone knows we're headed in that direction. He probably just wanted to give an answer to a question at a dinner party. Why am I feeling cornered?

"Wrong? Of course not! Vivian just called me after because she heard you say something about it and she was mad I hadn't told her already. You know how she is."

Landon can't stand Vivian. He thinks she is *the worst*. Self-satisfied. Opinionated. Bossy. Whenever he tries to elucidate her faults for my benefit, I just laugh and tell him he doesn't like her because she's too much like him, and that usually puts an end to his litany.

He slows down on the path and then stops and turns to face me. I am not paying attention, and I stumble into him. He takes both my upper arms in his strong grip. I think for a split second that he might ravish me in the forest after all, and I sway into him, hoping to encourage him, I guess.

Alas. No.

He shakes me and says, "Do you even want to move in with me?"

The hesitation is probably answer enough, but I make it worse. "I don't know," I whisper.

It just slips out! I am feeling loose and honest and foolishly think we might be able to have a forthright discussion about my unfamiliar apathy. Unfortunately, Landon isn't feeling quite so loose and honest. He is pissed.

"Are you fucking kidding me?" He squeezes my arms harder. He's passionate, all right, but it is not sexual passion. He is working up to a fury. "You *don't know?*"

I feel the press of tears. I am not going to cry! I can't very well drop a bomb like "*I don't know*" and then think I can whimper my way out of it. I stand up straighter. "I just don't *know!*" I say with defiance. "You seem so sure about *everything*, and I'm not! Wouldn't you rather know now instead of after I move in?"

"Yeah, I guess. But when I *really* would have rather known is, like, a year ago—that I was putting all my effort into something with *no long-term benefits.*"

Does he have to make me sound like an annuity? And a poorly performing one at that?

"What has gotten into you?" he asks. I think he feels a bit guilty as soon as he says it. "I'm sorry. I didn't mean it like that. It must have been really hard with your dad and everything that happened in Russia. And your uncle bugging you all the time now and not letting you get on with your life. I'm sorry. Maybe I haven't been understanding enough about how all that is affecting you."

I get the feeling he's talking to me in some conciliatory way he learned at medical school, about how to talk to people suffering from post-traumatic stress or something. He loosens his grip on my arms and starts to smooth where he was holding me. "I'm sorry. I just never thought of you and your father as all that close. Maybe you need more time to deal with it."

Shit. Now I really *am* going to hell if I pretend my father's death is the reason I'm acting like a flip-flopping airhead. I look down. I kick the pine needles at my feet.

"Maybe you're right," I agree. "I think I need some more time."

He lets go of my arms. "Shit," he curses under his breath, and turns away from me but doesn't go anywhere. I reach out to touch his back, then stop before I actually make contact. Do I really want renewed intimacy, or am I trying to withdraw? I let my hand drop. I need more time. That's the simple truth.

He takes a deep breath, then turns to face me. "Right. Okay." He exhales slowly. "Do what you need to do." He smiles—or tries to smile—then leans in to kiss me, a light, sweet kiss on the lips. I sigh and we hold hands as we walk farther down the path, until it narrows and we go back to single file.

The ride home is mostly quiet. It's not horribly uncomfortable, and I figure Landon is trying to go with the flow, but he's obviously having to work at it. He is not a go-with-the-flow kind of guy. When the Saab pulls up in front of my house in the funky Abbot Kinney neighborhood of Venice, Landon puts the car into park, pulls up the hand brake, and turns to face me. *Uh-oh, here we go.*

"Miki . . ."

"Yeah?"

He looks at my house, then back at me. "I really think you should call your uncle and tell him you're not going to be able to help him with any of the Voyanovski stuff anymore. He shouldn't be making you do that." For some reason, Landon has decided that my new role at Voyanovski Industries is the main reason I'm wavering about the future of our relationship. He's brought it up a couple of times over the course of the weekend. He rubs his cheek with the palm of one hand, a nervous gesture he always does when he isn't getting his way.

"Lan, he's not making me do it. I *want* to do it."

"No, you don't."

Okay. This is the part of Landon I like the least. In fact, *hate* might not be too strong a word.

"Yes," I answer patiently, "I *do*."

"Look, Miki." His veneer of being cool with everything is beginning to crack. "I think you're being a bit too *que sera, sera* about this whole thing." He gestures between himself and me; I guess we are *this whole thing*. "I don't want to be a jerk, but I'm thirty-five years old, and I want to be married and having kids, and I don't think it's expecting too much that the person who's doing that with me feels equally committed to the idea—enthusiastic, even—about one day being my wife."

I look out the window. He's right, of course, but why does it sound so wrong? If he had said it in a different tone, I might feel slightly guilty or sympathetic or whatever—I'm certainly not standing on any moral high ground lately—but the way he says *"my wife"* makes my skin crawl. It's about as far from "you deserve perfect" as one could possibly get. He says it like I should be grateful, that I should feel lucky—which, I suppose, with a different man, maybe I would. But the way Landon says it feels very much like he is doing me a favor.

I also feel like there's a much deeper problem that Landon will never see, and that I'm probably guilty of perpetuating on some level because, until very recently, I thought it was how I wanted to live my life as well. His life is all about what he *does* and not at all about what he *feels*. Of course I want to *do* things—I thrive on accomplishing projects at work, and I love taking care of my own house and enjoying the day-to-day world I've built—but something clicked in Russia, and now I know I also want to feel things. I want to surf harder; I want to have spontaneous sex in the back of a car if I feel like it.

And not as some self-destructive, thrill-seeking kick, either, but to feel alive. Even if I were to quit my job and become the perfect doctor's wife with two-point-something kids and an SUV someday, with the right person by my side, I would *feel* the joy of my day-to-day life. I would love my life. I'm still holding out a thin hope that maybe Landon and I could try really hard to have that life, but the way Landon is looking at me right now? There's not a whole lot of life loving going on.

I don't want to lose my temper. I told him I needed time to think, and I want to leave it at that for now. There's no way I'm going to be drawn into another argument. "I'll think about it," I hedge.

Landon leans over and kisses me. "Good." He is matter-of-fact, but I also sense a possessive thrill underpinning that kiss, as if he thinks he's won—as if my thinking about it means I will automatically do what he tells me to do.

I unbuckle my seat belt and reach for the door handle.

"Don't forget we have the big black-tie thing Friday night, okay?" he reminds me.

I get out of the car, then reach into the backseat to grab my bag. I swing it over my shoulder and shut the door. "I won't forget. Have a great week."

He flips down his sunglasses and smiles that Captain America smile of his. "You, too, sunshine."

I wave good-bye and turn up the narrow stone path that leads to my front door. I like how he calls me sunshine. He is like a really great older brother.

Ugh. I shake my head, dig my house keys out of my bag, and walk inside without looking back.

CHAPTER NINE

I drop my bag by the front door and take a deep breath. I love this little house. It's kind of quirky and holds a mishmash of country-casual furniture that I've picked up at garage sales, mixed in with a few modern glass side tables and chrome reading lamps. One wall is all shelves, packed with tons of books and Russian knickknacks and black-and-white photos in small, mismatched frames. I also made a copy of the picture I found in Russia, of my mom and dad, and put that on one of the shelves last week.

I walk into the kitchen, pour myself an iced coffee, and stare out the French doors leading to my small backyard. On either side of the doors are two beautiful fauvist paintings that my mother gave me, and I feel a pang of longing for her.

She is so generous, but it's always in the most impractical way. Or maybe I'm just ungrateful. This house is the perfect example. My mother bought it on her eighteenth birthday, or so the family lore goes. I think she may have already been sleeping with the producer who made her famous and he may have given her the house. But she likes to tell it this way. She started modeling in Paris when she was fifteen. Her real name was Marie Simone Durand, but she renamed herself Simone. Just Simone. It's pretty ridiculous that my mother has only one name, like she's Madonna or something, but that's how it is.

Simone got a combined print-and-TV modeling job in Los Angeles when she was seventeen and made a name for herself as an early-'80s It Girl. On her grand piano in Bel Air, there are silver-framed photos of her hanging out with Sting, for example.

Anyway, she unexpectedly hit it big as the face and voice of a new men's cologne that had a silly—but damnably catchy—tagline, "Roulette: Take Your Chances." When it came out in her throaty, French-accented voice, from her wide-eyed, innocent face, apparently people went crazy. Simone made a small fortune.

Despite her father's careless parenting in some respects, he was an excellent attorney and incredibly shrewd and attentive when it came to her career. He used Simone's popularity in France to leverage an unheard-of deal with the American cologne company. Namely, Simone got a percentage of the profits on the product in perpetuity. A year later, wanting to wrest a bit of independence from her father's control of her finances, she bought the house in Venice, California.

Either she knew what she was doing in terms of real estate (or that producer did) or she lucked out, because the house is a gem. It's a two-bedroom Cape Cod, with a rickety white picket fence out front and a tiny studio building out back. It's right on one of the nicest canals and walking distance to all the galleries and restaurants on Abbot Kinney.

For a few years, she pretty much lived the life of a Brat Pack idiot, partying in Venice Beach or flying around the world on the arm of one producer or another. Then she met my father and had me, which put a bit of a wrench in her wild youth, but only a bit. By the time I was two, Simone hit it big with her first feature film. It wasn't a really significant part, but it established her as a young actress, rather than a young partier. After that, she could no longer afford to be seen as some flake living on the beach with a baby. She needed to entertain in style, so she bought The Monstrosity.

We moved to Bel Air when I was two and Simone was a Real-Life Movie Star. Our house is on all the star maps.

I won't go into any Norma Desmond foolishness about how grim and melancholy it was to grow up rich in Bel Air. Other than the aforementioned normalcy fantasies, I had it pretty damn good. There were a few hiccups. My mother was gone most of the time, and she always hired irresponsible, pretty nannies. One of them left me at the movie theater when I was eight.

My mother laughed over the crackling phone line from Budapest and told me to quit crying. "In certain countries, girls are married when they're eight! Be a big girl!" As if that were supposed to make it all better. In Simone's world, there was always a starving eight-year-old getting married against her will. Whatever.

Then, on my eighteenth birthday, she gave me the house in Venice. I don't think she ever really knew what to do with me when I was a girl, but when I turned eighteen, she kind of got the hang of it.

The following week is hectic like the last. I burn the candle at both ends, as spring term ramps up at work and Alexei pulls me deeper and deeper into the everyday running of Voyanovski. To be fair, he's no longer having to pull very hard. I start looking forward to my ten o'clock calls. I start volunteering ideas for some new projects, without his prodding. I start becoming far more interested in what's happening in Segezha than I am in what's happening with my whiny graduate students' final projects.

And I'm trying to respect Landon's justifiable wish for me to make a decision about our next step. I decide to go all out for the party on Friday night. It's a hospital fund-raiser, and I know how much he loves to squire me around at those sorts of things. I don't even resent it—if he wants arm candy, I'm perfectly willing to give him arm candy.

I leave work early, waving to one of my colleagues about having a doctor's appointment. Well, it's only a white lie. It is an appointment. At my mother's favorite salon.

Three hours later, I'm feeling like a goddess (and looking like one, or so they tell me). My hair's been blown out in long, sexy waves; I'm all waxed and buffed and shiny. I even go over to my mom's house and rifle through her closet and borrow a vintage Pucci gown. It's long and stretchy and wonderfully sexy without showing much skin, which is a bit of a sticking point with Landon when we're out with his stodgy colleagues.

I call a cab to take me to the hotel and feel like a million bucks. Or a billion. I don't know what the exchange rate is for fabulous anymore. Anyway, I'm cruising along really well, seriously schmoozing all the board members of and major donors to the hospital, but I sort of feel as if my face is going to crack right off after about an hour.

While we're all standing around, having multiple conversations at the same time, I overhear Landon tell someone, "Yes, she's also a professor at USC."

It kind of makes me cringe, that *also*. If Bill Gates were hot, would anyone say, "He's *also* the founder of Microsoft"? I try not to let my feminist hackles get up on Landon's big night, but he's bugging me. I tell myself to get over it; he's happy and proud of me, so I try to leave it at that.

Unfortunately, in the next breath he refers to me as "the whole package." And I kind of snap.

This is not the first time he has referred to me as "the whole package," and I used to think it was kind of funny and endearing. Suddenly, when I hear him use that phrase at the Beverly Hilton, while he is all puffed up in his tuxedo and bragging to a bunch of likewise-tuxedoed cardiologists, I can't stand another minute of it.

"Hey, honey," I say, pushing my way gently into his conversation. He looks at me and smiles, waiting for me to add something to his witty banter. "The whole package, here. Present and accounted for. I'm standing right here."

He looks at me like I am trying to be funny and not quite succeeding. One of his asshole colleagues, James Galmoy, *EMM-DEE*, shakes the ice in his glass of scotch and gives a low whistle. "Uh-oh. Someone's in trouble."

Give me a break. Seriously? Am I Landon's mother? Now I'm really peeved. I look at James, try to bite my tongue, but he winks, the stupid bastard, and I blurt, "Hey, Jimmy, you know what? *Someone's* being a prick."

Landon puts his hand on the soft part of my arm above my elbow and squeezes. "Miki?"

"Yes?" I turn and give him my mother's best megawatt smile. If he wants "the whole package," he is damn well going to get it.

"Why don't we go dance." It isn't a question. He leads me away from the jerk posse and then pulls me aside before we get anywhere near the dance floor. "What the *hell* are you thinking? James is about to set up one of the most important specialty practices in Los Angeles, and we might become business partners. What is the *matter* with you? Have you been drinking?"

I look down at the untouched champagne I've been carrying around for the entire endless hour. I have never felt more clearheaded in my life. "Barely a sip." I stare into his eyes. They are perfect. Sparkly blue. And empty. In that moment, I know I would rather be alone than be with this man. "I think we're finished here, Landon."

"What? We haven't even gone in to dinner yet."

"I mean we are *finished.*"

"You're going to break up with me at a fucking cardiologists' fund-raiser at the Beverly Hilton?"

"Would you rather I call your receptionist and schedule a more convenient time?"

Turns out Landon might have a bit of a violent streak. Through clenched teeth he whispers, "How dare you make fun of me at a time like this?"

I shake out my long hair. I *am* the whole package, damn it, a 100 percent American woman. Well, technically half-Russian, but whatever. I'm channeling Lenny Kravitz.

"I'm not making fun of you, Landon." I unhook the diamond necklace he gave me for my birthday and hold it out to him. He won't take it, so I end up slipping it into the side pocket of his tuxedo jacket. I reach up to touch his upper arm. He isn't really a bad guy; he's just completely wrong for me.

He pulls away from my attempt at a conciliatory touch.

"Fine." I shrug. "Think what you want."

He looks around the party, probably to see if we're making a scene. "We need to talk about this, Miki. How can you go from wanting to move in together to wanting to break up in the course of a month?"

I look up at the ceiling—absurdly ornate, fake Italian Renaissance rosettes—and count to five. I exhale and look him right in the eye. "I do not want to marry you, Landon. It's just that simple. I'm sorry if you feel I led you on, but it has taken me until this moment to really know my own mind. I'm sorry, again, for what you see as a waste of your time."

"You are such a cold bitch."

Well, that pretty much seals the deal. I extend my left hand and ask for my lipstick.

"Your what?"

"My lipstick. I asked you to carry it in your jacket pocket because it wouldn't fit in my narrow clutch. May I have it, please?"

"Miki, honey, come on. This can't be over."

"Landon. You just called me a cold bitch. Let's not go down this road. I'll call you in a couple of weeks, and we can go to a movie or something and try to be normal so we're not awkward at our friends' parties. All right?"

"I don't even know who you are anymore. Ever since you got back from Saint Petersburg, you've been this judgmental, arrogant cun—"

I hold up my hand and put two fingers over his lips. To anyone across the room at the party, it will look like a gentle, momentary passion. Maybe I do have a drop of my mother's theatrical blood in my veins after all.

"You really, *really* do not want to finish that sentence, Lan. You know what they say—some things can never be unsaid." I let my fingers come away from his lips. "Keep the lipstick."

I turn on my very high, very sexy heel and walk out of the ballroom. I cross the lobby and pull my cell phone out of my too-slim purse. I loved that lipstick. I am going to miss it.

There is only one thing I need to do.

I hop into a cab in front of the hotel and hit the speed dial for Vivian.

CHAPTER TEN

It is loud in the background when she picks up. "Hello!" she screams into her cell phone.

I raise my voice slightly so she can hear me. "Viv? It's Mik. Where are you?"

"Wait! I'm stepping outside! Hold on!"

I wait about a minute, then hear the sound of a loud door banging and the relative silence of a sidewalk full of people. Vivian is an executive producer at Paramount. Her husband, Peter Travkin, is a viciously successful entertainment lawyer. So it's entirely likely that one or the other of them has some fancy party going on.

"Mik? What's going on? Where are you?"

"I just broke up with Landon."

"Oh, honey, where do you want me to meet you?" Vivian takes life by the balls. She has probably done more in her thirty-three years than most people do in three hundred. She even plans her vacations like Rommel planned for Egypt.

"Where are you? It sounds loud and irresponsible, which is exactly what I need right now."

"It's totally grubby, but you should come. Are you wearing that purple-and-yellow vintage Pucci dress?"

MEGAN MULRY

"Vivian. Only you would give me fashion advice at a time like this. *Where are you?*"

"Peter's cousin is in that stupid band, and we came to support him. It's a bunch of rich kids pretending they're skate rats at Whisky a Go Go. Get over here. We'll stay for a set, then go have proper drinks at the Rainbow. Landon's a dick."

"Oh, cut it out. You said he was '*husband material*' just last week." Peter loves to tell people about their meet-cute—it was an adorable fender bender on Mulholland that threw them together—mostly because he never loses his sense of awe that he was able to convince this brilliant, beautiful woman to marry him. Vivian knew she had found husband material.

"Well, I know how you look up to me, and I wanted it to be your own decision."

I tell the patient taxi driver the address and then turn my attention back to Vivian. "Thanks. I guess. I'll be there in ten minutes. See you soon. And, Viv?"

"Yeah?"

"Thank you."

"Oh, you're welcome, sweetie." Then she's gone.

I disconnect the call and begin to wonder what the hell just happened in that hotel ballroom. I think of the Bob Dylan lyric about mathematicians and carpenters' wives, and I realize my overwhelming feeling is plain old relief. I am simply relieved that I am no longer on the road to ever becoming Mrs. Dr. Landon Winslow Clark III.

I am free! I am as light as a bubble. And maybe as fragile, but I am free, so I don't care about fragility at the moment. I want to get falling-down drunk.

I succeed.

I wake up the next day with my face pressed into the sofa cushion of Vivian's playroom with her youngest child, six-year-old Eli, dragging a neon-pink feather across my forehead and down my cheek.

When I open my mouth to speak, I almost throw up on him.

"Hi, Aunt Miki. You look like a scary monster. Your eyes are all black like the mean girl on *Pokémon*."

"Thanks, Eli," I say in a scratchy whisper.

"You're welcome," he answers politely, then goes back to his meticulous block-building project.

I groan as I sit up and hold my face in my hands. There is something final about being this hungover. I definitely threw out all the babies with the bathwater last night, that's for damn sure.

I stand up on wobbly feet and practically float, Chagall-style, into the kitchen, following the aroma of freshly brewed coffee. Vivian must have changed me into one of her T-shirts, I realize as I look down at myself. I vaguely remember peeling off my dress in front of a roomful of faceless people and suggesting we all go skinny-dipping.

"Hey, sunshine!" Vivian cries in a too-loud voice. She hands me a coffee, and I scowl at her. "Okay," she says more quietly. "I'll try to be nice. That was a stellar performance, by the way. Your mother would be proud."

I growl into my coffee and take a big sip. Heaven. I put my other hand around the warm ceramic mug and lean my hip against the white marble countertop.

"Did we stay at Whisky a Go Go?" I ask casually.

Vivian turns from the scrambled eggs on the stove and puts one hand on her hip while she holds a black spatula in the other. She has on some crazy, domestic, frilly white bathrobe that makes her look exactly like June Cleaver. Her straight red hair and porcelain skin complete the wholesome facade.

"You're unbelievable," she chides. "Whisky a Go Go? You're lucky you're even in the United States, much less still in Los Angeles County." She turns back to the eggs and keeps talking. "At first you just wanted to get up onstage with the band; then, after we convinced you that was a bad idea, you wanted to go to a bar over in West Hollywood, because someone told you there was a French torch singer or something. Then we ended up going for martinis at the Hotel Bel-Air, because you said you missed your mother. Then you said you were going to get on a plane to Acapulco to go visit her or your cousin Olga, and we had to convince you again that *that* was *not* a good idea. Then you had a few *more* martinis and told us you were on your way to Paris." She turns back again to face me. "To marry Rome de Villiers."

I take another sip of my coffee and look at her over the rim of the mug. "Wow," I say. "Sounds like I was really drunk."

She points the spatula at me. "You were drunk, but you're not getting off that easily. Go jump in the pool and borrow something of mine." She turns back to the stove. "Peter went in to the office, so you don't have to worry about bumping into anyone . . . not that you left anything to the imagination with your striptease—"

"Please," I beg. "Please have mercy on me. First, let me suffer my physical humiliation. Then we can begin the emotional portion of our show." I shuffle out of the kitchen, toward the pool, and try to rejoin the living. I can hear Vivian laughing at my expense as she calls all three of her children in for breakfast.

I float around in the pool for a while, the heavy T-shirt clinging to my body in a morbidly comforting way. I feel like I am being mummified. Maybe that's what is happening to my life: a slow, asphyxiating death.

Maybe I'm reenacting Sunset Boulevard after all, I think as I float like a corpse facedown in Vivian and Peter's pool. Either that or *The Graduate*, neither of which bodes well for my future. I get out of the pool and drag myself to the outdoor shower on the side of the small guesthouse. I am starting to revive, and I turn off the shower with a renewed faith in my own abilities to act like an adult. I have a great job. I have great friends. I have an amazing house in a vibrant, thriving neighborhood. I need to quit obsessing about dudes for a while and get on with my life.

My pretty awesome life, now that I think about it. I've been ready to give Landon the boot for weeks, and I was just too much of a coward to admit it. Now that he's officially out of the picture, I can really focus on work and do some of that joyful life living I'm supposedly after. I towel off with a renewed sense of life's grand possibilities and walk upstairs to Vivian's room, where I stand for a few minutes in her insanely vast and organized closet. I grab a purple T-shirt and a long peasant skirt from Calypso.

When I get back to the kitchen, the kids are nearly finished with breakfast and Isabel, my ten-year-old goddaughter, looks up.

"Hi, Aunt Miki. What are you doing here?"

"I had a sleepover."

"Aren't you kind of old to be having sleepovers?" Isabel has entered the not-always-charming double digits, marked by sarcasm with a dash of ridicule.

I reach for the chair next to her, pull it out, and sit down. "I hope I'm never too old for a sleepover."

"Me, too," she says through a smile. "I just wish you had come earlier last night. We could have watched a movie or something." She takes another bite of her eggs.

"Well, why don't we hang out today?" I realize it's the first Saturday I've been free in ages and hope she bites. "Do you have anything going on?"

Isabel looks at her mother. "You'll probably say I have to practice the piano or do homework."

"Oh, please. Would you cut it out with the aggrieved-preteen thing? I have never told you to practice the piano or do your homework. Go spend the day with Miki and say mean things about me behind my back. I was mean to her long before I was mean to you."

Isabel smiles, gives me a clandestine thumbs-up under the countertop, and whispers, "Yay!"

"Viv, do you have time to take us back to my place to get my car, or should I call a cab?"

Vivian looks up at the wall clock above the sink and then out the window. "I think if we all hustle I can drop you off and still make it to Ryan's soccer game."

"I do *not* want to be late, Mom!" Ryan is eight going on eighty. We all joke that he was born in a coat and tie.

"Then go upstairs and get ready. And just because we need to move quickly does not mean you don't have time to brush your teeth. You, too, Eli and Isabel. Go!"

All three leap from their stools and run upstairs.

"Thanks for that," Vivian says. "I can't believe the I-hate-my-mother phase now starts at ten. I don't remember hating my mother until I was at least twelve." She rinses off the breakfast dishes and loads them into the dishwasher. A few minutes later, she has wiped down the counters and the kitchen table, answered a couple of emails on the large Mac that sits at the end of the counter, and fed the dog.

I sit staring at her, ashamed of my own domestic uselessness. I can barely keep a plant alive.

"What are you staring at?" she asks, without turning around from the computer screen.

"You're just ridiculously productive."

"Don't start with the wonder-mom crap. You know I have a nanny and a housekeeper every minute of every day except Saturday. It's not like I do this on a regular basis. And you're basically teaching some kind of statistics that Albert Einstein would have had to think about *and* running a Russian paper empire—"

"It's hardly an empire—"

"Whatever," she interrupts with a quick eye roll. "Don't start being modest with me. It's far too late for that, Ms. Supermodel Brainiac."

I smile and finish my coffee in silence. Vivian goes into the laundry room and comes out two minutes later in a pair of bike shorts, sneakers, and a zip-up hoodie.

"Let's go."

"Okay, chief," I answer with a small salute. Vivian is unstoppable.

We all pile into the enormous Escalade (that Vivian drives only on Saturdays, when her nanny is off), and Isabel and I go back to my place. We walk all around Venice Beach. We have lunch down near the pier, eating lots of food that is bad for us—that Vivian would never allow—and laugh about how we're being *sooooo* bad. We drink too much soda and eat fried dough and feel sick after. I suggest we go to LACMA for one of its afternoon drawing classes for kids. Isabel is just on the verge of that age where she doesn't want to do anything specifically geared toward children, so it is only after I agree to participate that she gives in.

We drive across town and walk through the lamppost forest to find a group of parents and children convening near the information desk. The teacher is a handsome young college professor named Mark. I think he might be sweet on me. I look down and realize I probably look like a teenager myself. Vivian's too-small purple top and flowy long skirt make me look as if I've just been airlifted in from Coachella.

Something about wearing someone else's clothes makes me feel like someone else. Like someone who flirts with a docent. I smile at cute Mark, then follow him as he directs us through several galleries, until he stops in front of the piece we are going to discuss and draw this afternoon.

Perfect. Just perfect. The Matisse.

This particular Matisse and I go way back. An ultra-wealthy family who lived near The Monstrosity commissioned this tile confection in the 1950s. They have grandchildren my age, and I used to go over there to play, not realizing that it was rather unusual to have Picassos and Giacomettis scattered around the house. What I would now call the more aggressive pieces in their collection always made me nervous. The Picasso over the piano was downright terrifying—not the image itself, but the painting sort of radiated its priceless importance to the point that none of us even liked to walk anywhere near it.

But *La Gerbe* is different. As ten-year-old Isabel would say, "Le sigh."

I sit cross-legged on the floor next to Isabel and start sketching. Of course, all I can think of is Rome leaning into my neck and talking to me about the red painting in the Hermitage. I force myself back to the present and focus on the shapes of the leaves, the joyful explosion of color and motion.

But I also think about that woman who is arranging the fruit bowl back in Saint Petersburg, frozen in time. It is hard to believe the same artist created both pieces. This is one of the last things Matisse did before he died, and it feels entirely free—bright ceramic leaves explode across a pure white background in a carefree, joyful array. It's as if the woman cocooned in her red and blue–vined cell has escaped. She's flown. I worry that I will squander my life, busying myself at a table like that. This one, with all of its white openness and free-floating expression, makes me think of Rome. It makes me think of how Rome makes me feel.

My pencil slows and then stops. Isabel is really into it, drawing the outline of each leaf with precision. I feel the tears on my cheek and reach down to the silly bohemian skirt and use it to dry my eyes.

"What's the matter, Miki?" Isabel looks genuinely worried, more on her own behalf than as a sign of concern for my potential sadness. Nothing is worse for an aspiring teenager than being mortified by an accompanying adult. She is already like her mother, I think with a smile: letting me have it. I finish drying my tears and pat Isabel's bare knee two times to reassure her.

"Sorry about that. Nothing's the matter. Don't you worry."

"I'm not worried," she replies easily. "I just don't want you to freak out. Landon's not worth it." She looks at her paper and then back up at the ceramic wall sculpture as she speaks.

What a pal. "Yeah. Well, not that you care about my tender sensibilities, but if you must know, I wasn't crying about Landon." That seems to get her attention. Her pencil pauses.

"Well? Then what were you crying about?"

I whisper (in what I think is a pretty cool tone of teen complicity), "I think I have a crush on someone."

Isabel rolls her eyes. Exactly like her mother. "Oh, Miki. Crushes are so over."

I laugh and kiss the top of her strawberry-blond head, then resume the calm, restorative motions of looking up at the wall, then back at my paper, as I do a fairly good depiction of the Matisse.

Crushes are so over. Out of the mouths of babes.

CHAPTER ELEVEN

Vivian calls me at work Monday morning and asks me to meet her for lunch at the Polo Lounge.

"Seeing you drunk and naked on Friday night was a treat—as always—but you and I need a proper sit-down, Mik."

I sigh. I know she is going to ask me all the hard best-friend questions, and I am not sure I'm ready.

"Quit stalling and meet me there at one," she presses.

"Ugh. Fine!"

She hangs up on me before I have a chance to change my mind.

Vivian is flipping through the latest copy of *Women's Wear Daily* while she waits for me to arrive. I am not much of a lady-who-lunches type, but Vivian totally is. The nails. The hair. The impatiently kicking Louboutin.

I lean down and kiss her on both cheeks, an inside joke that we both started, mocking how phony the gesture is, but we've never stopped doing it. So, as often happens, we have become portraits of what we formerly ridiculed. She gives me a quick extra hug, looks deep into my eyes, and says, "I'm so sorry about your dad. In the midst of all the recent mayhem, I don't think I've really said it outright."

"Thanks, Viv," I say as I sit down.

"But you're good, right?"

She, of all people, knows the last thing I want is some gory emotional autopsy. I nod. "It was a drag, but it was fine. It was good, actually—I mean, that I was there when it happened." I pull my napkin onto my lap, and she nods once to let me know she is listening but isn't going to push.

Vivian pauses before closing the magazine. "I mean . . . would you look at this guy?"

I look across the table and down at a montage spread of fashionably dressed couples and eye-popping headlines: PIPPA IN TROUBLE AGAIN! THE FALL OF ROME!

My heart feels like it is tumbling out of my chest. Right there in front of me—with Vivian's perfectly manicured, bright-red fingernail tapping repeatedly over the image—is a picture of Jérôme Michel de Villiers with his . . . his . . . brand-new . . . *fiancée*.

"May I see that?" I ask, trying to sound casual. The waiter comes over just then, so my shock is lost on Vivian. She is launching into her very specific requirements for the preparation of her salad (basically, everything on the side, in separate containers) while I stare in stark disbelief at Rome holding another woman, his soon-to-be-wife other woman. He holds her just like he held me, close and inside, protecting her from the elements. Aziza Mahdi. She looks fantastic. She's Somali, apparently, tall and exotic, but also youthful and adoring. The way she looks at him—*dear god*—like he's her savior or something.

Vivian is finished with her lettuce lecture, and, without looking up, I tell the waiter I'll have the fish of the day. After he walks away, Viv grabs the magazine back.

"I mean, seriously, could he be any hotter? He's like a frickin' pirate. And four graduate degrees? And speaks five languages or something. And he's rich as anything. And just look at his wife—"

"Fiancée," I correct, with far too much vehemence.

"Well, whatever, fiancée. She's like Iman, for chrissake." Vivian looks up. "You okay? Don't you think he's hot? In your state of drunk-enness on Friday, you certainly had plenty to say about his supposed hotness."

Vivian has always been like this. Ever since she was thirteen and I was ten, Vivian has always been boy crazy.

"Sure, he's fine." I take a sip of water to stall.

"Fine? I'll say. He's *damn fine*. What's up with you?" She looks at Rome one more time, makes a clucking sound of appreciation, then folds up the magazine and tucks it into her way-too-expensive handbag. Then she stares at me with those laser-beam best-friend eyeballs. "What gives?"

"He's a client."

"Did you start an escort service while I wasn't looking? What do you mean, he's a *client*?" We both laugh, and I try to look out toward the piano player and set the conversation in another direction.

"How's Isabel doing on piano?" My tween goddaughter is already showing amazing musical promise. Most parents love to bore people with their children's soaring accomplishments. Not Vivian. Not today, at least.

"Nice try." She takes a sip of water, then her eyes widen. "Oh my god. Have you actually met him? In real life?" Her eyes are shin-ing as if I might be able to introduce her to Rome in time for prom.

"Yes. I met him in Saint Petersburg. His company, Cla—"

"Clairebeau. I know, I know! Go on—I don't care about any of the CV stuff. What is he *like*?"

"You're unbelievable."

She rolls her eyes and takes another sip of her water. "You're totally trying to change the subject. He's obviously *all that* if you can't even talk about him without blushing."

"I'm not blushing. Cut it out."

Vivian raises her eyebrows and shrugs. Point taken.

"Okay, okay. Yes, I met him. Turns out my father did business with him and I needed to renegotiate the terms of a three-year contract that had come up—"

Vivian is shaking her head right to left, letting me know she stopped listening sometime around *renegotiate*.

"What?" I ask, trying to be normal, which is so not possible.

"Backtrack. Are you crazy? *You met him?* What is he like? I want details! He's like a modern-day Renaissance man. Apparently he has this huge art collection—including one of the Matisses with the palm tree in Nice—and a place in the South of France that's to die for, and he's a major donor to that human-rights coalition, or whatever it's called, where his fiancée works."

I try to look away again, because I just don't know how to make sense of all the lofty qualifications and accomplishments that Vivian is describing and then to make them fit into the friendly, charming man I was with in Russia. Even now I can picture him with perfect clarity, laughing on the bridge, smoking a cigarette. At night, I relive the feeling of him pulling me close against him while he slept. He still feels so *real*.

And now he is engaged.

Fuck.

Vivian stops talking, and the silence yawns between us. Usually when we get together, we fill every breath with updates and juicy bits of gossip. Her silence is unnerving.

"Oh. My. God. You slept with him," she whispers, but it sounds so loud to my ears that my *shhhhhhh* reply is like a hiss. Several heads turn in our direction.

"You broke up with Landon for him, didn't you? Oh my god!" Her voice is quieter but still high-pitched. She takes another sip of water, and her eyes brighten again, like I am a really good movie script and she has won the option.

"Stop it. I never . . ." Well, what can I say? She's my best friend. I can't outright lie to her. But I don't want to tell her, either. Obviously, it really is nothing after all, and if I start talking about it, that will mean it is still something. And really, it is none of her business. "Oh, all right, so we fooled around. But I did not break up with Landon because of Rome."

She represses a squeal behind her napkin, then chokes a little when she tries to talk. "*Rome?* You call him Rome? I can't believe you finally get in touch with your wild side a week after Landon asks you to move in with him. Priceless."

The waiter has just taken the order of the table next to us, and Vivian practically trips him to get his attention. "Two martinis. *Pronto.*"

"Yes, Ms. Steingarten. Right away."

"Thanks." She smiles at the waiter, then lets the courtesy evaporate from her expression as she stares back at me. "So . . . you know he's a total snake, right? A complete player?"

I stare at my water glass.

"Holy shit. Did you fall in love with the French pirate or something? What the hell got into you? I told you you needed to slut it up more in high school! You were supposed to get it out of your system *then*, when it didn't matter. Wild oats and all that. Not now, when you're *thirty* and . . . well, you're gorgeous, obviously. But you're a responsible adult now. You can't go around sleeping with . . ." Her eyes turn dreamy again, and she completely loses the plot. "Was he just so amazing in bed?"

My eyes must have softened, because she realizes her mistake before I have a chance to answer.

"Forget I asked that! What were you thinking?" She shakes her head and takes another sip of water, then plows ahead. "You were always so afraid of being trampy, like your mother . . ."

At least she gets a smile out of me on that one; my mother may sleep around, but she is still one of the most elegant, sophisticated women on the planet—the idea of her ever being something as pedestrian as *trampy* cheers me right up. The martinis arrive, and we both take a happy sip.

Vivian continues apace. "It's just sex, Miki." She looks down toward her purse as if the French pirate is curled up in there for real, then looks back at me. "I imagine it was pretty *great* sex. But seriously? That is not the stuff that dreams are made of, sister. That's the stuff of bad gossip rags and splotchy makeup behind too-big sunglasses snapped as you're whisked away in the back of a darkened limousine."

"God. You are so in the right business. Listen to you. The drama."

"What?" She takes another sip of her vodka and looks all innocent.

"It's all a big story to you."

"Look, it's *always* a story. If you tell yourself the story long enough, it usually becomes true. If you are in there"—she swirls her hand toward my forehead—"telling yourself that maybe, *juuuust* maybe, it could be all unicorns and moonbeams with this guy, you *will* start to believe it. You can pussyfoot around all you want, but hear me now. Rome de Villiers is a wild man. He is the quintessential rake. He is *not* husband material. This thing with the Somali woman is just the latest in a string of engagements, I'm sure."

"You think?" I ask hopefully, the martini making me forget that I'm supposed to be getting over the guy, not having some dreamy fantasy about him falling madly in love with me after our one night in Russia.

Vivian scowls at me like I am the stupidest ingenue on the planet.

"Right," I say with renewed confidence. "He is totally ridiculous. Not even worth talking about. It was nothing."

I'm a bit shifty-eyed as I take a healthy slug of liquor to strengthen my resolve. I have the conviction (albeit fleeting) that Rome is my good, good friend and he needs my protection. Am I not allowed to feel slightly protective about my new, good friend?

"Oh. My. God." Vivian is the picture of sisterly despair. "This is ten times worse than wild monkey sex in Saint Petersburg. You're actually thinking this could *mean* something?" Viv drains her martini and nearly kicks the poor waiter in the shin as he passes. "Again," she says, without looking up.

He nods quickly and scurries off.

"I'm a big girl. It was just a fling, nothing life-altering." Okay. That's probably a lie.

Now she has her arms crossed and is kicking her pointy high heel in an impatient motion again. "Stop," she orders.

"What?"

"Just stop. I won't bring it up again. I can tell that talking about it just puts it back into the realm of possibility for you."

I take a big sip to finish the first martini just as the second round arrives. I feel better already. Warm and safe. With my best friend. My real best friend. Not my imaginary new best sex friend who is engaged to someone else. My real friend who will be logical and talk me out of these tiny, incipient fragments of hope that—she is right— I have been harboring since he drove away from me on that cool morning on Nevsky Prospect after typing his number in my phone.

"Okay," I say, fortified. "Let me have it. You left off at *rake*. I want a complete character assassination. Go!"

At first her insults are like lashes against sensitive skin, but I feel myself hardening as I accept the truth.

"He's a horrible misogynist. He sleeps with every woman he lays eyes on. He's filthy rich, and who knows how he *really* got all that money? He's probably involved with the Russian Mob and arms dealers—"

"Now, now," I interrupt. "He can't be a paragon of Human Rights Watch and a duplicitous, money-grubbing arms dealer. I'm not giving you that one. Go back to the misogyny."

We both feel the effects of two martinis too fast on an empty stomach, and we both warm to the task of discrediting de Villiers. By the end of lunch, I am too buzzed to drive and I decide to reschedule my afternoon meeting with one of my colleagues at USC. Vivian's driver takes me home in my car, and I collapse into bed at four in the afternoon and sleep straight through until Tuesday morning.

I awake refreshed, rejuvenated, and entirely over the rat bastard Jérôme Michel de Villiers. I go in to work and try to mind my own business.

CHAPTER TWELVE

I admit I've been a bit out of it at work. I was jet-lagged after Russia, then distracted by Landon and everything. Voyanovski *is* taking up a huge part of my time and energy, but when I get called into the department head's office a week later and see the academic dean of the entire university also sitting there, I snap to attention.

"Bill. Sanjay." I look at both men in turn, then sit down. I smile brightly as I speak. Neither returns my chipper tone, or even fakes it.

"Here's the thing, Mikhaila." No preamble, either. "You're really good at what you do, and we were really close to offering you the tenure-track position. But, after much consideration, we finally decided to go with Andrew instead."

Were really close? Past tense? *Andrew*? Who the hell is Andrew? And what does Sanjay mean by *really close to offering*? Before I left for Russia—when I asked if it was *okay* for me to be away for two weeks this close to the final decision-making phase—Sanjay used the words *in the bag*.

In.

The.

Bag.

"Gentlemen," I begin with genuine assurance, "I think there must be some mistake. I'm the most qualified person in this field, not just here at USC, but in the state of California. I have the most published papers—"

Bill, the department head, holds up his hand to silence me.

My voice peters out.

"Mikhaila. Not that we're under any obligation to relay to any applicant the nature of our praise or misgivings, but I will do you the courtesy. You're uninspired."

I am dumbstruck. *Uninspired*? What does that have to do with anything? I *strive* to be uninspired. I am ambitiously uninspired! "Bill," I say carefully, "the type of statistical analysis for which I've developed a keen understanding and excellent reputation does not benefit from inspiration. What are you even talking about?"

He stares down at his single manila folder. He is staring down at my rapidly telescoping future, I think lamely. Then he looks up. "You've just proven my point. Again, only because I truly believe you show great promise in this field, I'm telling you to take a few months or even a year off and rediscover what fires your creativity. Whatever it is, it will inform your academic performance. Until then, Sanjay supports my decision to keep you on salary as an associate professor. We will review your potential tenure status in one year's time."

I am beyond speech. I have spent months preparing a grant application for the upcoming five years and am awaiting only Sanjay's signature to send it in. The bastard is probably stealing my entire thesis. I stand too quickly, and both men jerk up their heads to follow the unexpected movement. Everything seems so obvious all of a sudden. For so long, I have been clinging to all these ideas of what my life *should* look like, when the reality can be so much brighter than any idea. Voyanovski Industries is real! I don't need to live in this shadowy world of academia, tamping myself down all the time. The real thing is right there for the taking, and I've spent enough time trying to shoehorn myself into this life. I want that other life! I want to go to my friend's wedding in the South of France! I want to run my father's company! I want Rome—

Well, I skip over that last part and toss my long blond ponytail over my right shoulder, take a deep breath, and then almost laugh as I say, "I quit."

I'm not even doing it out of spite. It feels glorious! I'm not just quitting USC; I'm quitting my entire habit of living life on a Habitrail. These two men have unwittingly shone the light on this golden opportunity. I can actually *choose* to stop running away from my father's company and admit that it's what I really want to do.

"I'm moving to Russia to run Voyanovski Industries. Thank you, gentlemen."

I watch both of their jaws drop before I turn and walk out of the office. I pack up my desk in under an hour. I make loose plans to meet up with three of my colleagues with whom I have developed real friendships. It is otherworldly how simple it is to wave and smile at the remaining fourteen people in the department, with whom I have never developed the slightest rapport whatsoever.

I throw my cardboard box in the backseat, then get behind the wheel and simply breathe.

Oddly, I want my mother.

I take out my cell phone and dial her number before I turn on the car. She picks up right away. "Simone," she answers, identifying herself by her single name.

"Hi, Mom, it's me."

"Darling! Are you here in LA?"

"Yes. Where are you?"

"I'm here! Come to the house right this instant. I want to see you. Come!"

"Okay." *I'm fine; thanks for asking.* "I'm just leaving USC." *Forever.*

"Let me drive over to your place, and I'll see you soon. It's probably going to take me a good hour at this point."

"An hour? That's too long."

This is one of my mother's favorite tactics: accuse the world of being round, then act affronted.

"Look, Mom, if the 10 is backed up, it could be longer. Do you want me to come or not?"

"Yes, yes. Of course I want you to come! I'll see you when you get here." I think I hear voices in the background just before she disconnects the call.

I slip my phone back into my purse and try to prepare myself for Friday-afternoon traffic. And my mother. And probably Jamie What's-His-Name.

An hour and twenty minutes later, I pull into the vast courtyard that spreads out before the front door of The Monstrosity. Mom comes gliding out, dressed in something totally age-inappropriate. It is sheer and sexy, and she has a bikini on underneath. Maybe I am becoming a prude, but I'm sorry, I just don't need to see my mother nearly naked. Luckily, Jamie is noticeably absent.

"Darling!" She holds my cheeks in her palms and stares into my eyes. Her blond hair is cut in her signature short style, and her near-black eyes are piercing. She always tells this silly tale about her gypsy ancestors and loves to pretend that her Romany blood gives her deep, accurate insights into the hearts and souls of others.

I shake her hands off. God forbid any of that insight stuff is true. The last thing I want is her looking into the present state of my discombobulated soul. I switch my computer bag to my other shoulder to put some additional distance between us. We walk up the wide front steps and cross into the marble foyer.

God, how I hate this house. It is worse than a mausoleum. Worse than a football stadium. And, as if the total lack of human scale weren't bad enough, Simone has gone to the expense and inconvenience of covering every inch of the vast halls with loads of crap. Mementos. Awards. Black-and-white photographs of her in various states of undress.

As usual, my mother ignores it all and heads into her cramped study. I have attempted more than once to point out the fact that she spends all her waking hours in the smallest room in the house, so selling it might be a good idea.

"When are you going to sell this place?" I ask. As usual.

That does not go over well. At all. "This is a movie-star house, and I am a movie star."

Whatever. I am in too good a mood to argue. "Why did you want me to come over so quickly?"

"Well . . ." She stops and stares at me. "Are you okay? You look different. What's gotten into you?"

Damn her and her fake Romany blood. "Nothing. Well, I broke up with Landon. And I quit my job today, but other than that, nothing much has been going on." I'm not about to tell her I'm moving to Russia to head up her despised baby-daddy's company. And the crazy part of how ridiculous that sounds—about those things being nothing—is that they *are* nothing compared to the fact that I finally know what I want to be when I grow up, and I am pretty sure I fell in love with Rome de Villiers after spending a day and a night with him in Russia. And damn if she doesn't see that— just glides right past all the abandoned boyfriends and tenure-track positions and right into emotional territory.

"What else?" she asks, more serious than I've seen her in years.

"Isn't that enough?"

"There's something else. You don't sound upset about either of those supposed devastations. Your job? *Pffft.*" She practically hisses. "The bland decoration in your office alone would have made me quit. And I never liked Landon."

I widen my eyes. "What? I thought you told me just a few weeks ago it was the life you always thought I wanted."

"It certainly wasn't the life *I* wanted for you! But"—she shrugs—"I thought you were in love."

"Mom! You're the worst. You've spent the past year telling me to settle down and . . . ugh. I don't even know why we're having this conversation. I should go."

"Look, sweetheart, we both know you always do the opposite of what everyone says. Do you really think I would want that for you?" She brings her hand to her neck and reenacts a choking motion, eyes bulging, tongue lolling from her mouth. It is over a split second later and she is beaming her famous smile at me. "Kill me now!"

I laugh. I haven't laughed with my mom in ages. Years, probably. She isn't reliable at all. She might be all insightful and clever with me for the next few minutes or hours, or even days, but then she'll be on to the next thing with no warning.

On the other hand, I am no longer an eight-year-old who's been left at a movie theater. Maybe this is the little bit that she can give.

"I met someone else," I say, looking down at my hands clasped in my lap. I am sitting across from her in the small office.

That gets her attention. She *loves* love stories. She collapses farther back into her big desk chair, a swiveling leather number from the 1960s. She got it at a yard sale in the late '80s from some washed-up producer in Bel Air, and she loves every crack and tear in the leather. She says sitting in it makes her feel like Louis B. Mayer.

"I knew it!" She also loves being right, so I let her enjoy it. "You've fallen in love!"

"Yeah. Well, lust, at least. And don't get too excited. Nothing will ever come of it."

Simone sweeps the papers (probably important financial documents that needed her immediate attention four months ago) to one side of the large mahogany desk, puts her elbows down, and rests her chin in her hands. "Tell me all about him," she beams. "Or her!" she adds with equal enthusiasm.

I can only imagine how much *more* thrilling it would be for my mother if I'd broken up with Landon for a woman. She will have to make do with an already-spoken-for French pirate.

My mother may not be the most dependable person in some respects, but she's never betrayed a secret in her life, and when she's actually able to pay attention for more than five minutes at a stretch, she's got some pretty amazing life experience to share, especially when it comes to sordid love affairs. I decide to tell her all about Rome and my fling in Saint Petersburg.

I leave out the intimate details but tell her all about the Matisse, and the romantic dinner, and the kiss on the bridge, and how handsome he is, and how his voice kind of makes me weak just thinking about it.

"Oh. He sounds positively delicious . . . and he smokes? How horrible." But she winks and probably adds that to her mental list of things to adore about Rome de Villiers. "So, when are you going to go after him?"

"What? Never." Looking out the window behind Mom's desk, I stare at the oversize pool in the backyard. The audacity of the man who built this place never ceases to amaze me. An Olympic pool? In the middle of Bel Air? I shake my head and meet her eyes. "He's engaged. Didn't you hear me?"

She shrugs her shoulders and purses her lips, just like Rome. Just like every arrogant Gaul since the beginning of time. "Engaged is not married. You were thinking of moving in with someone only last week, remember? And you're not anymore. And married is not always unavailable, either."

"You're horrible. I'm not going to break up his relationship. His fiancée looks like a wonderful person. She's a humanitarian, for goodness' sake. And forgetting all that . . . Why am I even defending myself to you? Just because I fell for him . . ." I pause, and then I sigh.

"*Yeeeessss* . . ." My mom loves every minute of my ignominy and is encouraging my descent into blind passion.

"Well, just because I fell for him doesn't mean he fell for me. It was probably just lots of rolling in the sack, as far as he was concerned." And that is all I am going to say about that. My mother has never had a proper understanding of boundaries when it comes to my sexuality, or her own, for that matter. She was always asking me about my period and who I liked during high school and if he was a good kisser, despite my often-repeated opinion that it was gross—*gross!*—and she needed to cut it out. I think Vivian's mom finally intervened and told her she was going to scar me if she didn't back off. That put an end to it.

"Was he—"

I hold up my hand. "Don't you dare ask me anything about his lovemaking. I swear, I will walk out of this room right this instant."

She clenches her teeth. "Oh, fine! But you are such a spoilsport. He sounds dreamy."

I am momentarily disgusted as I realize that Rome is probably around the same age as my mother's latest boy toy and that if my mother ever met him, she would probably flirt with him. Hard.

"Seriously, Mom, this is getting into Freudian-wing-nut territory. Cut it out."

"Oh, okay, okay. Sex. Off-limits." She pretends to seal her lips and throw away the key.

I smile and I'm actually glad—for the first time in forever—that I have a crazy, loving mother. I know in that moment that whatever other goofy mayhem she might get up to, she really, *really* loves me in her wonderfully nonjudgmental way.

"So what will you do now?" she asks gently. "Are you going to move to Russia?" The way she asks makes it sound like maybe it wouldn't be so horrible after all.

"I might. I haven't decided yet. Everything's been happening so fast. I want to go to France for a couple of weeks. The time zone is much better for my work in Russia—instead of waiting until late at night for their workday to start, like I do here, in Paris I'll be only two hours earlier—and I can go to my friend Margot's wedding and just sort of regroup for a while. Alexei will be thrilled to have me that much closer, and besides, I should get out of LA for a while."

"Oh, that Alexei. He got his hooks into you after all, didn't he?" The words are harsh, but she sounds almost sweet on him.

"He kind of did. It's not all bad, you know, Saint Petersburg is—"

She swipes her hand to stop me from talking about Russia, as if the mere mention of it will put her over the edge.

"Enough about that. I have big news." She looks excited; then her eyes cloud slightly. "Jamie and I broke up, by the way—"

"Oh, Mom. I really am sorry. I know I made fun of him forever, but I know you cared for him."

She clenches her jaw for a few seconds, the way she does when she is changing scenes and needs to let go of whatever emotion it is that came before. Her face clears. "It's over now. And that's not my big news."

"Okay. I won't dwell on it."

She plows ahead. "I've been offered a wonderful part. Filming begins next week. In Cairo."

"Cairo?"

"I know! Isn't it incredible?"

For a second, the child in me relives that hint of being abandoned; then I'm genuinely happy for her. "It's wonderful, Mom. Congratulations."

"Oh. We'll be on location in Egypt for only a few months, but I just can't wait. They're finally going to make an English film based on one of Naguib Mahfouz's books."

"Will it be dangerous?"

"Oh, probably. Who cares? Like that ever stopped me from doing anything." The sun is starting to set, and Simone turns to look behind her, toward the pool. "Do you want to go for a swim?"

"Sure."

"Oh, good. Why don't you stay for the night, and we can eat popcorn and watch movies in my bed?"

"Okay, Mom."

"And we'll buy tickets to Paris and spend a few days together there. Then I'll go to Cairo and you can go to your friend's wedding and everything will fall into place. You'll see."

I roll my eyes and follow her out to the pool. The odd thing is, she's managed to live her entire life this way, hopping from one lily pad of excitement to the next. I realize I may not want to be a mousy academic married to a cardiologist, but I also know I don't want what she has, either, living in a constant state of upheaval like this.

Despite everything, I have to hand it to her. She is in amazing shape. She slips out of her sheer whatever-it-is and dives into the pool. She does a few laps at a rapid clip while I change into my suit in the pool house.

CHAPTER THIRTEEN

Later, we have a delicious dinner that her French chef has left on the counter and then eat microwave popcorn and watch old Cary Grant movies in her enormous bed with the pillows and all the scents and textures that remind me of my strange childhood. These wonderful times of maternal intimacy are so bittersweet, because they are always punctuated by such long separations.

When I wake up the next morning, my mom is already in a flurry of packing.

"Where's the fire?" I ask with my throaty morning voice.

She turns to look at me. "Oh, good! You're awake. Let's go to Paris today! It will be so much fun. Tori was able to get us two seats in first class on the 9:35 p.m. flight. I thought you'd need the day to get everything in order."

I sit up straighter and plump the pillows behind me. "A whole day?"

She has the good sense to laugh. "Well, she could have put us on the 3:45, but I figured that would be too hectic for you."

"Mom, I can't just up and fly to Paris tonight."

"Why not? You're such a fuddy-duddy. This is the perfect time to up and fly to Paris! You already said you wanted to go to your friend's wedding . . ."

"But that's not for another ten days. I was going to take some time to—"

"Oh, come on!" she interrupts excitedly. "We'll go to your house and make sure everything is okay. You'll get packed and everything. The whole point of having a small beach house is that it's turnkey. Come on! Be spontaneous with me!"

I hesitate because it actually sounds like fun and I *can* mix a bit of fun into my life now if I feel like it. It's my life! There's no academic review board or stuffy doctor boyfriend making me worry about what kind of *impression* I'll make. Voyanovski has offices in Paris, and I can easily have Alexei meet me there. He'll probably be thrilled at the idea.

"You know what?"

She stops shoving a completely impractical taffeta ball gown into her huge bag and turns to face me. "What?"

"I think it sounds like fun. Let's do it!"

"Oh, how wonderful!" She actually clasps her hands together and twirls around like a girl. "We are going to have so much fun! We'll go shopping and dancing and—"

"Let's just start with going to Paris on the spur of the moment and work our way up to shopping and dancing, okay?"

She comes over to the bed and hugs me when I stand up. "Okay! One spontaneous thing at a time."

I go to the bathroom and brush my teeth. When I come back into her room, she's sitting on the side of her bed, near her bedside table. "What are you doing? We need to hurry."

She looks up quickly from a snapshot in her hand and then stares at me in that damnable gypsy way of hers. "Come here for a minute, *chérie*."

When my mother *chérie*-s me, it's usually bad. I cross the room slowly and sit beside her on the bed.

"There's more to your father and me than either of us ever told you."

The air stills around us.

She gets up nervously and tries to busy herself with more packing, attempting to shove some sunscreen into the side pocket of her suitcase.

I get up. "Mom. We are going to Paris, not the Riviera." I take the sunscreen from her unsteady hand. "You don't need sunscreen. Let's deal with one thing at a time." I take her shoulders in my hands and turn her to face me. "Tell me about you and Mikhail."

She sits down on the edge of her bed again with a defeated sigh. "I never stopped loving him. I guess I hated him for making me move back to the United States, when I would have died to stay with him."

I sit down with a thud on the bed next to her.

She continues slowly. "It was still Soviet Russia, Miki. You can't imagine what it was like for us. We were simply mad for each other. I was willing to give up my career—what little it was at that point— for both of us to live in Russia, and he wouldn't hear of it. But I was getting close to convincing him. I still had my French passport; I hadn't received my American citizenship yet. I told him I wanted to be with him and that I didn't care if we lived in some horrible Soviet shoebox. I'd almost convinced him . . ." She looks away for a couple of seconds, then continues. "He knew changes were afoot; he was probably the agent of a lot of that change, truth be told. But when I learned I was pregnant . . . it was misery."

I put my face in my hands and shake my head.

"Oh, goodness!" she cries, reaching her arm around my hunched shoulders to pull me in close. "Not like that! We were both *so* happy. He was older and he never thought he'd have a family. He had devoted his life until then to his political work and his business ideals, building that damn company with Alexei. But when he realized there was now a new life to consider, he absolutely forbade me to return to Russia with him. He would not be swayed. He was so autocratic and . . ." I can practically feel her gritting her teeth and reliving all the anger she obviously still feels toward him beyond the grave.

Jesus. This is bittersweet news. My parents actually *loved* each other at one point? Yay.

My arrival was the wedge that drove them apart? Ugh.

I wipe away tears. "Oh, Mom."

She is weeping quietly also. "He was too stubborn!" she says with angry vehemence. "Why didn't he leave all those stupid Russian people to clean up their *own* messes? Well." She clenches her jaw tighter and swipes at her tears as if they are making her cross. "No point in despising the very thing you adore about someone, eh?" She looks so young to me in that moment. So vulnerable.

I reach my arm around her waist and hug her close. "I'm so sorry, Mom."

"Oh, honey. It all seemed to make sense at the time. He wanted to protect you from that world. It was so dangerous, and your father was right there in the thick of it, both at the KGB and with the paper company. I don't think you can really even imagine it. After Brezhnev died, before Gorbachev, it was just a mess. And then after the wall came down and you were able to go visit him in the summers, and political tensions had eased, well, I just couldn't forgive him, I suppose."

"Oh, Mom."

She stares into my eyes. "He loved you so much, Miki."

"He loved you, too, Mom." I get up and walk around the bed to pick up my handbag. I come back to where she's sitting and riffle through the crowded bag to pull out the small red leather photo case from my father's apartment in Saint Petersburg. "I found this in his bedside table. I have a feeling he was never with anyone else."

She takes the leather and rubs her fingertips lightly across it, remembering the feel of it, before she opens it. She gasps and covers her mouth when she sees the picture of herself in his arms, laughing and free, in love.

It's a bum deal. If I am really a love child, why wasn't there more *love* to go around?

She hands back the photos, and I hold up my hand. "No, you keep it."

She gives me a watery smile, then stands up and opens the drawer in her bedside table. She lifts a false drawer bottom, which I never discovered in all my years of snooping, and pulls out an identical red photo case.

"Oh," I say. There isn't really much else to say.

She opens it and shows me what's inside. The one that I found in Russia has the hugging picture on the left and Simone on the right. In the one that she's pulled from her bedside table, the left-hand photo is the same, but the right side has a picture of my father. It's probably weird of me to think so, but he looks incredibly handsome. He is looking up from a sun lounger, probably in the South of France, and his face shows the delighted surprise of someone who is very happy to see the person taking the picture. His hand is partially covering his eyes, the shadow slanting across his face. But his smile is glorious—wide and adoring.

"Oh, Mom."

She's crying again. "I know. So silly of me, after all these years, to still pine for him. Isn't it?"

"No, it isn't. But . . . why all the foolish liaisons? Why Jamie? Why didn't you settle down with another man after you and Dad split? Or why didn't you reconcile with him?"

She shakes her head again to clear it. "I could never love another man the way I loved your father. I tried. And I could never forgive him." She sounds bitter, as if it were my father's fault she was never able to love anyone again with the same passion. In her mind, it probably *was* his fault.

I have a flash of myself blaming Rome in the same way. I am starting to feel like it *is* his fault that I fell for him so quickly and easily. He didn't need to be *that* wonderful, after all. He shouldn't have been so alluring if he didn't want me to be lured in.

"So. In the absence of a good man," she says, clearing her features again, "I settled for boys. Jamie was just the last in a string of . . . diversions."

"Oh, dear."

"Yes." She smiles weakly. "I liked Jamie. Of course I liked him. But when we were in Acapulco and I learned that Mikhail had died and Jamie caught me sobbing in the bathroom . . . well, it turns out Jamie had actually fallen in love with me, and it didn't sit well with him that I never really stopped loving your father."

Here's the thing: The whole illegitimacy issue never really mattered to me one way or another—I had a mother and a father, after all. I had two parents, and they each loved me in their way, and I never wanted for anything, so I knew I was far better off than many other kids out there. I forced myself to be grateful. But I grew up believing my parents hated each other and that I was the result of an ill-advised, short-lived affair; I didn't realize until this moment how much I internalized all that strife.

They are both guilty of perpetuating that stupid story about how frivolous and foolish and deluded they were when they met in France, in the '80s. What else was I supposed to think? When your parents tell you things about your childhood, you tend to believe them.

"I'm not going to make the same mistake," I say.

Simone is instantly angry. She grabs back her photo case. "You would see it that way, Mikhaila. Here I am, trying to be honest with you at last, and you are as self-satisfied and arrogant as your father."

I sit with my mouth open. "Mom." I reach for her forearm and speak softly. "I didn't mean it like that at all. I meant I don't want to have the regret that you have right now because I didn't try hard enough to be with Rome. I am agreeing with you."

Her shoulders fall. "I'm so sorry, sweetheart. I'm terrible. You make me so nervous sometimes. You're so much like him with that mechanical brain of yours; you terrify me." She grips the photo case more tightly. "All that damned conviction."

I know she is upset, because even after all the speech coaches and years of mastering every nuance of the English language, she still lapses and turns her *th* into a *z*—"all *zat* damned conviction"— when she is losing control of her emotions.

I laugh darkly. "I am so far from conviction, you have no idea."

She calms and pats my leg. "All right. We both have a lot to learn about each other. For now, some of it is clearer, yes?"

I reach for her and pull her into a hug. "Yes."

She pulls back and tucks a strand of hair behind my ear with rare maternal tenderness. "Paris, here we come."

I smile in return and then help her finish packing.

Leaving my car in Bel Air will be safer, with my mom's caretaker to look after it for me. He also drives us to my place in Venice, and he and my mother help me sort through everything that needs to be dealt with in my absence. In the end, just like it was at my office, it's kind of unnerving how easy it is for me to close up my sweet house.

The gardener is happy to stop by more frequently to check on the plants and the yard; my mother's caretaker is happy to drive over every day or two to pick up the mail and forward everything to Paris. I pack up two big bags with clothes and toiletries and all my electronics. My mom informs me that she will be throwing most of my mousy clothes into the incinerator when we arrive in Paris. I think her first glimpse of the new-and-improved, spontaneous Miki is like a maternal dam bursting for her. She is completely enamored with this idea of going on some wild Miki-makeover shopping spree when we arrive in France.

I realize I'm not totally opposed, either. I call my friend Margot from the airport lounge at LAX and give her a very truncated version of events. She's thrilled that I'm able to attend her wedding after all and is sweet enough not to ask a bunch of difficult questions when I tell her that Landon and I have broken up and I'm no longer working at USC.

She gasps slightly, then sounds really happy for me. "I have to say, you sound really good, despite all that. And, selfishly, I can't wait to see you, Miki, whatever the circumstances."

I call Alexei next, and, as I expected, he is delighted that I'm on my way to Europe and we will get to work together in person. He promises to meet me in Paris the next day, and his enthusiasm is actually quite contagious. As I settle into my luxurious first-class seat an hour later, I take a sip of champagne and realize I'm going to work in Paris! In my company's offices! And this is my new life!

CHAPTER FOURTEEN

My mother and I are both tired when we arrive at her three-bedroom apartment near the Musée d'Orsay the next night. We order in a light supper and then sleep through to the next morning, until we are awoken by the sound of insistent knocking on the front door.

Mom wraps herself in a long ivory silk robe and saunters down the front hall. She looks through the peephole, then pulls the door open and grabs Alexei into a fierce hug. I stand at the far end of the hall that leads back to the bedrooms.

"Hi, Alexei." I wave.

They both turn and stare at me, and I can tell immediately that something is going on. Alexei shuts the door behind him, takes off his trench coat, and hangs it on the antique coatrack.

Simone speaks first. "I'll make coffee. You two go into the living room."

I walk down the hall, and Alexei pulls me into one of his big bear hugs. He mumbles all sorts of apologies in Russian near my ear.

"Slow down." I pull away and then tuck my arm through his. "What's going on?"

It sounds pretty bad. Pavel Durchenko claims my father signed a transfer agreement for the Segezha plant, with Kriegsbeil serving merely as the front so Durchenko isn't publicly involved. But it's still *his* in his mind. And Alexei is claiming there is no such agreement. Durchenko is pissed, to put it mildly.

"Alexei . . ."

He looks guilty. "Yes?"

"Well?"

"Well what?"

"Is there an agreement?"

I can see the wheels turning in his Cold War head. He tries to be all reassuring. "Don't worry about it." He pats my knee.

I move his hand away. "Are you *crazy?*"

He opens his mouth to speak, and I hold up my hand. "You know what, don't answer that." I get up and walk over to the front hall and pick up my computer case. I pull out my phone and scroll to the private number Durchenko gave me at my father's funeral service. I don't have any reception in this part of my mother's apartment, so I reach for the old black telephone on the antique side table. "I'll simply tell Durchenko there's been a misunderstanding and we accidentally mislaid the document." I start to dial.

"Miki, no!"

I continue dialing.

"I shredded it!" he blurts.

I set the phone back down slowly. "You did *what?*"

"When we were going through your father's desk that last day you were in Saint Petersburg," he says quickly, as if saying it really fast could make me skip past my rising fury. "It was in one of the private files I was sorting through, and, well, I shredded the agreement. It wasn't notarized or anything. It was just a handwritten—"

"Damn you, Alexei," I interrupt.

At least he has the good grace to hang his head in shame, but only for a few seconds. "I knew you would be mad at me."

I shake my head, because me being mad at him is the least of our worries. Durchenko killing us, on the other hand, might be more of a legitimate concern.

Then Alexei fists his meaty hand and punches his own thigh. "No! Damn Pavel Durchenko! Your father—" Alexei's voice catches on the emotion, and I think he is about to cry. Then he shakes his head. "Your father was being practical. Just give me two weeks."

"Two weeks to do what? To figure out a way to cover up your lies?"

"To reason it out?" he asks tentatively.

I've been feeling the power dynamic changing between us over the past few weeks, but his tone just now makes it feel official. Alexei is asking my permission, in a way he never would have—and obviously didn't—a month or two ago.

"Alexei," I say with a sigh. "You of all people know Durchenko is not *reasonable*."

"Two weeks—that's all I'm asking. Come on, Miki. I know I can get a better deal sorted out by then, and we also have Clairebeau to think about now."

I stare at him. "Is Clairebeau in on this with you?"

"What? No. You negotiated that deal with Clairebeau."

"With your encouragement, if I remember correctly. You've been trying to mess with Durchenko this whole time, haven't you?"

He looks mildly guilty but hardly remorseful. "It all presented itself."

"My negotiating my first deal with one of the most powerful publishing conglomerates in the world—under false pretenses—just *presented itself*?"

"Miki, we—"

"You totally used me, Alexei. Which I get . . ."

He smiles like he did this really clever thing.

"No!" I yell, then calm my voice. "I mean, it's fine because no one is dead yet. It's not fine that you manipulated me into negotiating that deal with Rome de Villiers when you *knew* Durchenko already had a claim to the property—"

"I didn't technically know that . . ."

I stare at him with as much disdain as I can muster.

"I mean, I didn't find the document until after . . ."

"Alexei, just stop. You got what you wanted. You threw a wrench into Durchenko's plans by using me and Clairebeau."

"Just two weeks, Miki. Kriegsbeil is almost ready to deal without Durchenko."

I scoff. "Well, they're idiots if they cross him. I'm sure he's thrown people out of planes for less."

"Those stories are highly exaggerated," Alexei tut-tuts.

"You realize what you're asking, right?" I stare at him for a few seconds. "Exaggerated or not, Durchenko is a man who can tap my phone, break into my house . . . *kill me*! And you're asking me to wait around while you try to cook up some backroom deal with one of his silent partners?" I'm beginning to sound shrill. "And to keep Rome de Villiers in the dark as well?"

"This has nothing to do with Rome," Alexei snaps.

"I suspect he'd take a different view."

"Look." He rests his palms on his knees and tries to calm down. "It's just a small factory in Segezha."

"Exactly. So what is this really about, Alexei?" My voice has softened, too.

"It's ours, Miki. Your father and I built that plant. We hired those workers and the workers' children. We have kept it running all these years, through so many lean times. And that man—"

"Stop making it personal."

He sighs. "Fine. I'm sentimental. I admit it. I don't want Durchenko to have it. He doesn't deserve it. He doesn't care about people."

"Then why did Mikhail make the agreement with him?"

"Your father saw the future of the business in our timber holdings, in the land and the trees." Alexei sighs again. "We had a major disagreement before he died. Mikhail was going to phase out all the paper factories."

"But, Alexei . . . I agree with my father." My voice is even gentler, because I wish there was some way to soften the facts, but he knows that's what I intend to do.

"I know." He looks like he is almost crying. "I know in time that's what we will have to do, but please let me have this one thing. For a short time longer."

"Oh, god, Alexei. Please don't get emotional. You're going to make me cry."

Alexei looks so tender that I don't say anything more.

"Eventually Durchenko will get his hands on everything, but please, let's at least try. If I can get Kriegsbeil to get on board—which I think I can—and Clairebeau is already in, then it will be as if the document between your father and Durchenko never existed. He can still be in on the deal, but he won't be able to shut down the plant and sell it off in pieces."

"Regardless, what you're suggesting is completely unethical. The agreement was real."

He furrows his brow and shakes his head, as if ethics are such silly, childish things at a time like this. I think he's actually convinced himself that shredding the contract was the ethical thing to do. "Two weeks, Mikhaila. That's all I need. Let's not be overly dramatic."

My mother has returned from the kitchen and is standing in the arched entry to the living room. She listened to the tail-end of our conversation, and that last bit makes her break into infectious laughter. "Oh, Alexei, you are the one who needs to quit being such a drama queen."

Unexpectedly, I burst out laughing, too. The man is the epitome of brawny, scowling, hirsute manhood, and the idea of his being a queen is priceless. His thick beard and heavyset stature make him look as if he could fight a bear without a weapon. But I have to hand it to my mother—she's right. It is as if Alexei wants this caper to remind him of the "good old days" of his Cold War heyday. Simone is having none of it.

"If anyone can get to the bottom of this," Alexei continues, "it's Jules Mortemart."

I raise an eyebrow for further explanation, feeling like the name rings a bell, though I'm not sure from where.

"He's a brilliant attorney who practices here in Paris. Your father and I have had him on retainer for a few years." He hesitates for a moment in that sheepish way of his. "For when we have issues that we don't want to handle in Russia. You probably saw his name on one of the old deal memos."

It turns out Jules Mortemart is thrilled to take on the top-secret investigation into whether our company is obligated to Durchenko in the absence of a cosigned contract. He is also willing to pursue our various options and work with us for the next two weeks.

We put Jules on speaker and talk for an hour. He puts my pesky ethical questions to rest almost immediately by explaining there are all sorts of legal reasons the shredded document might not have been valid in any case, given how it was executed in such a hasty manner—perhaps under duress—and how soon before my father's death it was signed. I get a recurring chill up my spine when I realize I am speaking as the head of the company, that Alexei and I are talking about the Segezha deal as equals. Alexei gets up a couple of times to refill his coffee, impatient with not getting his way more easily. I've pretty much assumed my father's position—taking the long view against Alexei's clever but often shortsighted plans—and I begin to see why they had such a successful, enduring partnership.

Eventually, Jules and I decide to let Alexei pursue some of his more questionable alternatives with the Germans, but we also agree that Jules and I will work on drafting a proper agreement with Durchenko in the meantime, in case Alexei fails. We all agree to postpone contacting Clairebeau for the moment. If the deal I negotiated with Rome becomes null and void because of a preexisting agreement, we will deal with that mess next.

I try not to think about how I've been secretly looking forward to casually touching base with the CEO of Clairebeau while I just happen to be in Paris. We're business colleagues, after all, and it wouldn't be totally inappropriate for me to give him a call, I've been rationalizing. But, once again, the universe is trying to help me squash my foolish lust, and I try to see the self-imposed gag order as a blessing in disguise. Of course, as soon as I think of the word *gag*, the foolish lust pulls right back into the lead.

Alexei is watching me have this absurd internal battle while Jules drones on about how he is familiar with Clairebeau and how it shouldn't be a problem keeping them on the sidelines for two more weeks.

"Are you okay?" Alexei asks quietly.

I nod and shake off the stupid thoughts. Rome is *engaged*, I remind myself. But my mother's words still poke at the edges of my mind: *engaged is not married.*

After we hang up with the attorney, I tell Alexei point blank I am calling Durchenko. He growls and grumbles but ultimately gives in. I'm nervous, but probably not as much as I ought to be.

In fact, I feel sort of exhilarated. The private number gets answered after one ring.

"Durchenko."

"Hello, Mr. Durchenko," I say in my most formal Russian. "Apparently we have a misunderstanding about a Segezha contract."

"I have no misunderstanding. I am holding a copy of it in my hand right now."

"Yes, well, as you can imagine, we are concerned that we do not have my father's signed copy. Please give us some time to sort through the rest of his documents, if you would?"

He breathes heavily into the phone. "This is a totally legitimate contract, *Dr. Durand*."

It ruffles me a bit that he knows my real name, and that he is *trying* to ruffle me. Not that I kept it a secret or anything; it just sounds mildly threatening in his rumbling Russian drawl. "I very much hope we will all come to an agreement on that," I add carefully.

He exhales, not sounding pleased. "Be careful what you wish for, Mikhaila. Two weeks. Then I will take what is rightfully mine." The call ends without another sound.

"Wow. That was interesting," I say to myself as I disconnect the call.

I look up to see Alexei clasping his hands expectantly.

"Well?"

"You got your two weeks."

"Yes!" He starts to do his new favorite thing, the fist pump.

"Don't you dare fist-pump! We're on thin ice; we're not celebrating. I just lied to one of the most intimidating people I've ever met."

"It wasn't a lie, exactly," Alexei tries.

"You've got two weeks, Alexei. Don't gloat!" But I smile to soften the blow, and he does a mini–fist pump, like a kid who's been told to quit kicking the back of the seat and gives it one more tiny nudge for good measure.

I feel a firm zing of excitement that I try to tamp down. Going toe to toe with Russian Mafia men shouldn't be this exhilarating. But it is.

Afterward, Simone orders a lovely lunch brought in from Fauchon, and Alexei seems much calmer when he leaves the apartment a few hours later. Everything is complicated and potentially dangerous, but somehow I feel like things are looking up. At least, on some level, everything is coming out into the open. I am well and truly the CEO of Voyanovski Industries, and I can't help but feel a deep thrill about it.

CHAPTER FIFTEEN

I work from my mother's apartment for a few hours after lunch, until my mother's nine millionth interruption finally forces me to shut my laptop.

"Are you finished now?" she asks sweetly. "Ready to go shopping?"

This afternoon, my mother heard from one of her old modeling friends. Madeleine has reinvented herself as a woman of a certain age who hosts all sorts of soirées and salons and always manages to make them fun and edgy, rather than stuffy and pretentious.

"Before we meet up with Madeleine," my mother announces, "you need clothes!"

It's probably impossible to overstate my mother's love of clothes shopping. Now that I know the Russian Mafia isn't going to attack me with a knife in one hand and an AK-47 in the other—for the next two weeks, at least—I decide to ride the wave of Simone's enthusiasm. As Rome would say, I am ready to have some fun.

I stand up from behind the desk in the guest room where I've been working, and Simone shakes her head dramatically.

"What?"

"That goes in the garbage," my mother says, pointing at me from head to toe. I know she is talking about my clothes, but still, her expression leaves me with the feeling that my whole being needs an overhaul.

"Okay, okay. I'm on board."

She folds her arms and assesses me further. "I mean, darling, look at yourself."

I look down, as ordered. I don't think I look all that bad. When I am in work mode, I tend to dress in earth tones. I look down at my chocolate-brown pencil skirt and cream blouse. I don't need to draw a lot of attention to myself when I'm running four hours of statistical analysis. "I think I look professional."

"You look like a very tall turnip. Let's go." She pulls on a black three-quarter-length raincoat and ties it at her waist. She tops it off with a jaunty black rain hat and looks like she's ready for a Mary Quant photo shoot. Lickety-split.

I realize she's right. There's no longer any reason—maybe there never was a reason to begin with—to divide my wardrobe into sexy, fun on one side and very-tall-turnip on the other.

She turns to see why I hesitate. "What's the matter? Just grab one of my coats from the closet, and let's go have some fun."

Fun. *Remember fun?* I think of Rome again. That seems to be happening a lot lately. Pretty much consistently. "Count me in."

We find a taxi, and Simone tells the driver he'd best take us to the rue du Faubourg Saint-Honoré, as if he must also agree that my appearance is in need of a rapid, extreme transformation that can be accomplished only at the most expensive, most exclusive stores in the world.

First stop: Lanvin.

Okay, I admit it: On one level, it's disgusting, so much money for a few scraps of fabric. The two T-shirt dresses my mom insists on buying come to a total amount greater than my monthly salary at USC. Well, my *former* monthly salary. But the fabric is like the softest caress against my skin. I think of Rome. Again.

From there we go to Hermès, where I flatly refuse to carry a $9,000 purse, no matter how much money I'm now making at Voyanovski. Simone is crestfallen, then buys one for herself—in purple—just to spite me. We settle on Galeries Lafayette to get the rest of my new look rounded out. We are there right up until they close at eight p.m., and need two assistants to help carry all the bags out to a taxi.

Clearly, I am a late bloomer. At the age of thirty, I am finally getting around to the squealing delight I should have embraced when I was thirteen. I don't need to limit myself to borrowed Pucci dresses and a blowout every six months for a black-tie event—I can actually look this good every single day if I choose to.

When we get back home (yes, I am already thinking of it as home—crazy but true), Simone pours two generous glasses of a jammy Bordeaux, turns on Édith Piaf, and makes me do a full fashion show with all my new acquisitions.

For the most part, she sits on the silk-upholstered chaise longue in the corner of her bedroom, and occasionally jumps up and pulls out insane accessories from the back of her closet: a mid-'80s, three-inch-wide snakeskin belt that somehow works with the black silk shift from agnès b. Or a pair of purple suede stilettos that are perfect with the pleated silk dress from See by Chloé.

Around midnight, we go to a hip new place called Beef Club in Le Marais with Simone's friend Madeleine. I don't know if it's because I am speaking French, or because I am wearing thousands of dollars' worth of designer clothes that feel like Rome's hands trailing across my body, or because I am so jet-lagged I don't really know where I am, but the whole night is a dreamlike fantasy. My mother encourages me to wear my hair loose and hanging down my back. Turns out, I feel loose all over after the removal of one simple hairband.

I'm wearing a pair of her vintage Moroccan earrings that are huge and spangled. I dance in the crowded upstairs room with men and women from all over the world. I don't drink too much. I laugh. My mother is beautiful and joyful, and we are just happy to be with each other. Why have we never done anything like this in Los Angeles? Why have I never wanted to, I suppose, is the better question.

I spend the next week shuttling between the Voyanovski offices, where I work with Alexei in the first arrondissement in the mornings, and the office of Jules Mortemart, whom I see every afternoon. The handsome attorney bears a passing resemblance to Rome— dark hair, sparkling eyes—but I try to ignore it, since I feel like I am seeing Rome's likeness everywhere: in the height and breadth of every passing man, or the loose curl of dark hair across the forehead of a stranger sipping his coffee. Thursday afternoon, as I am sitting across from Jules in his office, his cell phone rings, and he looks up and asks if it is all right to take the call. He is very polite that way, not wanting to interrupt me.

"It's my brother, down in the South. Do you mind?" he asks.

I stand up to leave, to give him privacy, but he motions for me to stay, so I sit slowly back down at the small worktable where I've taken up temporary residence.

I am not eavesdropping, but it is a pretty small space, and my head shoots up when I hear him say the name Margot Montespan. It's not a common name; in fact, I don't think there can be more than one in the world. Jules senses my interest and asks his brother to hold on for a moment. He looks at me.

"Do you know her?" he asks in his formal French.

I answer likewise. "Yes!" I beam. "She was my roommate at MIT. But maybe it's a coincidence? Is your brother her fiancé? I'm actually here in France for her wedding. I don't know why I didn't put your last names together."

He speaks to his brother, and his face lights up with humor. "She is the same!" he says in his funny English. "Do you want to speak to her?"

"Sure!" I've talked to Margot a few times since I got to France, but never about work, and we both laugh at how small the world is after I take the phone from his outstretched hand.

I tell her a bit about how Jules is on retainer for Voyanovski, and she laughs again and says, "So perfect! We were all worried he would miss his train and forget about the whole wedding weekend. Why don't you take the train down with him tomorrow and stay for a while?" She lowers her voice to a conspiratorial whisper. "He's kind of dishy in a nerdy, academic way, don't you think? A rebound romance, maybe?" I look away from Jules just then so he doesn't suspect Margot is talking about him.

"That's a great idea for us to take the same train tomorrow," I say into the phone, but I catch Jules's eye. "Sound good?" I ask him.

"Oh, is it tomorrow already?"

"Yes, Jules. It's tomorrow," I rib him.

He gives me an embarrassed smile. "Yes, then. That's sounds good." And then he goes back to the spreadsheet he's been working on.

"It's gorgeous here," Margot continues. "Why don't you and Jules work from here for a couple of weeks? Just stay and stay!" I hear her shoo away her fiancé with a sweet "cut that out," and I am suddenly desperate to see my friend and see what a normal, loving relationship actually looks like.

"Perfect! I would adore that."

"Really?" Margot's attention is back on me. "I can't believe you are really your own boss. But yay! That's fantastic. You sound so good, Miki."

I smile through my words. "I feel good. I think running Voyanovski is going to be amazing." I start to laugh, sort of hysterically, again. "Amazingly scary, but still amazing." She laughs with me, and then we both settle down again. "Do you have everything set for the weekend? Is it going to be very formal?"

"God, no! It's more like muddy boots and Barbour coats down here. Lulu and Trevor are like a pair of hippies, hanging around in flannel shirts and Timberland boots. She can't wait to see you, by the way."

"I'm excited to see her, too. Is she driving you crazy?"

During college, we used to joke that I had my wild mother and Margot had her wild younger sister, Lulu. Our crosses to bear.

"She's pretty great, actually." Margot's voice softens. "How's your mom? Still driving you crazy?"

"She's pretty great these days, too. Maybe we were uptight after all?"

Margot barks a laugh. "Maybe! Is your mom still there, or has she left for Egypt already?"

"She leaves for Cairo today, so I've got the Paris apartment to myself for a while."

Someone in the background asks her something about flower arrangements, and I remember she must be swamped with last-minute details. "I'll let you go, Margot."

Her tone switches quickly from warm interest to all business. "Thanks, sweetie. It's kind of hectic."

"I can imagine."

"But it's going to be really fun, I promise. No wedding stress! I can't wait to see you tomorrow. And you're definitely staying here at the farm, right?"

"Yes, I'm planning to."

"You might have to share . . ."

"Margot, please stop trying to set me up," I say with a laugh.

"Oh, nothing like that. I can hear from your voice Jules isn't your type anyway. There are two beds, so it shouldn't be a big deal. It's one of Étienne's cousins. She's kind of a pain, but she means well. I'll see you tomorrow in Avignon. So exciting! Bye, sweetie!"

The phone goes dead, and I pass it slowly back to Jules.

"What a fun coincidence. Turns out your brother is about to marry my college roommate."

"How nice," Jules is only half paying attention, his mind already fully consumed by the intricacies of international law. He is an academic, as well as a practicing attorney, and he makes my brain look like pudding by comparison. He is fluent in all things Russian—not just the language, but the law, history, and philosophy of the country. I feel a bit out of my league.

I get up to stretch. "I think that's about it for me today, Jules. Do you mind if I head out?"

He looks up slowly, keeping his finger pointed at the document so he doesn't lose his place. "Of course. Off you go." He starts to look down again.

"Jules?"

"Yes?"

"What train are you taking to Avignon tomorrow?"

"Oh, let me see . . ." He flips through his day planner, leather and paper, like my mother's. He tries to find the train information. "Maybe three o'clock . . . or perhaps seven o'clock . . ."

I smile at him. I love that he has a brain that can hold vast amounts of information but cannot recall a train departure time. I pat his forearm. He is only about five years older than I am, but he seems to require the care and feeding of someone thirty years my senior. "Never mind. I'll check with your secretary, and then I'll be here tomorrow with plenty of time to spare."

"Oh, that would be helpful. I do tend to miss trains with appalling frequency."

"Good. I'm glad I can be of service." He realizes *I mean I am glad to be of service* since my intelligence is rather pale compared with his in terms of all the other, *real* work we are trying to accomplish.

"Oh, you've been very helpful, Mikhaila. You are quite decent at maths."

Quite decent. Sweet man. "Thanks, Jules. I'll see you tomorrow."

Jules would undoubtedly have missed the train to Avignon if I hadn't shown up at his office the next day to physically tear him away from his work. I finally have to yell, "Your only brother is getting married! Let's go!"

Once he is away from his desk, Jules opens up considerably. We talk the entire three-hour journey about his childhood and how he developed his interests in genealogy and the law. And mathematics. And languages. He seems shy about his accomplishments.

Even though I've known him for only a little over a week, I've come to admire him. He is awkward but also incredibly kind and thoughtful. He is the type of person who might have been dropped on his head—half a bubble off the level when it comes to interacting with other people—but no less endearing or intelligent.

The high-speed train pulls into Avignon station at 5:18 p.m. exactly.

Margot is waiting for us at the end of the long, sloping ramp that leads from the upstairs platform. The sun is cutting through the white slats that line the enormous barrel roof of the modern structure. She looks so beautiful, and so relaxed—so unlike her former, ambitious New York City self.

She's always been a dark beauty, but very erect and full of purpose. Rigid. Her time in Provence—or, more likely, her time in the presence of the man who loves her—has loosened and softened her. She's wearing a colorful, multipatterned scarf around her neck and a bright orange cotton coat. She exudes vitality.

"Oh! Miki! You're really here!" She pulls me into a hard hug, then holds me at a slight distance to get a better look at me. "It's so good to see you! Someone rational!" She turns to Jules and gives him a similarly forceful embrace, which he pretty much tolerates. "Make that *two* rational people!"

Margot's eyes skitter over my shoulder. "Zoe! How are you?"

I turn to see a petite, fashionable woman walking toward us. Her red hair is smoothed into a chic bob, and she has a stunning slash of matte red lipstick across her lips. I hear Jules mutter something disparaging under his breath.

"Miki, this is Jules and Étienne's cousin Zoe Mortemart."

I shake her hand, and she seems nice enough, except for the whole sizing-me-up-from-head-to-toe thing. "Hi. Nice to meet you," I say.

"Oh, hey! Are you Simone's daughter? I heard you were in town!"

Oh, hey indeed. "I am, actually. Have we met?" I'm trying to stay cheerful, but with Jules rolling his eyes behind the woman's back and Margot trying not to laugh at my obvious discomfort, it isn't easy.

"We have now!" she chirps. "I work at *Paris Match*. It's great to meet you! Wow. This weekend just got a whole lot better. Would you be willing to do a quick interview at some point?"

"Zoe!" I've never heard Jules raise his voice before now, and he sounds pissed.

"What?" she replies innocently. "Don't act all aggrieved. I'm just doing my job."

"Now, now, you two." Margot smiles at the bickering cousins. "It's our wedding weekend. Zoe, you promised to keep your newshound instincts on a tight leash, remember?"

"Oh, fine!" She rolls her eyes. "Only for you." She leans in and kisses Margot on both cheeks. "Congratulations, by the way. You look fabulous, as always."

"Hardly!" Margot says, looking down at her bright but casual outfit. Then she turns to Jules and says, "Now, wipe that scowl off your face, and let's go. We can't all be introverted geniuses." Margot slides an arm through mine and leads us out to the parking lot.

CHAPTER SIXTEEN

The May air is crisp and clear when it hits my face. So unfamiliar. The air in Los Angeles often makes me feel like I am in need of a squeegee to wipe away the thick pollution, or just the human congestion—all those exhalations. The spring air in Paris felt fresher, but still wet and thick.

The Provençal air feels brand new. As we cross the promenade, I take a very deep breath. This will be perfect—a clean slate.

"Isn't it incredible?" Margot asks. "I think that was the first thing I fell in love with when I got here: the air. It's like a drug. Be careful; it's very addictive." She pulls me along, and Jules smiles some small, knowing smile and keeps up with Margot's leading pace.

The drive east out of Avignon is slow with after-work traffic, but Margot talks the whole time, asking Jules all sorts of questions about the land dispute he's working on for her and Lulu, and then she laughs with Zoe about the latest scandals in Paris. Then she is interrogating me as best she can about Landon.

"You broke it off with a hot cardiologist?" Zoe asks with disbelief, as if I declined the Nobel Peace Prize. She is twenty-five, and apparently the idea of being purposely single at thirty strikes her as appalling.

"I think it's for the best," I answer slowly.

"Maybe you'll have the same luck I did," Margot says, catching my eye in the rearview mirror. "I met Étienne soon after I moved here." She returns her attention to the road ahead.

"Right after she broke off her engagement in New York," I add with a smirk.

Jules looks up. "You were engaged to be married?"

Margot nods.

Jules looked affronted on his brother's behalf.

Margot laughs and pats his thigh. "Oh, Jules. Look at you, all protective of Étienne's honor. Seriously, we need to get you a girl to take your mind off things. Miki's available," she adds.

Poor Jules. He turns bright red.

I reach from the backseat and squeeze his shoulder. "Don't worry, Jules. I understand. She's the sister I never had, always saying the very thing that will make you feel the most discomfort imaginable."

"I do not!" Margot gasps with false innocence. "That's Lulu!"

We all laugh. Apparently, Jules and Zoe have both visited numerous times and know the dynamic Montespan sisters already.

Margot turns to Jules. "On the other hand, if we're going to make *everyone* uncomfortable, shall I ask the question that's on everyone's mind? Is Miki already in love with someone else? Is that the real reason she broke it off with her boyfriend and quit her fabulous job at USC?"

"Margot!" I cry. I lean between the two front seats and say, "Do not answer that, Jules. She's baiting us."

Margot hums and nods her head knowingly. "That's a definite yes."

Zoe perks up from her endless texting at the sound of that. "Oh! You broke up with the cardiologist because you met someone else? Now I get it." She nods her head. I need to stay away from this woman, or she is going to drive me nuts.

"Oh. My. God." I blush in the backseat. "Cut it out, you guys. I'm a single woman at a foreign wedding. I need a good old-fashioned fling."

Zoe continues, "Agreed! I'll fight you for one of those sexy bad boys coming in from London!" She elbows me in the upper arm, and I nod vaguely. Charming.

Jules tries to sink even lower into his seat. Making him cringe is apparently one of Zoe's favorite pastimes.

Margot smiles in the rearview mirror again as she changes the subject. "Here we are, Miki. This is the village where we go for coffee and the bakery." She is navigating the car through a narrow, steep street that leads to a medieval town square. She pauses for a bit, pointing to the café and the *boulangerie* in the opposite direction. She drives down another narrow street, and, after she makes a hairpin turn, the entire valley spreads out before us. Margot pulls the car to a halt in the middle of the deserted street. "Isn't it unbelievable?"

I stare. There isn't really anything else to do. Jules and Zoe stare, too. The sun is setting and the surrounding fields and trees are etched in gold and copper and hints of ochre and fiery orange. Some of the spring fields are still fallow, but every cropped stalk creates a shadow and reflection of the setting sun. It is van Gogh and Cézanne and Monet and Millet all rolled out at our feet.

"It's incredible, Margot." I turn to look at her serene profile and feel her happiness like a punch in the gut. I sit back quickly so she won't see my threatening tears. I fear I will never be that happy, in that carefree way. We wind our way under the arch of trees, and I am once again reminded of my fantasy of being on the back of Rome's imaginary scooter, with the spring leaves just beginning to refill the canopy over the curving road.

Margot slows the car and turns down a rocky dirt lane that leads for about a mile through more scraggy oak groves, and then the panorama opens wide again, this time to the south, across the valley in that direction.

When we come to a stop in front of a stone farmhouse, Lulu comes running out of the house with two tall, handsome men. I wonder which one is Margot's fiancé; then I don't have to wonder, when the taller, dark one comes to Margot's side as soon as she steps out of the car. He pulls her into his arms and swings her around. She laughs and kisses him quickly on the lips, then pushes him off. "Cut that out and come meet Miki."

Of course, Étienne Mortemart is yet another stunningly handsome Frenchman. Is it in the water? Deliver me.

He bends slightly in a formal greeting. Margot says my full name when she introduces us. "Mikhaila Voyanovski Durand, please allow me to present Étienne Mortemart, my fiancé." Margot shivers visibly when she says the word *fiancé*, and I cast aside my own selfish thoughts about scooter dreams that are very obviously *not* going to come true. I decide, instead, to dive headlong into Margot's ocean of nuptial excitement. I grab Étienne into a brief hug.

"I'm so happy to meet the man who does this to Margot!" I say, then point at her.

He knows what I mean, and I love him even more on Margot's behalf. He leans in slightly. "She does it to me also," he confides in a throaty French accent that makes me feel as if I am never going to escape the whispering reminders of that single night in Saint Petersburg.

I smile at the sweet concession and then try harder not to see his resemblance to Rome. His height, the spread of his shoulders, something about the way he smiles that inclusive, mischievous pirate smile. It is distracting. And Margot notices. I think for a minute she thinks I'm coming on to him.

"What is it?" she asks.

"Oh, god, sorry. Nothing. Étienne just reminds me of some-one, that's all. Sorry." I shake my head and smile again. "It's really a pleasure to meet you."

Lulu is bouncing up and down, just as I've always remem-bered her. She and Zoe are babbling about some gallery exhibit in Avignon they both want to see, while Jules and Étienne take our luggage out of the trunk.

While I was at MIT, I spent most of my holidays at the Montespans' house in the Berkshires. Rather than flying back to Los Angeles to what might very well have turned out to be an empty house—or, more accurately, a staffed house—I became the Montespans' de facto third sister during those visits. Lulu was still a teenager then, irresponsible and wild, and Margot clung to me like a raft. Her family was notoriously bohemian, and Margot . . . wasn't.

I hug Lulu and marvel at her new maturity. She is still her same Tigger-ish self, but she seems more grounded somehow. Then I see why.

"Hi, I'm Trevor McCormick. Nice to meet you, Mikhaila."

I take the British man's offered hand. Lulu answers for me before I can speak. "Oh, she's Miki, silly. No one calls her Mikhaila!"

He smiles and finishes shaking my hand. "Okay, then. Hi, Miki."

"Hi, Trevor, nice to meet you." He is kind of scruffy around the edges—rough-cut, light-brown hair that hasn't been trimmed in a few months; a few days' growth of beard—but the sharp eyes give him away. He looks like he is playing at being louche, more than anything.

We turn toward the house, and Étienne pulls Margot into a one-armed hold. It is exactly how Rome held me when we walked down the street. This is going to be a hell of a long weekend with all these swooning young lovers everywhere if I persist in translating every gesture into a Miki-and-Rome reenactment.

Thankfully, the sight of a little girl, probably two or three, who comes bounding out of the house, takes my mind off Rome. She runs up to Margot, who bends down to grab her and swings her into a wide turn and tosses her in the air.

"*Mar-mar . . . vous êtes revenue!*"

Make that young lovers *and* love children. *Hell.*

"Uh . . ." The stunning revelation that Margot has a baby makes me lose my poise. My open-mouthed shock sends Margot into a fit of laughter. Étienne takes the baby and holds her easily on his hip.

"How could you not tell me you have a baby?" I ask, eyes wide.

"Miki," Étienne says, "this is my daughter, Ariel. From my first marriage."

Jules and Trevor are smiling at my attempt to recover. "Oh."

"Why don't you and Margot catch up and we'll get dinner ready?" Lulu offers. "Obviously, a lot has been going on, and she needs to fill you in."

"Zoe," Étienne says, "you and Miki are going to share the small bedroom. Hope that's okay."

"Of course!" Zoe replies.

"Perfect," Margot says. "Let's get a glass of wine and go sit by the fire in my study. It's starting to get cool. Come on, Mik." She pulls me next to her, and we all trail back into the house.

Margot's study—her refuge—is a rich, book-filled sanctuary. Two comfortable leather chairs are angled in the cozy bay window, and a low fire crackles in the small grate.

"Wow, Mar, this is phenomenal."

She closes the door behind us with her hip. "I feel so lucky. It still doesn't feel like this is really my life." She hands me one of the glasses of wine.

We both sit down, and I let my eyes wander over shelf after shelf of books and box files. "I love it in here."

"Me, too," Margot agrees. "Come in anytime you want to hide if it gets too chaotic this weekend, with my crazy parents running around, or Étienne's glamorous cousins from his mom's side or his British ex-in-laws. It's going to be only about forty people . . . forty very strong personalities, if you know what I mean." She winks and takes a slow, appreciative sip of the wine.

"I feel bad taking you away from all your guests like this," I say.

"Don't be silly. You're a guest, aren't you? I can see those people anytime. When my mom and dad get back from Aix tonight we'll hang out with them, but until then I'm all yours." Then her tone changes. "So. What the hell's going on?" She looks so concerned, so earnest, I just kind of collapse into the safety of a very old, very trustworthy friend and burst into tears. Margot leans forward and hands me a box of tissues from her desk.

"The doctor is in," she says with a supportive smile.

"Oh, Margot. What a mess. I mean"—I try to smile—"everything is so amazing. I am so excited about Voyanovski and all the new opportunities that are coming my way." I sort of sputter through the words, as surprised by my outburst as she is. "I'm so relieved to be free of Landon, and even giving up my place at USC feels like this huge weight off my shoulders. But . . ." I take a deep breath.

"You *have* met someone else, haven't you?"

I nod slowly. "It's just so stupid." I wipe the tears away and sit up straighter. "I thought it was going to be this one-off, a kind of . . ." I stop, distracted. I look out the wavy glass panes of the bay window behind Margot's shoulder and watch the last edge of the sun fall behind the mountains to the west. Even the red of the sunset reminds me of him. It's becoming ridiculous. I refocus. "I thought it would be a spot of fun. We both agreed it was just going to be *fun*."

"Was it?" Margot asks.

"Was it what?"

"Was it fun?"

I picture his eyes when he kissed me on the bridge; I picture his lips when they trailed down my stomach in the shower. Rome was definitely the most fun I've ever had in my life.

I whisper, "He was so damned hot, Margot. I become sort of weak when I think about him."

Margot smiles as if she likes the sound of that. "Sounds dreamy. So, what's the problem?"

"Yeah. Slight problem. He's now engaged to someone else."

"Ouch. Well, it's not like any of us are strangers to botched engagements. Why doesn't he just call it off? It can't be impossible."

I let out a self-deprecating laugh. "Yeah, maybe if I had ever spoken to him or seen him after our tawdry one-night stand, that would be the perfect time for me to tell him to break off his engagement to Miss Perfect." I take a sip of wine and shake my head at my own foolishness. "It was just a stupid fling."

"Then why can't you stop thinking about him?"

"Hell if I know, but that's what I need to do. He's a business colleague, so I just need to think of him as a business colleague and nothing more. I'm trying."

Margot swallows another sip and stares at the fire, then sends an assessing look down the length of my jeans to my expensive high-heeled boots.

"So, he hasn't seen the new, hot you?"

"Margot, stop!"

"What? You look gorgeous. I mean, you always were gorgeous, but you seem . . . cooler somehow, more comfortable in your own skin."

"It's just the clothes and stuff. My mom took me on a wild shopping spree in Paris."

"Really? It was all your mom's doing?" Margot widens her eyes suggestively.

"Okay, fine, I may have purchased a few things myself. It probably sounds superficial, but I feel stronger somehow when I'm in beautiful clothes." I lift my free hand as if I am posing for a photo. "It's the new me: Glamorous Miki."

"It suits you. You look great."

"Thanks."

Margot's smile slips, and she looks serious. "How are you handling things since your dad died?"

I burst into tears again.

"Oh, Miki." Margot leaps up and hugs me awkwardly; she's half standing and I'm half sitting. I pat her back.

After I finally settle down again, I say, "It's okay. I think I might still be in shock."

Margot sits back down in her chair and reaches for her glass of wine on the round table between us. "You think?"

We both smile. I wipe away the new tears and shrug. "I thought I was so tough, about my dad and everything, but I feel so devastated sometimes, without even realizing it. I keep thinking everything is just a little off kilter, but really, my life has completely changed in so many meaningful ways. Between all the stuff that's happening with these negotiations and the crush I have on this guy, I feel like my dad is sort of with me in spirit. I can't really explain it."

"All right. One thing at a time. Tell me what happened with your dad."

We spend the next hour going over all of the insanity of the past six weeks, everything to do with the paper business and my (old) job at USC. Margot used to be a really successful forensic accountant at KPMG in New York, before she moved to France, and it's fun to talk to someone who understands that part of what's happening. She totally gets my excitement about taking over the company and applying all the things I was only theoretically good at. She is happy that I am finally realizing I was never going to be professionally satisfied in a university setting.

"We are so messed up," she says. "You go from being a researcher to being a businesswoman, and I go from being a businesswoman to being a researcher."

"You are?"

She looks over at her desk, piled with documents and history books. "It's so weird, but yeah, after I got here and I started letting go of the idea that I was only on a leave of absence or a hiatus or whatever . . ." She shrugs. "I got really into it. I've started doing all this research into our family history, and we found a bunch of documents that might prove historically important." She smiles. "But what the hell do I know about seventeenth-century French history?"

"I bet a lot."

She smiles again. "Well, I'm learning. It's been really great. Anyway, back to you. What happened after your dad's funeral?"

The conversation circles back to Rome. I still haven't referred to him by name. Margot finally presses. She's holding her wineglass close to her lips. "So, are you going to tell me this guy's name or keep him as some big, bad secret?" She starts to take a sip.

"You've probably heard of him. His name is Jérôme de Villiers."

CHAPTER SEVENTEEN

She flies into a fit of coughing, nearly breaking her wineglass when she sets it down next to her with a crash. Then she's thumping her own chest to alleviate the choking. There is a quick knock at the door, and Étienne pokes his head in with a smile, then frowns when he sees Margot struggling. He rushes into the room and lifts her up, patting her back. "Are you okay, sweetheart? What happened?" She's waving her hand in front of her face.

"Nothing! Nothing!" she wheezes, catching her breath. "Totally fine!" She's talking way too brightly.

I am frozen in the chair. "You know him?" I whisper.

Margot is still watery-eyed and trying to collect herself.

"Know whom?" Étienne asks kindly.

"Jérôme de Villiers . . ." I say, hoping the name will ring *no* bells after all.

"Rome? Of course," Étienne says with innocent joviality. "He's my cousin! Our mothers were sisters. We're actually sort of related to Trevor, too, by marriage. Trevor's older half-brother, Luke, is also our cousin . . ." He realizes he is rambling a bit and stops talking into the silence.

I take a slow sip of my wine and nod, which Étienne sees as some cue to elaborate. "Really?" I add. I figure if he talks, I won't have to.

"Yes, there were three Rothschild sisters. Estranged, of course. What else?"

I smile and pretend I didn't know any of this. "Interesting . . . I think I may have seen something about that," I say lightly, as if it has nothing much to do with me. "He and I negotiated a deal in Russia, after I inherited my father's company in March."

"Oh, great. Right, so you've met him?"

"Mm-hmm," I answer as I take a sip of wine and try to avoid Margot's best-friend laser eyes.

Étienne senses something more is going on, but he's a good guy, so he natters on. "Right. Yeah, so Rome's mother was the oldest—brilliant, apparently—but she ended up being a crazy socialite in Paris, gallivanting everywhere, but really sharp, you know? I think she was probably the brains of that operation—her husband, Rome's father, was a total lush, nearly destroyed the whole company—but Rome doesn't really talk about it. His parents died about ten years ago. That's when he took over Clairebeau. But you probably knew that already." He is starting to seem like a caged animal, looking from Margot to me.

I nod and act as if I don't know anything about it, as if I never held poor Rome in my arms as we exchanged every sordid detail about our parents, very late at night in a Russian hotel room. "What a coincidence," I say.

Margot is sitting back down again, rubbing the pad of her index finger against her thumbnail like she always used to do before finals at MIT.

"So you met him in person, then?" Étienne asks politely.

"Only briefly."

Margot widens her eyes, and I shake my head at her.

"Oh." Étienne purses his lips. "Oh, I see." Then he smiles. "A passing fancy, then."

Margot stands up and pats his solid upper arm as she walks him across the room and tells him the two of us will be out to dinner soon. She closes the door quickly and kneels on the floor in front of me. She pulls the wineglass out of my hand and sets it on the table next to us, then takes both of my hands in hers. Very serious.

"I mean this in the most loving way possible, Miki: Rome is *bad news*. He's a terrible flirt. He's an international *playboy*, for goodness' sake. Étienne loves him, obviously, because he's funny and charming and all that. But like you said, it's just best to forget about him and move on."

"I know," I whisper, even though there is that treacherous part of me that is clinging to the absurd idea that he is The One or my soul mate or something equally ludicrous. I stare at her and nod yes.

She looks so concerned, I almost feel sorry for her. "Miki"—she squeezes my hands more tightly—"he is not a good man. I know I sound overly dramatic, but I'm afraid for you. We joke about what a rat bastard he is. *He* jokes about what a rat bastard he is. Seriously. What are you *thinking*?"

It is like lunch with Vivian all over again. But worse, somehow, because Margot actually knows him and still thinks he's a *bad man*.

"He's coming to the wedding, isn't he?"

Margot nods. "He's actually hosting the whole thing."

"Oh, god. Maybe I should just go." I try to pull my hands from hers. "I don't want to make your wedding awkward."

"No! I'm so sorry. I didn't mean to make you defensive. I'm just . . . Oh, Azi's coming, too. Does she know about you?"

"Know about me?" I laugh at the absurdity. "What's to know? I was probably one of the seventy-four women he slept with in the first quarter. Oh, hell. I am such an idiot. Promise me you won't make a big deal of it. Can you do that?"

"Of course I can do that, but I'm worried about you. Are you really okay?"

"I swear I'm okay. More than okay."

We both stand up, and Margot hugs me. "Miki, you deserve to be happy. You will meet someone so much better than Rome."

I pull away slightly. "I refuse to be your pet project for the weekend!" I say with a smile as I set her farther away from me. "It's your wedding, for goodness' sake! You don't need to be worrying about me."

"I know. You can take care of yourself." She looks at me in that penetrating way of hers. "For now, it's only two days of seeing him with her. You can deal with it?"

"Sure, I can handle it." I hope I'm not lying.

"Good! And you'll stay here for a couple of weeks. Please? You can work from here. Trevor's a mad technical wizard, and we have massive bandwidth, so you can do whatever you need to do and it would just be great to be with you."

"Okay, okay!" I smile. "I'd love to. I have everything I need with me, and I'm my own boss. That has such a nice ring to it, doesn't it?" We walk to the door, and she rests her hand on the knob before opening it.

"Showtime?"

"Let me rinse off my splotchy face. I'll meet you out in the kitchen. Thanks, Margot. I'm so glad to be here."

"Me, too." She looks at me hard one last time to see if I'm just covering up or if I'm rallying. "Me, too," she repeats, then pats my upper arm one last time and pulls the door open. "Let me show you where your room is. Sorry you have to share with Zoe," she whispers. "Hope you don't talk about Rome in your sleep; she'd file that story with her editor in about five seconds."

Great.

Margot leads me out into the living room, then down a short hall to a small room with two narrow single beds. "It's pretty tight. Sorry."

"It's perfect. Are you kidding?" The pale yellow walls and terracotta tile floor are the epitome of French country comfort. "I love it."

"Okay. The bathroom's just here, outside your door. I'll see you in a few minutes."

"Thanks again, Mar," I say as she leaves.

I close the door for a bit of privacy.

Two hours later, Margot's family and the rest of us are sitting around the rough refectory table in the kitchen, laughing loudly and pouring more wine, surrounded by plates and platters and bottles and glasses from the delicious meal that Lulu and Trevor and Étienne and Zoe prepared while Margot and I were catching up with each other before dinner. Margot's parents have returned from Aix, and Ariel has been put to sleep. All nine of us are feeling loose and happy. Trevor is sitting to my right, and Jules to my left.

The too-loud engine of a too-expensive car roars outside the kitchen window, and Trevor jumps up, almost slipping backward as he underestimates his drunkenness.

"That must be Rome and Azi." He walks out to open the front door as I feel the blood drain from my skull. Margot looks at me as if she is my Victorian governess, her entire posture demanding I be strong, no matter what. She mouths the words *I didn't know* and then turns to look toward the entrance to the kitchen.

Zoe practically falls off her seat, she's so excited. "Oh! Rome is here with his fiancée? How fun! I didn't think we'd get to see them until tomorrow!"

Rome fills the room like he always does as he comes in. He's laughing—the familiar deep roll—and holding Trevor's shoulder with one hand and his fiancée with the other. A tall, model-thin black woman with enormous turquoise earrings walks next to him, laughing at something Trevor says and smiling at the general company.

"We made it at last!" she calls in her elegant British-African accent, going around the table and kissing everyone on both cheeks. Lulu is thrilled to see her, unfolding herself from the farm table and standing up to give the stunning woman a big hug.

"How are you, gorgeous?" Aziza asks Lulu. "Introduce me around!" Lulu introduces her parents to Aziza, then turns to me and Zoe.

"This is Miki Durand, my sister's best friend from university. And this is Étienne's cousin Zoe Mortemart. She works at *Paris Match*, so don't say anything around her unless you want it on the front page," Lulu jokes. Aziza shoots a quick smile in Rome's direction, and I feel myself die a little with each breath.

He is staring right at me.

Aziza shakes hands with Zoe first. She is polite but cool, especially compared with Zoe's unveiled curiosity.

Then Aziza turns to me.

"Hi, I'm Aziza. So nice to meet you."

Lulu is smiling with her usual puppy-dog enthusiasm. "You two will love each other!" She points at me and looks at Aziza. "Miki is *so* fabulous, Azi! She's part Russian and part French and brilliant and lovely!"

Rome's eyes widen when Lulu's higher voice cries out my name. He has the audacity to look angry. *At me!* As if I somehow orchestrated this debacle. I keep my cool. I deserve an Oscar.

Trevor is staring at Rome staring at me.

"Do you two know each other?"

Aziza looks from me to her fiancé, then back at me. "Are you Mikhaila Voyanovski? Of course! They are business colleagues; isn't that right, Rome?"

Man, she is definitely the daughter of a diplomat or someone equally tactical, because she's got this whole grace-under-pressure thing down pat.

"Yes." Rome comes around the table and actually kisses me on both cheeks, because it would be ridiculous not to. But does he need to be this good a faker? My treacherous body wants to hurl itself at him. "How are you, Miki?"

"Fine, thanks." *The smell of you is making me faint.* "So nice to see you again."

"Come on, everyone—let's get more wine and move to the living room!" Étienne (my hero!) calls over the melee. Margot's parents and Jules start to get up and clear the table.

"I'll get that!" I say a bit too loudly, taking Jules's plate from him.

Aziza tries to help with the plates. "Are you staying here?" she asks with kindness.

"I am. Are you?" I try to sound casual, but I can tell my voice is strained.

Rome's voice cuts through the sound of glasses and dishes. "No. We're staying at my place in Lioux."

"It's a château." Aziza winks and gives me a little nudge with her elbow, new friend to new friend.

Of course it is. I smile weakly. "Sounds like fun."

"Oh, you'll see it tomorrow," Aziza continues merrily. "Didn't Margot tell you that's where the wedding reception is going to be? It's all tucked up in the mountains, with this incredible view over the valley, and—"

"That's enough, Azi." Rome sounds like he's embarrassed, which is impossible—I would have thought the only thing better than bragging about his own châteaux and jets was having someone else brag for him.

Aziza looks surprised and then bursts out laughing. "Since

when have you ever been modest, Rome?" She is still laughing at him. "Please don't start now. It doesn't suit you."

Margot finally returns from the living room. "Oh, Azi, quit it with being so helpful. Go sit down with Lulu and Trevor and everyone. Miki and I will get this cleaned up in a few minutes. My parents would love to talk to you. They were both in the Peace Corps in Somalia, and they're dying to hear how it's changed in the past thirty years."

Azi's smile falters. "Not enough, I'm afraid. But I'd love to talk to them." She wipes her hands on a kitchen towel and heads toward the living room. "You coming, darling?" she asks Rome when she catches him staring at me.

"What?" He looks back at his fiancée. "Oh. Yes. Let's just stay for one drink and then head over to Le Cloître."

I sigh my relief that they won't be staying long. Rome looks equally relieved when I catch a glimpse of his face before he turns to leave the kitchen.

Margot and I are the most assiduous, painstaking dishwashers in history. I don't think I have ever cleaned a stack of plates with more purpose and conviction. After everyone is resettled in the living room, Rome comes back into the kitchen, ostensibly to get a glass of ice water.

He looks at me, then at Margot. Something must flash across Margot's face, because Rome smiles. "Margot knows, right?"

"Knows what?" I try lamely.

"Miki," he whispers, and I feel it like a caress, damn him.

"Why don't you two go out back?" Margot lifts her chin toward the laundry room, where a small door leads to the terrace.

"Good idea." Rome smiles.

"Bad idea." I scowl and keep washing the dishes.

He leans his hip against the counter and pulls a clean kitchen towel from the drawer. He's obviously familiar with the house, and

I kind of hate that he's actually a normal person with friends and cousins, instead of a 24-7 playboy at some debauched BDSM château party every night. When he starts drying one of the plates and putting it up on the rack, I want to rip it out of his hand and smash it on the tile floor.

"What are you doing?" I grind out.

He raises an eyebrow. "Helping with the dishes. Where's Landon?"

Margot turns off the water on her side of the sink. "I'm out of here. Please don't break any of the china, all right?" She kisses me on the cheek and nearly snarls at Rome. "You are a very bad man."

He gives her saucy wink and says, "And you know you love it!"

Margot shakes her head as she walks out of the kitchen, but damn if she doesn't have a reluctant smile on her lips.

"So?" he prompts, taking another plate from my hands and letting his finger trail suggestively along the back of my wet hand.

"So what?" I ask.

He looks down the length of my body. "You look fantastic, by the way."

"I'm in blue jeans and a white T-shirt, doing dishes," I huff, as I pass him another plate. His fingers touch mine again, even more slowly this time, and said blue jeans suddenly feel all tight and confining. I shift my thighs and he totally notices.

"None of these old places has air-conditioning. It can get a little close." His hands are strong and deft as he dries the next plate, and I start to feel very *close* as I watch him. He puts up the plate and then reaches in front of me and turns off the faucet, since I'm just standing there, wasting water.

"Miki," he whispers close to my ear. "Where is Landon?"

"I don't know. LA, probably." My voice is shaky because all I want to do is lean into Rome and press myself against his hard chest. I take a deep breath to fortify myself. "What difference does it make?" I straighten up and try to pull away from him, but he grabs my wrist and pulls me toward the back door.

Next thing I know, we are out under the stars and the pool is twinkling in the background and the cicadas are sawing away and if it were any more romantic we'd be in a Russell Crowe movie. "Rome, stop. You're engaged. What are you doing?"

"I just want to talk to you . . ." He sounds sort of desperate, and I hate to admit how much I love the longing in his voice. The idea that he's been thinking about me, maybe even pining, does incredible things to my insides. He's rubbing the tender part of my wrist back and forth as he looks into my eyes, as if he can somehow caress the truth out of me.

"So talk," I whisper.

He slams his lips into mine and uses his free hand to press into the small of my back and push me against him, against his . . . oh, god. He's so turned on and we're under the stars in Provence and it's so tender and hot all at once and . . .

And his fiancée is in the other room.

I shove him away and scrape at my lips with the back of my fist to wipe off the taste of him. "What the hell are you doing?"

"Kissing you. And it's even better then I remember."

"You're sick, you know that?" I point toward the house, from which the sound of light laughter and conversation is wafting. "Your fiancée is sitting in there. Are you insane?"

He reaches for me again, and I try to pull away, but he gets hold of my wrist in that incredibly tender way again. "When it comes to you, I think I *am* insane, Mikhaila."

My heart starts to pound, because I think he's talking about feelings and not just one-night-stand sex feelings, and he's looking at me like he looked at me in the museum and over dinner in that hole-in-the-wall—like we understand each other, like we're different from the rest of the world. And I want him so badly in that moment that I have to close my eyes and just inhale him because I can't touch him or actually do anything about it.

"Rome." My eyes are closed. I want to imagine for a few seconds that I'm allowed to say his name like he belongs to me. But then I open my eyes; it's all too much, just stupid passion, like my mother always falls prey to. Meaningless panting and groping, maybe with slightly higher stakes because of our work and Aziza and all of that, but nonetheless just a game to him. Still, I want to cry, because the way he's looking at me—so hopeful, innocent, even—doesn't feel like a game at all. It feels real and powerful.

But I force myself to see him for what he is. The spoiled manboy who does whatever he wants whenever he wants. Gets engaged on a lark. Sleeps with women and never calls them again. Buys and sells companies like new toys. Flies his jet to his château. Or to bring a girl coffee.

I tell myself he's ridiculous, and I think he sees the moment I think it.

His face shutters, and he drops my wrist. "Fine. You pretend this is nothing between us if it makes you feel better." He turns to walk away, and I practically rip the sleeve off his blue oxford shirt to stay him.

"Feel better?" I nearly shriek, but somehow manage to keep my voice to a strained whisper. "You think this feels good, you asshole? Knowing you're sleeping with that beautiful, loving woman—"

He pulls me into his arms, and I let him. I hate myself a little, but not nearly as much as I should, because, god, he feels like heaven wrapped around me like this, kissing my neck and telling me how much he missed me and how angry he was that I never called and he didn't want to interfere and how Landon was putting all that shit about us moving in together all over social media, and it's all mixed together with his hands roaming all over me and kissing me and me just melting into him.

When his hands grab hold of my hips and my ass and he pulls me against his erection, all the melting comes to a halt.

"Stop." I may be kissing him when I say it, but at least I say it. "Just stop."

"Miki—"

"I mean it, Rome." My voice is still damnably breathy, but I'm pulling away from him inch by inch and I am not crying, so that's a bonus.

He releases my hips and stares at me a few seconds longer, then drags both of his hands through his hair, and all I can think is how jealous I am of his hands. I turn away slightly so I don't have to torture myself by staring at his parted lips and his turquoise eyes glinting in the reflection of the moonlight and the pool.

"This is *not* over." He sounds almost threatening, like he did on the phone the first couple of times we were negotiating.

I shut my eyes. "Just go. I'm never going to be some girl on the side. You made me want way more than that, you bastard. I deserve perfect, remember?"

He swears in French, and I hear his steps in the moist grass as he heads back toward the house. A few seconds later, I hear voices in the kitchen. Everybody is saying good-bye. I just stand there like a statue under all those stars until his arrogant sports car roars out of the driveway, and then it finally quiets down and Margot comes out and gives me a hug.

"You okay?"

I nod. "I think I'm okay." I turn to face her. "He's so hot, right? I'm normal to be confused by his hotness, right?"

Margot laughs at my attempt to reduce my feelings to some teen summer blockbuster. She pulls me into another one-armed hug. "He's very hot, Miki. But . . ."

"I know." I sigh and smile back at her. "But. But. But. I know all the buts. I can handle it." I take a deep breath and start to feel slightly normal again. "We're grown-ups. It'll be better next time I see him. I knew I would have to see him for work and everything. It's just sooner than I had anticipated. And it's probably better he's engaged, because now it's really not even a possibility."

"Oh, sweetie." Margot takes a deep breath, too, like she's leading a yoga class. "You'll get over it. He didn't say anything about breaking it off with Aziza, right?"

"No, he didn't."

"And you probably wouldn't want him to anyway, right?" Margot presses.

"Well. I wouldn't go *that* far. If he *wanted* to break it off with Aziza the Perfect Woman, I certainly wouldn't spend too much time trying to keep them together." I laugh at the absurdity of it all, and Margot laughs with me.

"You're going to be fine. You're smart and grounded and honest, and he's . . ."

"Hot?" I offer.

She smiles again. "Not . . . emotionally available."

"Right. Not available. That's what I meant to say."

Étienne comes out a few minutes later with another bottle of wine and three glasses.

"Everyone good?" he asks cautiously.

"Yes," I answer. "No need to walk on eggshells. The first awkward meeting is over. Thanks for everything, Étienne. I promise there won't be any drama to ruin your wedding tomorrow."

He puts the three wineglasses on one of the small tables between the pool loungers and opens the bottle with familiar ease. "Wherever Rome goes, there's bound to be drama." He shrugs as the cork pops free. "I'm used to it after a lifetime of watching him misbehave." After he pours the wine, the three of us stay outside for a while longer, staring up at the sky from the lounge chairs and talking about silly things to do with the wedding and the photographer and the flowers.

Margot and Étienne are holding hands and smiling while they talk, and I start to feel less maudlin. Rome is just a philanderer; I don't need to turn it into some torrid misadventure. I take another sip of wine and enjoy the simple pleasure of being with my old friend on her wedding weekend at her beautiful new home.

Near midnight, after I wash my face and brush my teeth, I'm too keyed up from this roller-coaster day, so I reach into my bag, pull out my e-reader, and fire up the book I was reading on the train. About fifteen minutes later, my phone vibrates. I look down at the unfamiliar number and answer it, thinking it might be Alexei.

"What are you wearing?" Rome whispers.

His voice is low and sexy, but it doesn't make me any less furious at him. "What am I *wearing*?"

I thought I was whispering, but Zoe pulls out one earbud and leans up on her elbow. "Everything okay?"

"Yep. I'll just take this outside." I slip out of bed. "Sorry to disturb you. It's my uncle in Russia." I roll my eyes as if it is *such* a drag and then pad through the living room and out the front door.

"Are you crazy?" I whisper hotly into the phone, once I step out of earshot of the house.

"Obviously, yes. I am completely mad about you."

"Where are you calling from? What's this number?" I ask.

"It's the landline at my place."

"Your château, you mean?"

"Yes," he answers happily, and sounds like he is settling back in bed. "I'm in my château, looking at my Matisse and thinking of touching you—"

"My god. I feel so sorry for Aziza. You're not even married, and you're already cheating on her?"

"Oh, darling, this is not even close to cheating."

"You're disgusting."

"So you've said. Yet you're still on the phone, aren't you?" he taunts. We both breathe into the silence.

"Silk pajamas," I whisper, wanting to torment him.

His voice is thick when he finally replies, "Don't even . . ."

"You started it," I nearly snarl. "You want me to be an immoral hussy? This is me being an immoral hussy, flirting with a man who's probably in bed with another woman—"

"She has her own room."

"That's totally none of my business. I'm hanging up now. I thought I could flirt or whatever, but this is so far out of my league, my mousy-statistics-professor league. Good night, Rome."

But like some panting teenager, I don't actually disconnect the call; I hang on just to listen to his goddamned breathing.

"*Je t'adore*, Mikhaila," he whispers, and heat flares up my chest and neck and my breasts ache and then the phone goes dead and I am standing barefoot on the rough gravel in my friend's driveway in the middle of the night.

Oh, god.

I tiptoe back into the house and try to go to sleep.

CHAPTER EIGHTEEN

Saturday morning passes in excited preparation. Lulu is the most nervous of anyone. She flutters around Margot until their mother has to pull her aside and tell her to relax. Étienne and Margot are getting married at noon in a tiny church in the nearby village of Saint-Martin-de-Castillon. The wedding luncheon will follow at Rome's château, a former cloister that he renovated a few years ago.

The few of us who are staying at the farmhouse have some mimosas with breakfast, so I am feeling properly festive. When we get to the church, I am laughing with Jules and feeling like I might be able to survive after all. There are a few photographers snapping pictures of Rome and Aziza. I roll my eyes—my decision to see him as utterly absurd is once again legitimate. He smiles right into the camera and jokes with some of the photographers, shaking hands and grinning when one of the paparazzi asks whether he saw the latest news that he was recently voted the sexiest man in Europe.

"So, no more Woman of the Week, *hein?*" one of the reporters quips.

I look away in disgust. Jules escorts me up the medieval church steps, the sun bright and promising. Some of Étienne's tall, handsome British cousins have also arrived, and Zoe is right that there's a fine flock of them to choose from. I decided to wear one of the fabulous Lanvin minidresses my mom helped me pick out in Paris, and it shows a lot of leg. I'm pretty close to a Viking maiden to begin with—tall and broad-shouldered—so when I sport really high heels, I sometimes feel like I run the risk of looking mannish. This morning, Lulu and Margot made that sound like the most preposterous thing they'd ever heard, and they forcefully encouraged me to wear bright-gold four-inch heels from Giuseppe Zanotti.

Anyway, I am feeling all Amazonian and powerful, towering over Jules, and I am starting to believe some of the hype about the power of clothes. I feel fortified. Jules settles me into the second row, along with Margot's cousins who flew in from the States, and I am grateful that I am squarely on the bride's side of the church, so I won't have to worry about any of the groom's French relatives being overly *close* in the seating arrangement. Despite all my efforts to the contrary, I am afraid if I am near Rome, I might just hurl myself at him.

I sense him in the church before I see him. When I turn to look, he is insanely gorgeous—dark-blue suit, black hair slicked back from his forehead but already coming loose. Irresistible.

In the end, it doesn't matter that he is on the opposite side of the church. I can feel him staring at me from a distance just as easily as I felt him breathing on me under the stars last night. I dig my fingernails into my palms. He is so totally off-limits. I do not have an addictive personality, so why do I feel like a junkie?

The one or two times I allow myself to look in his general direction, he is blatantly watching me. I feel my body swell and spark in response. I spend the rest of the ceremony staring at my clenched hands, trying to let the wholesome joy of Étienne and Margot and sweet Ariel, the ring bearer, wash away my egocentric lust.

Jules and I ride with Trevor and Lulu to Rome's château. Lulu cheeps like a songbird about how much I'm going to love it, how amazing the architecture is, and what an incredible job Rome did with the renovation. I know she means well—she is a furniture designer and restorer by trade. Then she's on about how great it's going to be to have Rome and Azi so close when they come to visit more often in the summer, after they're married, and how they'll all hang out by the incredible pool that's built into the side of the rock face, until I get peevish and tell her I'll see it for myself in ten minutes, so she can stop talking.

Trevor and Jules both look out the window to avoid getting drawn into the tense conversation.

"Sorry. I know I can be overly enthusiastic." Lulu is quiet for a few seconds, and I feel like such a jerk.

"I'm sorry, Lulu. I'm just stressed about work and Landon, and I guess I got emotional at the wedding."

"Oh! I'm so sorry." She turns from the front seat to look me in the eye. "That was really insensitive of me. I keep forgetting everything you've been going through recently."

"No, you're right to be excited," I add in apology. "I'm sure it's going to be a beautiful reception."

As Trevor's car hugs the tight turns that take us higher into the mountains, I try to keep my heart rate steady. We pass through a cool rock formation and come out on the other side, then pass through a tiny village.

"We're almost there," Jules says.

After a few minutes, we make another hairpin turn, and then the view opens up and fields of early lavender stretch out in endless rows. I gasp because the cloister in the distance is one of the most beautiful views I've ever seen—and because it belongs to Rome and it's obvious it isn't the result of some check he wrote to an architect or fling he had with a designer.

"Right?" Lulu asks over her shoulder. "Amazing, right? I wasn't being overly enthusiastic, was I?"

"No, you weren't," I answer quietly.

Trevor pulls the car into the big courtyard and parks it under one of the enormous plane trees to the right. A pair of huge, ancient wooden doors—which have likely been there since carriages passed through the entrance—are held open with two topiary trees that have been festooned with white silk. Other than that, it's just a beautiful day at a beautiful country château, without any real indication that it's a wedding reception.

Then we turn into the inner courtyard and I see that the perfectly orchestrated symphony of casual elegance continues. Waiters pass champagne, and there's a three-piece group near one of the lemon trees, playing American bluegrass. It should be totally incongruous, but it all works seamlessly. Round tables are set with gleaming silver and bright-white linen and white wildflower centerpieces, and tiny white lights have been strung up everywhere, flickering like fairies' wings within the ancient walls.

I turn to see Margot hugging Étienne, and she looks blissfully happy, like this day—this man—is everything she ever hoped for. I'm still on a contact high from their love when my gaze moves a few feet to the left and I see Rome, staring at me, lifting his flute of champagne, and toasting me from across the enchanted courtyard.

His attention is diverted when Aziza comes up beside him. She looks upset, and I turn away, not wanting to see them together or get caught staring back at Rome or whatever. I grab a glass of champagne from one of the passing servers and try to look busy observing all the decorations and architecture. Margot's parents arrive a few minutes later, and I spend a while chatting with them about the ceremony and how beautiful the day is.

I feel my phone vibrating in my small clutch and excuse myself from the conversation. Wending my way into a shadowy part of the house for a bit of privacy, I see that it's Alexei and listen to his brief message, then call him back.

"Hey, Alexei, what's up?" I take a sip of the (obviously) exquisite champagne and hope Alexei's not calling about anything urgent, though I doubt he would be calling me on a Saturday if it were something minor.

"Have you heard from Durchenko?"

"No. Why would I have heard from Durchenko? It's been only a week."

"Well, he's got some bee in his bonnet that you're trying to work out a side deal with Clairebeau. Are you and Rome together?"

"What?" I look around, as if I'm being spied on at that very moment, and go farther into the house, until I find a smallish office and shut the door. "I'm actually at his house right now, but . . ." I look around at the artwork and try not to choke on my champagne. The Matisse with the palm tree from the hotel room in the South of France; a Léger nude; a few small statues—I think one might be a Picasso goat. *Well, that figures. Randy bastard.*

I turn my attention back to Alexei. "What was that?"

"Miki! What the hell are you thinking? No contact, remember? We agreed no contact with Clairebeau until after the two weeks—"

"Alexei! I couldn't help it!" I turn angry, instead of defensive. "And how could Durchenko know any of this, anyway? I'm at my friend Margot's wedding, and it turns out her husband and Rome are cousins. It's nothing to do with business."

"It's always to do with business, Miki." Alexei sighs and sounds like he is ready to explode. "Please tell me Aziza Mahdi is not there."

"Of course she's here. She's Rome's fiancée. What does she have to do with anything?"

"Rome is such an idiot," Alexei says under his breath.

"Well, at last we agree—"

"Oh, not in that way. I mean, I kind of admire him, I must say. But he's playing it a bit deep, don't you think?"

"Playing what deep?"

"Didn't he tell you?"

"Tell me what?"

"Miki, what are you doing in here?" Rome enters the office and shuts the door behind him. I am so screwed.

"I have to go," I snap quickly, turning off my phone and shoving it back into my purse. "Nothing," I reply to Rome. I try to casually walk toward the door. "I just needed to take that call, and I didn't want to be rude at the party."

Rome is blocking my way, kind of nonchalantly but with a hint of menace that prevents me from leaving the room. His strong, wide chest is like a wall between the exit and me. "Landon checking in again?"

"Damn it, Rome. I broke up with Landon, okay? Would you just drop it? Why do you even care?"

He looks startled and then furious. "Why do I care? I guess that's the question, isn't it? Why do I care about a woman who thinks I'm ridiculous—"

"I don't." He looks so *not* ridiculous right now, in his bespoke suit fitted so beautifully to his amazing body. And his eyes are so serious.

"A woman who thinks I'm a womanizing playboy—"

"But you are!" I want to sound full of conviction, but my voice cracks, because he doesn't look at all like a womanizing playboy right now. Instead, he looks like he wants to pull me against him and never let go, until we're both soldered to each other. The rest of the world can go to hell.

He reaches for me, and I'm actually afraid of how much I want him, so I recoil from the power of our connection. I will hate myself if I give in to him like this. "You're engaged," I whisper.

He reaches out one hand and rests it against my cheek, and my eyes close involuntarily as I lean into the small touch. "What if I were free?"

My heart—my stupid heart—pounds to the galloping beat of what-if-what-if-what-if. "But you're not. You're not free, Rome." I pull his hand gently away from my face.

The door swings open, and it's Aziza and she's definitely been crying this time, not just disturbed-about-something crying, but actual puffy-eyed bawling. "Oh! I'm sorry to interrupt!" She starts to pull the door shut.

"No!" I practically shout. "Come back. I was just finishing a phone call, and I didn't realize it was Rome's study. I'm sorry." I walk to the door, cutting a wide berth around Rome. "I didn't want to talk on my cell phone in the middle of the party. I'm just leaving."

"Okay," Azi says softly, then turns to look at Rome as he's looking at me, and I want to slap him hard across the face. Aziza looks so desperate and sweet. I feel like the worst person in history—or at least like I've been influenced by the worst person in history. I scowl at Rome and close the door behind me.

I start to walk away, but I pause when I hear Rome yelling at Aziza about how foolish she is and how she has no sense, and I am tempted to go back into the room and bash him over the head with one of those priceless Giacomettis I spied in the corner while he was asking me stupid questions about Landon. What kind of bastard yells at his fiancée when she's just walked in on *him* coming on to another woman?

I can still hear Aziza crying as I turn toward the entrance of the house. I want to get as far away from all this chaos as I can. My phone vibrates again, and I pull it out and lean against a large door near the kitchen. I hope that the bustle of the catering staff will drown out my conversation.

"Alexei, what the hell is going on?"

"Pavel Durchenko—"

"What about him? I am at my best friend's wedding, and I've had enough of this bullshit. We will get back to him in a week. Just tell him to back off—"

"He and Aziza Mahdi have been together for the past year . . . secretly."

"What?" My voice is more like a high-pitched, strangled squeal.

"Shhh," Alexei hisses into the phone. "No one knows. Well, I suspect Rome knows and that's why they're getting married, to help her get out of a terrible situation. And now Durchenko thinks you're in on that or something. He is so livid, Miki, I honestly thought he was going to whip out his gun and shoot me just because we're related—"

"He's there in Paris?"

"Yes. And he has photos of you all at some church a few hours ago. He's obsessed with spy photos. Well, that part was quite good, actually."

"Alexei!"

"Sorry. I just mean he's got all the latest gadgets and the best people working for him, so be careful—"

"Be careful?" I half whisper, half squeal again. "How the hell am I supposed to be careful?" I look down at myself. "I am at a wedding in the South of France in a skimpy silk dress and a pair of way-too-high heels—"

"I saw in the photos. You look very pretty."

"Alexei. Seriously. I meant I am in no position to defend myself if Durchenko loses his temper about all this. I refuse to get dragged into some sordid love triangle. Does any of it have to do with Segezha?"

"Yes, I get the feeling it's all somehow related. Apparently, Clairebeau's been trying to make a side deal with Kriegsbeil, and now Durchenko is yelling about how Rome had better mind his own business. I'll get to the bottom of it. Don't worry—"

"I'm already worried! Do you want me to come back to Paris? I was going to stay a few extra days, but I can be on the train tomorrow."

He hesitates. "Maybe I should come down there instead, and we can all work together. Is Rome staying in Provence, too?"

"How should I know?"

"Oh. I thought maybe—"

"Well, don't think, all right? There's nothing going on with Rome and me, and there never will be!"

And of course that's the moment Rome happens to walk down the hall and turn to face me in the alcove, like I'm some interloper in his house, his beautiful house—because I *am* an interloper in his house. He shakes his head slowly and keeps walking, as if my words are just one more Judas kiss in an infinite receiving line of Judas kisses.

I curse myself and Alexei and tell him I'll call him later. He tells me he'll be back in touch about whether he's coming down to Provence. When I go back out to the party, I try to put on my happy face for Margot's sake. Other than avoiding Rome—which isn't too hard, since I can tell he really wants nothing to do with me at this point—I end up having a pretty great time. Étienne's cousins from London are tons of fun. Trevor's brothers are really interesting—one of them is a horse breeder who splits his time between Ireland and Dubai and who's going to buy some horses in Ojai later in the year. We exchange phone numbers and agree to meet up for dinner if we're both in LA at the same time.

Unfortunately, Zoe, the reporter, is relentless. She asks me all sorts of inane questions about my mother, and I keep trying to steer the conversation back to Margot and Étienne. She keeps trying to fob me off.

"Oh, no one really cares about Étienne's second marriage." She moves in closer to let me in on her secret. "The real reason I came was to get a closer look at Jérôme de Villiers and Aziza Mahdi." Zoe's look is scheming as she takes a sip of wine and stares at Rome across the grassy area where he is talking to Margot's father. I watch as he inhales on his cigarette, and I want to rip it out of his hand. I've noticed he's been smoking a lot this weekend, the stress of everything probably getting to him. Just because he's a dishonest bastard is no reason he should die of lung cancer.

"Really?" I try to act disinterested.

Her head swings around to face me. "Of course, really! He's impossible to reach; he never gives interviews, even though I'm his cousin's cousin!" She seems genuinely affronted. "It could really launch my career to get some sort of exclusive scoop about him and Aziza. I'm thinking maybe she's not really going to marry him at all, right? That she's just using him to get out of some old-fashioned arranged marriage back in Somalia or some other sticky situation. There are tons of rumors going around that she's a real trollop—sleazy Russian-billionaire boyfriends and all that."

I just won my second imaginary Oscar.

"I mean, sorry—I forgot you're half Russian, aren't you?"

"Just the sleazy half."

She bursts out laughing. "Good one. You got me. Sorry—just a slip of the tongue. You know how it is."

She laughs again, retelling the joke to herself, probably committing it to memory for future reuse. She keeps staring at Rome, then lets her attention slip over to the other side of the party, where Aziza and Lulu are laughing at something Trevor is saying. "They don't look very in love for two people who just got engaged, do you think?"

I take another sip of wine and make some sort of grunting, noncommittal reply.

Zoe shrugs. "Oh well. You're no help. And Étienne has already told me he'll never speak to me again if I publish anything without his permission, but it's my life, too, right?"

I don't know why Zoe has latched onto me as her working-girl partner in crime, but I need to break off the conversation before I let something slip. "Sorry, Zoe. I just remembered something I need to tell Margot. I'll be right back."

"Sure, sure." She is already distracted, watching Rome like a shark circling slowly until she smells blood in the water.

I know I am probably getting tipsy, because my visits to the bathroom are becoming more frequent. By eight o'clock, it is starting to get dark and people are getting ready to leave, so I go for one last time before the four of us—Jules, Trevor, Lulu, and I—make the drive home.

I am humming and wending my way up the narrow stone stairs at the back of the hall near the kitchen, when I feel the air shift. I swing around. Rome is standing right behind me. He looks over one shoulder, then shoves me up the rest of the stairs and into the tiny bathroom, until the two of us are enclosed in the small, private space.

I back away from him a pace, but he closes the distance between us in an instant and grabs the flesh of my inner thigh with one hand. I bite down on my lower lip to stop myself from groaning.

"This dress is too short," he says in a low, menacing voice. His hand begins to knead its way up my thigh.

"What do you care?" I taunt him. I've had one too many glasses of champagne, and suddenly I don't give a fig if he's engaged or if I'm going to get mown down by some angry oligarch. I just want his hands my body. Everyone else can deal with their own problems.

He puts his face right in front of mine, staring at me desperately, looking at my eyes, my lips, down the front of my dress, then back into my eyes. I think he is going to talk, but he just keeps staring at me like that. My breath is short; I just want to smell him all around me, to breathe him in. I shut my eyes and lean into him, shifting my thigh to force his hand even higher up my leg.

"Kiss me, Rome, please," I beg.

"Miki," he whispers in my ear, then licks the tender edge with the tip of his tongue. I moan and push my hips against his hand. He reaches his other hand up and grabs my loose hair into a rough hold. "Look at me . . ."

I open my eyes. He is so heated, his eyes snapping and firing, those tiny yellow spindles bright. His lips are barely opened, but the glistening skin just inside his mouth makes me weak. I lean in to taste him. He tugs on my hair to stop me from slipping back into that dreamy state.

"Miki." Even though he whispers my name, it comes out with harsh finality. "Tell me . . ." He kisses me, and it's almost a punishment. "Tell me this is real." His hand fists more tightly in my hair. "Tell me you trust me."

God, I want him. So badly. But nothing feels real. And trust is about the last thing I feel for anyone right now. I shake my head slowly, wanting him and doubting him all at once. "I have nothing to go on. You're hiding things from me—"

"That is all bullshit, and you know it. Aziza has drawn me into a fucking viper pit with these stupid secrets, and I'm going to have to deal with it in my own way."

"What about the Segezha deal?"

He falters, but only for a second. "What about it? None of that matters. I am not hiding anything when it comes to my feelings for you. I have never—"

"Never what? Never wanted something and not been able to have it in five minutes or less?" My anger is starting to bubble up. "You're spoiled, Rome. You want me?" I lean in and kiss him, wet and messy and tipsy. "Want me to get on my knees again . . ." I start to bend down, and he whips me up so we are eye to eye.

"Miki, stop it."

"Because you know I want it, isn't that it? And you can't figure out why I keep trying to get away from you. Well, I'll tell you why: Because you are so bad for me, Rome, that's why! You make me want to beg and be a liar and a cheat. You want to take things from me that I can never get back . . ."

I'm sort of crying like one of those crazy women on late-night Spanish television by this point. He loosens his hold in my hair and tries to soothe away my hurt, and the slow intimacy is far worse than the rough passion. His tenderness feels far too real.

"Please don't," I whisper, but I think he can tell his kindness is going to break me.

He leans in and kisses me, so soft and gentle, his tongue a sweet promise that merely glances against my lips. "I meant what I said in Saint Petersburg," he whispers. "You deserve perfect." He kisses me one more time, then turns and leaves the bathroom, and I'm standing there gasping and breathless, unsure of what just happened. Is he going to be the one to give me perfect, or is he going to leave me alone so I can forget about him and find some imaginary future perfect?

I turn to see myself in the mirror and don't know whether to laugh or cry. I'm a wreck. We've all been dancing for hours, so everyone at the party is a bit mussed, but the kissing and the crying have made me look just like the crazy Telemundo woman I imagined earlier. I take a few deep breaths, then clean myself up as best I can. I splash my face with cool water and pat it dry with a linen hand towel, then go back to the party.

Luckily, Rome and Aziza have gone off somewhere in the house or garden by the time I wander downstairs. Margot is sitting on

Étienne's lap, and Lulu and Trevor are slow-dancing to the acoustic guitarist from the band. The rest of the musicians are packing up.

Diana, Margot's mother, is barefoot and swaying with her arms around her husband. Jules looks happy and tired. I go and sit down next to him.

"What did I miss?"

"Oh. Were you gone?"

That answers that. "No, not really, just to the loo for a few minutes. Looks like everything is winding down. Should we head back home?"

"Sure. Why don't we ask Lulu and Trevor if we can make our way back once they're done . . . you know . . ."

I look in the direction he is looking and see how Lulu is staring into Trevor's eyes under a stray beam of moonlight. The guitarist is playing a few sweet chords from that old Oasis song, and, Jesus, they look so happy, it gives me chills. Jules watches them like a science experiment. I wonder if he is even capable of imagining that type of intimacy. Probably not.

I know I am. I can still feel Rome's lips against mine. But even more devastating was the way he asked me to trust him, the way he looked at me like I was the first—and maybe the last—person he has ever asked that of. And I'm not sure I will ever be able to.

I am perfectly capable of imagining Rome's hands at my lower back, and lower still, like Trevor's are against Lulu. I can imagine looking into Rome's eyes with that longing. My stomach goes into free fall. Again.

I suppose I need to get used to these moments of profound longing. I'm beginning to see why my mother just indulged herself.

The musician finally strums the last chords and smiles up at Lulu and Trevor. The three of them speak quietly to one another and then say good-bye. Aziza and Rome come out of the house holding hands, and I try not to stare. God damn him. I have to get out of here.

Margot stands up, and we all smile and hug and look around to make sure no one has left anything. Étienne and Rome are arguing about money—Rome insisting he always meant to pay for the entire wedding when he offered to host it, and Étienne sort of furious and grateful and buzzed all at once. Margot simply beams with happiness. She hugs Rome and thanks him again and tells him he's *the worst*, but then I hear her tell him he's the greatest. I know the feeling.

I turn before Rome has a chance to say good-bye to me, and I walk to the outer courtyard with oblivious Jules. Lulu and Trevor take Jules and me in their car again, and the Montespans go with Margot and Étienne. The newlyweds have decided to postpone their honeymoon until later in the summer, once Étienne's current case-load is lighter. Meanwhile, Margot keeps saying she is thrilled to have an extended house party until then.

I hate to be so selfish, but after all that drama in the bathroom, all I keep thinking is that one day, one fine day, I will be driving home from my own wedding with a man holding my hand and look-ing at me the way Étienne was looking at Margot. Perfectly content, as if everything in the world in that moment is perfectly *enough*.

CHAPTER NINETEEN

Sunday morning I wake up to the sound of Zoe shoving all her stuff into her bag.

"What's up?" I ask, opening one eye and then slipping deeper under the cool cotton sheets. The windows are open, and the morning air is chilly and gorgeous. I want to stay in bed for days.

"Rome and Aziza are going back to Paris earlier than expected, and he offered me a seat on his private plane. Can you stand it?"

I feel like groaning but smile instead. "Isn't the TGV just as fast?"

Zoe turns to look at me like I'm some sort of imbecile. "Rome de Villiers's private jet? Did you hear me? I'll get to see the two of them up close and personal."

I smile because she's kind of adorable and I get what she's saying. It's her job and she's excited. "Oh, fine. Have fun chasing your big story."

I pretend to sleep until after I hear Rome's car peel out of the driveway and I'm sure they're all gone.

"You just missed Aziza and Rome and Zoe," Margot says over the rim of her mug. "Nice timing."

"Not too hard to figure their comings and goings when he drives a car that's louder than the Indy 500." I pour myself a cup of coffee and reach for the paper. "I can't believe you still get an actual newspaper."

"Trevor's old-fashioned—and an early riser. He always goes into town first thing and brings back croissants and a few papers."

"I'm not complaining." I flip through the pages and pause and smile at a small black-and-white photo of my mother in Cairo. She looks daring and happy with a *Lawrence of Arabia*–type white scarf wrapped around her head. I don't love how her daring personality affected my childhood, but at fifty-three, she kind of has it all going on.

Margot looks over my shoulder. "Is that your mom?"

"Yeah. Doesn't she look great?"

Margot stares at me, then back at the paper. "Yeah. Crazy, but great." Margot pats my shoulder and gets up from the table. "I'm going back to bed." She winks at me and points upstairs. "First day of my honeymoon and all that. Ariel is off with her grandparents for the week."

"Off you go, then. Can I borrow your car and do a little shopping? Maybe make some lunch?"

"Sure. That would be perfect. The shops are open for a couple of hours this morning, but then they close for the rest of the day. The keys are in the dish by the front door. Take my Peugeot. Lulu and Trev usually come back down around ten."

"Okay." I smile and go back to the paper. It is like a commune, for goodness' sake, all these happy people living under one roof.

I drive into town, park in the central square, and walk up the narrow street to the small market for cheeses and fruit. I flirt with the handsome young man behind the counter, asking him how long he's lived here (born here, of course) and his recommendations for the best bread and meats. I don't know what it is about a man in an apron, but I love it.

Next I go to the *boucherie* and buy a beautiful rack of lamb that I watch the butcher trim and wrap while his wife makes fresh sausages. Everything about this place makes me miss California . . . not one bit. Well, I miss the waves, actually, but everything about how these people live their lives *right now* and not on some treadmill to save up for the weekend or vacation or some other far-off *goal* kind of makes me shiver with happiness.

Then I go back down the narrow, steep street to the *boulangerie* to get a few batons of bread and a glistening apricot tart for dessert. I drive back to Margot's place, and when I walk into the kitchen, Lulu and Trevor are reading the paper and drinking coffee.

"Hey, did you find everything?" Lulu asks, looking up from the paper.

"Yes. Oh my gosh, it's so beautiful here," I say with a happy sigh as I begin to unpack all the things I bought for lunch. "You guys have landed in paradise."

"It's pretty great, right?" Trevor is smiling and looking at the paper at the same time. "Do you think you'll stay for a while?"

I take out the food and set all the packages out on the counter, then start looking around for a few pans and platters. "I would love to, but I think things are about to explode at work. My uncle's pretty much freaking out, so"—I pull my head out from under the counter and turn to face them—"probably not more than a couple of days, but once things settle down, I'm definitely coming back."

"Good!" Lulu exclaims. "I'm so sorry again for all my gushing about Rome's place yesterday."

I begin making a rub for the lamb while I talk. "It's okay. I don't know if Margot told you, but I've actually had some business dealings with Rome, and it was kind of awkward. But it's not a big deal. I just wasn't expecting to see him, you know, socially. But I shouldn't have snapped at you. I'm sorry again."

"Oh, gosh. It was totally my fault. And no, Margot hasn't said anything. I can't believe you're, like, this big, important businessperson all of a sudden."

I sort of laugh through my words. "Me neither. I'm trying to rely on my strengths—math and statistics and all that—but my uncle is pretty confident that I can handle the rest of it: negotiating with clients, all the other public stuff. It's just going to be a really steep learning curve."

"You should talk to Trevor," Lulu says. I have my doubts about how this British layabout can assist with my internecine business dealings, so I simply smile and nod.

"Yes, let me know if you want any help," Trevor offers, still reading the paper.

I'm rubbing the herbs into the lamb, when I decide to pry. "So, what do you do, exactly, Trevor?"

The paper goes down so I can see his face. "This and that. Like you, I'm interested in numbers."

Lulu punches him in the shoulder. "He's being stupid. He's a total financial genius. He trades everything from metals I've never even heard of to boatloads of copper and whatnot. Why are you so secretive about it?"

I stare at this man in his ripped Glastonbury T-shirt and Vilebrequin swimming trunks and start to laugh. "You're a commodities trader working out of a farm in the Luberon?"

He smiles and shrugs. "I guess you could say that."

"Excellent." I shake my head. Landon and that picket fence are starting to feel so faraway, so irrelevant. "I might have some questions for you after all. There's a factory deal in Russia that's been giving me some trouble—"

"Segezha?" he asks, with a partial smile.

"Yeah," I half laugh. "Segezha. You've heard of it?" I shake my head again and smile.

"Yes, I've heard of it. It's like a toy that all the kids on the playground suddenly want."

"Something like that."

I set some carrots and potatoes to roast in the oven and finish by making a big salad. "Shall we eat outside?"

"Definitely," Lulu agrees. "I'll set the table."

About an hour later, Étienne and Margot are downstairs in all their honeymoon swooniness and the lamb is almost done and we've opened a crisp bottle of rosé and we're sitting outside at the huge stone table, about to have lunch. I get up to check the lamb, which has been slow-roasting on the grill for about an hour and looks just about perfect.

And then I hear the roar of that godforsaken race car in the driveway.

"Oh! Is that Rome? What is he doing back?" Lulu perks up, then catches my eye and pretends to be disinterested.

Seriously. Is the man just going to torment me endlessly?

Étienne gets up and goes to the front door, and, sure enough, he returns a few minutes later with Rome, who is smiling and patting Étienne's back.

"What the hell?" I mutter as I lift the hood of the grill and put the meat on the wooden platter to set for a few minutes. He comes right over to me, the idiot, and kisses me on both cheeks.

"Miki. How are you this afternoon? I missed you this morning when I came by to pick up Zoe."

"I was asleep."

He smiles. "Sorry I missed that," he murmurs. And then turns to face Margot and Étienne. "I hope I'm not imposing."

"Of course not," Margot says cheerfully, then looks at me. "I mean . . . we have enough food, right, Miki?"

There's enough food for an army. I was extremely enthusiastic at the market with the cute shopkeeper. Everything's already out on the table—the roasted vegetables, the huge salad, several cheeses and breads. I nod.

Rome rubs his hands together. "Great. It smells wonderful. I didn't know you could cook, Miki." He's standing too close to me again, near the stone grill, and I want to spear him with the long fork.

"I just follow recipes."

He lifts his chin like he doesn't really believe me, but maybe he's done messing with me for a while.

"I thought you went back to Paris." It comes out sounding like he's a bad penny that keeps turning up, but that only makes him smile more.

"I just wanted to get rid of Zoe. And Azi had to get back for a work thing. So I figured it was only an hour or so to come on back and hang out with you all." He turns from me to face Étienne. "I also brought some wine. Let me go get it out of the car."

I take a deep breath when he's gone back into the house and he's out of earshot. I'm still holding the grilling fork and I'm using it like a conductor's baton—or an épée, I think viciously. I gesture with it while I talk. "What the hell is he doing here?"

"I think he likes you," says Lulu innocently.

"You think?" Margot razzes.

"But he's engaged to Azi." Lulu looks to Trevor as if he would know, because obviously the facts no longer make sense to her. She's always trying to believe the best about people. "So that can't be right . . ." Her voice trails off as she tries to figure out some way in which everyone can be a good person in this scenario.

I wave the fork. "Exactly! It is not right, Lulu. He just does whatever the hell he wants without—" I stop talking when I see him through the kitchen window, unloading the bottles of wine. He comes out a few minutes later with two unmarked bottles of red wine. I assume they're from the co-op at the bottom of the hill, but I'm quickly reeducated.

Étienne sits up straighter when he sees the bottles. "Should I put on a tie?"

"Very funny. It's just wine. A little wedding present." Rome removes the corks from the two bottles as he talks, and then he pours some of the wine into the empty wineglasses on the table. I'm still standing by the grill, not wanting to be part of whatever it is that's going on with this French wine foolishness.

Looking as if he'd dive into his glass if he could, Étienne takes a tentative sip and lets it rest in his mouth, then does a quick swish and swallows. When he opens his eyes, he turns to Margot and kisses her passionately, like he's already drunk after one sip. "I love you," he whispers.

"I need to have some of that," Margot says with a laugh, then takes a sip from her own glass. "Oh, Lord," she whispers.

"Good, right?" Rome says, still swishing and sniffing his around in his big glass.

Lulu and Trevor are the next willing victims, sipping the wine and swooning like fools. I think Lulu actually shudders.

"Miki?" Rome asks, holding his glass toward me.

"No, thank you. I'm fine with the rosé."

"Oh, Miki, you have to." Lulu is being Tigger again. My look silences her. "Or not. More for us—right, Trev?"

"Right, darling." He kisses her cheek, then looks over his shoulder to make sure I'm okay. There's something British and gentlemanly about Trevor that makes me feel safer than I would with all these seductive Frenchmen everywhere. "How's the lamb doing?" Trevor asks.

"Done." I pick up the platter and set it in the middle of the big table. "*Bon appétit*." At least I hope they can all enjoy it. I've totally lost my appetite.

"Looks gorgeous. Thanks for letting me crash." Rome slips one leg and then the other over the stone bench alongside the table and sits down. Of course, the only place left is between him and Étienne, and it would be immature and ridiculous for me to scurry off to my room and hide. Even though that's exactly what I want to do.

I sigh and sit down next to him. He pours me a glass of the

magical red wine and encourages me to have a sip with a nudge of his shoulder against mine. "Go on. It's just wine. Take a sip."

"Oh, fine." I reach for it with a snippy attitude, and he puts his hand on my arm to stop me.

Margot quickly starts serving the food and making small talk with Étienne and Lulu about how delicious everything looks, to distract them.

"You can be mad at me," he says softly, "but don't be mad when you take your first sip of this."

I set the glass down. "Are you going to try to tell me how to drink a glass of wine?"

Lulu laughs, then tries not to keep laughing. Rome smiles at her, as if I am the one who's such a spoilsport. I breathe in and try not to feel like I have a radioactive love machine sitting two inches to my left. "Fine." I smile thinly and reach for the glass. "Here goes." I take a sniff, and as much as I want to hate it, it's one of the most wonderful things I've ever smelled in my life. As with Étienne, I kind of want to burrow down into the glass and never come out. Just from smelling it.

Rome is still swirling his around and watching me be seduced by his damn wine.

I take a sip. At that moment, my bitterness flies away, because it is simply one of the most pleasurable experiences of my life—the taste of the natural embodiment of the earth and the sun. It makes me feel as if I am part of the universe or something extraordinary that people who write about wine probably have a better way of describing. To me, it just tastes like love. On my lips. Down my throat. Warm in my belly.

I open my eyes and realize the other five are staring at me. Margot looks a little guilty, despite herself, like she tried to warn me.

"Hmmm," Rome hums, kind of a question and a victory all at once. "So you like it?"

"Yes. Who wouldn't like it? It's delicious." I put it back down and pretend that I don't want to cradle it against me for the rest of the meal. It's probably obscenely expensive, and I don't want to encourage him.

Of course, Rome never needs encouragement.

"So?" Étienne prompts. "What is it?"

"It's the 1982 Pauillac," Rome explains.

"I knew it!" Étienne cries, smacking his fist on the stone surface and dipping his nose into the glass for another soul-satisfying sniff. "Damn it, Rome. You shouldn't have."

"It's peaking. We need to drink it. And you get married only once—or, in your case, twice, but I suspect this is a long-term hold. Am I right?"

Étienne smiles at his cousin, then pulls Margot close. "Definitely. But still, this is too much."

I begin filling my plate with salad and vegetables and slicing off a few pieces of the lamb, and then Rome is doing the same. After a few minutes, we've all piled our plates with food, and before anyone takes a bite, Rome raises his glass.

"To Margot. The perfect woman for Étienne."

"To Margot!" everyone chimes in, and Margot looks sweet and sort of embarrassed, then jokes, "Does this mean I can't drink if the toast is in my honor?"

Rome laughs. "This, you can always drink."

She takes a sip, and then we all dig into the food. I'm not a gourmet or anything, but I do love to cook when I feel like it. Everything just tastes fresh and delicious, and everyone is loving it. The wine doesn't hurt. Apparently, this is a family game the Rothschild cousins play, bringing unmarked bottles of Lafite or Mouton Rothschild and then trying to guess the vintages or vineyards.

It's good to be the king.

After he pours me a second glass and he's not pestering me too much, I turn to steal a glance at Rome while he's talking to Trevor about a deal Clairebeau is working on in Milan. I know he senses I'm paying attention, but he doesn't slow down the conversation. I take another sip of the wine and slip deeper into the wonderful lull of friends and food and this spectacular place in the world.

He turns to me slowly, his lips on the edge of his glass, and takes a sip. Margot and Étienne are all lovey-dovey—and why shouldn't they be, after one day of wedded bliss? Lulu and Trevor are talking about a piece of furniture she's working on. And Rome is staring at me while that enchanted wine slides past those lips.

Fine. I look. And start not to care about fiancées again. My heart tightens in my chest. I put the wineglass down and look away from him, out across the valley, beyond the swimming pool and the ancient hedges and rough ground.

"Miki?" His voice is mellow.

"Yes?" I don't want to face him.

"We need to talk."

"Fine." I look at my hands, then up into his eyes. "You want to go for a walk?" I suggest.

"Sure." He smiles at the idea. "Then we'll have coffee and that apricot tart."

"Okay." I stand up and pull my long legs out from under the stone table. I can feel Rome staring at my bare thighs, almost as if he has his actual hands on me. "Excuse us for a few minutes, will you?" I ask Margot.

She looks up at me. "You okay?"

I love her for that. She's not going to let me get hornswoggled by a bottle of wine and a few suggestive glances.

"Yeah, I'm good. We've got some business to discuss."

Rome rolls his eyes. He puts his hand at the small of my back and guides me toward a path at the far end of the pool. After Rome and I have walked about ten minutes, through the oak grove and then farther, into terraced rows of olive trees, he puts his palm on my bare neck and I stop walking.

"Miki?"

I turn to face him. "Are you engaged to Aziza or not?" I blurt. "No hedging. No story. Just the truth."

He looks up to the sky and shakes his head, then looks me right in the eye. "Yes, but it might not be for long."

I know it's immature, but my first impulse is to kick him in the shin. I don't, but I really want to. I want to throw sand in his eyes and pull his hair and do every angry, juvenile thing I can think of—because he is so awful. "Take your hand off me." His fingers have started massaging my neck where it meets my shoulder, and it reminds me of how he did that same thing the first morning in Saint Petersburg, and how good it felt.

He lets his hand fall away slowly. "Why can't you trust me, Miki? There are things going on with Aziza, and I'm just helping her through—"

"Alexei told me. I don't care if she's secretly in love with Durchenko and you're some sort of front or bait or some shit. It's all the drama. Don't you get it? You are an adrenaline junkie who thrives on all this chaos. That is exactly what I don't want."

He looks around, and I realize we are standing in a quintessentially bucolic and peaceful place. The trees sway gently around us; the cicadas are beginning to saw in the late-afternoon sun.

He smiles ironically and says, "Yes. It's very chaotic here."

My heart loves that shit. My romantic, fast-beating heart is trying to tell me this is a wonderful man and this is his strange way of courting me. My rational mind tells me he just wants what he wants. He wants to get me back in his bed, and maybe we'll even be a couple for a while, but then he'll get bored. We will peak, like one of those expensive wines, and then he'll be on to the next premium vintage.

"Rome, I like you."

He practically chokes on how trite that sounds.

"What?"

I'm trying to stay calm. "I like you. We had a sweet time in Saint Petersburg. We're obviously attracted to each other."

His eyes narrow like he can't believe what he's hearing. That he's being reduced to an episode.

"But seriously?" I shake my head cynically and fold my arms in front of my chest. He stares at me, and I think maybe I've succeeded in fending him off.

"Yes, Miki. Seriously."

Not quite. Not at all. He reaches up and touches the edge of my lower lip, slowly tracing his finger along the sensitive skin, and it causes a bolt of sexual excitement to shoot down my spine. That tiny touch, and I'm just . . . mush.

"Rome." I reach up and move his hand away from my mouth, but I'm still holding his wrist in both of my hands. I lean in and kiss his fingertips. "I can't. I can't be this crazy, free-spirited lover you're looking for."

"That's not what I'm looking for, damn it. I'm looking for *you.*"

My body goes berserk—tingling and desperate. "You don't even know me," I breathe out.

"That is such bullshit." He yanks his hand away, and I'm simultaneously relieved and bereft. "You're just scared—"

"Damn straight I'm scared!" I'm breathing heavily now, from a combination of wanting him and wanting to protect myself. "I'm terrified. You're everything that screwed up my parents' life—*my life*—all wrapped up in one super-hot, tempting package." I start enumerating, raising one finger as I begin. "One: blind passion.

Great—we were great in bed. So what? That always fizzles. That's not something to build a future on. Two: you are fucking *engaged.* That is not a maybe-I-might-move-in-with-my-cardiologist-boyfriend misdemeanor. That is you planning to marry someone I've met—and actually admire, from what little I know of her. And—"

He tries to interrupt, but I won't hear it.

"No! I don't want to know that it's some sham engagement to do with Durchenko. That still makes you the type of psycho who would actually agree to such a thing."

He recoils slightly at that. "Fuck you," he says.

"Well. That's better. I'm a bitch. Nice to meet you." I extend my hand in a mock introduction.

He slaps it away, and then it's his turn to point his finger in my face. "You never called me, Miki. Nothing. And don't you dare pretend you wanted me to call you! You made it perfectly clear in Saint Petersburg that you wanted me to *respect your real life*—I think was how you put it. And I did that. The past two months have been miserable! And not because you are some quick fix I want in my bed, damn you. I wish it were that simple. Let's fuck and get it out of our systems—is that it? I'm happy to try that route, by the way." He smiles for a split second, then scowls. "But you're a liar—if not to me, than to yourself. What we shared in Saint Petersburg might have been torrid, but it was still real." He pushes his finger into my chest on that last word. "Real."

"Stop," I whisper. "Just stop. If you weren't engaged . . ."

He grabs hold of his own head. "Then what?" When he lets go of his thick black hair, he looks kind of insane—still sexy, of course, but wacked. "Miki . . . Azi is really in a bad spot. She's pregnant with Durchenko's baby, and maybe he'll come through in the end—they actually love each other, for some fucked-up reason—but if she has this baby out of wedlock, her father will disown her. Literally. Disown her. Or have her stoned to death or some shit. He's a goddamned fundamentalist Somali warlord. He's already irate that she's refused to do any of his arranged-marriage crap, but she convinced him of that, at least. But if she has this baby?" Rome shakes his head. "He'll go off the deep end. And why should I break it off anyway, especially if you think I'm some playboy lightweight bullshit artist? Why would I abandon a real friend, someone who respects me, to be with someone who thinks I'm a two-dimensional buffoon? Who thinks I've agreed to marry a friend because I'm some sort of adrenaline junkie? So, yes, fuck you." He turns around and walks back toward the house.

My heart is racing from everything he's said, and I realize I'm crying because he's made up of so many parts I don't understand—but it doesn't make me want him any less. He also reveals parts of me that I don't fully understand, and he's right: I'm both afraid and lying to myself. I'm afraid of how much he makes me feel, even though we've been around each other only for these short, intense times. And I'm lying to myself because I don't think I would ever tire of waking up next to him, or going to sleep next to him, or working at a large partners' desk across from him. In fact, I can't really imagine a situation in which I wouldn't want to be near him. Tucked into him.

"Fuck." So now it's all on me to declare some undying faith in our burgeoning maybe-relationship? For that to be enough for him? For me to have faith in him?

Faith? I don't have faith in people. I was raised by faithless wolves. That's one of those learned human traits—nurture versus nature—that I most definitely did not learn. And he knows that about me, so why is he asking me to do the impossible?

I walk slowly back toward the house and dry my eyes with the edge of my T-shirt. Maybe there's some of that mystical wine left over for me to drown my sorrows in.

CHAPTER TWENTY

Alexei calls first thing Monday morning. "I didn't bother you on Sunday; did you notice?"

I stretch out, enjoying the quiet bedroom, with Zoe gone. But it's still really early.

"Yes, I noticed, Alexei. Thank you for that. But it isn't even seven—"

"Good. Okay. Now, back to work. Do you still want me to come down there? I'm happy to meet you in Monaco or wherever. We're going to need to do a press conference soon. The *Financial Times* has been in touch with the head office, and I've been getting a few calls from our PR department in Saint Petersburg. The board is also getting itchy about whether or not you are permanent. Maybe we can do that from Nice. Paris is gray and boring."

"Sure, we can work down here if you want." I dread the idea of willingly standing in front of a roomful of reporters, but I remind myself I'll probably be of little interest to anyone other than a few financial journalists. I force myself awake when I realize Alexei's not going to take a hint and let me go back to sleep. "Hop on the train, and I'll pick you up in Avignon this afternoon."

"Well, actually . . . Rome said he'd send his plane up for me."

"What the hell?" I'm fully awake now. "Is he running a shuttle service?"

"I think he'd just send the plane, you know, as a courtesy."

"I thought you weren't in touch with him. When did he offer said courtesy?" I ask suspiciously.

"Well, he and I were talking about the big picture . . ." Alexei's voice trails off.

"Really. The big picture. Enlighten me."

"Well, I was thinking . . ."

"Oh, god. You've been thinking again? What now, Alexei?" I sit up straighter in bed. "Maybe we should just merge Voyanovski Industries with Clairebeau and go head-to-head with Durchenko so all of us can spend every waking hour in close contact, arguing with each other."

"I knew you would already have thought of it."

I shove the sheets off me and leap out of bed. "I was being facetious!" I start pacing around the room.

"It makes sense, Miki. Listen to me. We need to at least start talking about it. Clairebeau has been angling to expand into some of the supply chain and manufacturing."

"Alexei. How could you enter negotiations of this magnitude without telling me?"

"We haven't entered into any negotiations! It just happened—"

"When?"

"Last night." He sounds like his stupid, sheepish self. "He called me here in Paris."

"Of course he did."

"Look, Miki. Your father and Rome talked about this on and off for years. He would definitely want to keep you on board—"

"I bet he would."

"I mean, he promises he'd keep the whole company intact."

Oh, god. Rome as my boss? If he can't have me in his bed, he'll just muscle his way into my life some other way. I try to separate out my feelings from the reality of what Alexei is suggesting. He's right that in the grand scheme of things, it makes perfect sense. Rome is a businessman at heart, and he would never do something specifically to spite me. If it happened to turn out that way, he'd just see it as a bonus.

"The world is made up of conglomerates, Miki—"

"I know that! Just stop. I don't want to hear another word out of you," I hiss. "I need to get my mind around this. Just give me a couple of hours to separate the personal crap from the deal, all right?"

"Okay. Yes, that sounds good. Take some time to start thinking, and then call me back."

"Alexei." I sit back on the bed and want to smash something. "We need to hash this out in person. And obviously I need some sort of initial deal memorandum from Rome."

"Yes, he wants that, too. He wants to work with us both. All the way through the deal."

Of course he does. The idea of working all the way through anything with Rome simultaneously nauseates me and turns me on.

"Where is he now?" I ask.

"He's still there in Provence, at his place."

His château, I want to add venomously, but I manage to stay silent.

"Miki, I know it's a lot all at once, but we need to act quickly if we are going to present a united front against Durchenko and Kriegsbeil. Our two weeks are up Thursday."

"I know," I mutter.

"So, I'll head down there?"

"Yes. And just take the TGV, would you? I can take only so much of his jet-carpool kindness."

"Fine," Alexei says with a laugh; then his voice softens. "It's all going to work out, my dear."

"I hope so. Just get on the train and text me when you're going to arrive in Avignon, okay?"

"Okay."

I disconnect the call and take a deep breath. Rome thinks he can get all saucer-eyed and passionate under the olive trees and then take over my entire company? That's a really clever way to show me how much he cares. I whip off my pajamas and pull on a swimsuit. I need about nine hours in the pool, but I'll settle for one.

I head out to the backyard and dive into the cool water. I feel better immediately. The water has always been my deliverance. I swim for a solid hour, slow laps with a few sprints mixed in, until I think I've worn out my body enough to settle my mind.

When I enter the kitchen, Trevor is there—in board shorts and another concert T-shirt—making coffee. It's just before eight o'clock.

"Sorry if I woke you," I say.

"I was up. I already went into town and got the papers. You okay?"

I'm rubbing my hair dry with the towel. "Yeah. I'm fine."

He looks at me after he's filled the *cafetière* with boiling water and put the top on to let it brew. "You sure?"

I slow down with the towel and stare at him. "No. I'm not fine at all. My uncle called earlier." I hesitate. "Are we in the cone?"

He quirks his lips with humor. "The cone of silence? Yeah, we're definitely in the cone."

"Okay, then." I flop down into one of the mismatched kitchen chairs and start spilling everything. Segezha. Clairebeau. Durchenko. I leave out about Aziza and Rome and Durchenko's personal mess, but I suspect Trevor has his own insights where they're concerned.

He starts talking about the different components of the Clairebeau bottom line, the physical plant of Voyanovski. It's obvious he's been following both companies very closely for quite some time.

"You just read annual reports for fun?" I rib him.

He turns his back to press the coffee, then pours a cup. "I guess you could say that." He offers me the cup of coffee, makes another for himself, and joins me at the table.

"Thanks," I say. After a few minutes, I continue, "So now Alexei tells me he and Rome have been having some talks without me—which pisses me off, of course—but, setting my ego aside . . ." I sigh and pull on the ends of the towel. I'm wearing a thin cotton Indian cover-up, and the moisture from my bathing suit is starting to soak through to the chair. "I think I'm going to have to actually consider it. Especially because I know deep down if it weren't Rome making the offer, I think I'd be pretty psyched. Our cash flow is precarious, to say the least, even though our net income is solid. Really solid."

His eyes brighten, as if the prospect of helping actually excites him.

"So, you want to work as my M-and-A advisor on the deal?"

He looks down at his messy appearance. "Do I need to put on a suit?"

"No," I laugh. "But . . . where do you work, anyway? You can't seriously do all this on a laptop in front of the TV, can you?"

He smiles again. "No. Let me show you my office. Lulu calls it the Batcave."

"Let me change into dry clothes. I'll be right back."

Lulu stumbles into the kitchen as I'm leaving. "Why is everyone up so early?"

"People to see, places to go," I say lightly, giving her a kiss on the cheek as I pass.

About ten minutes later, I'm cleaned up and Trevor and Lulu are leading me to a stone building about a hundred yards from the house. It looks like it used to be the stables or something, but while the original, golden-hued stone is still intact, it's obvious that it's been re-tuck-pointed. Modern windows and doors have been installed. We dip our heads beneath an overgrown vine that arches over the door, where it's beginning to blossom, and then climbs wildly along the edge of the roofline.

The first room is a huge studio overlooking the valley—Lulu's furniture studio—and it's amazing. I feel a thrilling rush when I see what's behind all their supposed lollygagging. I trail my fingertips along the edge of a perfectly smooth oval dining table. "It's so gorgeous. My gosh, Lulu. You're so good."

"Oh, cut it out."

"You are," Trevor says definitively, and Lulu looks like she wants to throw him to the floor and make love to him right then. I look away from their heated silent exchange and walk around the space, fingering a few tools and loving the smell of sawdust and shavings. There are also a few stone pieces. "What are these?"

"I'm starting to get into carving and sculpting, too. There's an artist over in Apt who's been helping me."

"They're so cool." I let my palm rest on an egg-shaped stone that comes up about as high as my chest. There's a perfect circle drilled into the center.

"That's going to be a fountain, maybe. I don't know."

"It's really great, whatever it is. The size and shape are so appealing." I let my hands feel the turn of the stone. It's incredible—solid and alive. "Wow." I turn to her. "You're really doing it, Lulu. I'm so happy for you."

"Well"—she shrugs self-consciously—"we can't all be smart like you and Margot."

I want to cry, because I don't feel smart in so many ways that count. I feel like I've been following rules my whole life, never taking any chances. Margot and I used to make fun of Lulu and how she nearly flunked out of high school and never went to college, and here she is with this beautiful creative spirit. Not to mention that she's also got a gorgeous man who loves everything about her. Trevor certainly isn't looking for a *whole package*. He's looking for Lulu.

I catch my breath when all that rolls through me. "It's really great."

"Are you okay?" Lulu comes over and puts her hand on my shoulder. "I feel like I keep saying the wrong thing with you lately."

"No, it's not you. I'm just so happy for you. You've really made this wonderful life."

She smiles sweetly. "It is pretty great. But your life is wonderful . . ." Her voice trails off.

"Lulu. I'm basically squatting in your guest room, and my company's about to be taken over by a man who—" My voice cracks, and Lulu pulls me into a tight hug.

"You're good, honey," she whispers, holding me close and soothing me. "It's all going to work out."

I get ahold of my emotions and almost laugh. "Everyone keeps telling me that, but I'm not so sure."

"It will. Just do what you love . . . and then this happens . . ." She spreads her arms wide and gestures around the studio.

"Okay. I'll try it. What I would really love right now is to see if we can get Rome de Villiers to pay an obscene amount of money for Voyanovski Industries while still letting me run it."

Lulu laughs. "You're a nut, but if that's what will make you happy, you should go for it."

"This way," Trevor says, continuing toward another set of doors at the far side of the studio. "You going to work, love?" he asks Lulu.

She's already picked up a sander and is rubbing her hand along the edge of that perfectly smooth table. "Mm-hmm," she says, barely paying attention anymore.

"She'll be out of it for hours now," Trevor says with a hint of pride.

"Amazing." I look back one last time before he unlocks a door with a pretty serious-looking coded-entry system.

"Holy shit," I whisper once the door opens. Ten large screens along the far wall flicker to life when he flips a switch near the entry.

"Welcome to my secret lair." He walks over to one of the keyboards on the long white table that runs the length of the room and taps in a few commands. One of the screens starts scrolling through the annual report from Voyanovski Industries. "I've been looking at Weyerhauser's decision to operate as a REIT, and I think what you should be considering about that . . ."

He continues talking, and it's as if I've entered another realm. Like Lulu's studio, it gives me a thrilling feeling of purpose and wonder, but this is the type of place I need. This is where my creativity resides. Numbers. Information.

"You like?" Trevor asks.

"So much." I turn to him. "You all make it feel so obvious. Do what you love. That's it, right?"

He smiles, and it's really contagious. "It helps that I inherited a boatload of money, so I can manage my own accounts, but yeah, it kind of makes sense that you'd be best at doing something you love . . . and I love this shit."

Sitting down in a black desk chair, he spins around and starts typing and looking up at a few different screens, checking the Nikkei index and a couple of other exchanges. "So, Rome is trying to bully you—is that it?" he asks while he taps and looks up at the different screens.

I sit in the chair next to him and start to take in all the information that's there for my delectation. "I don't know . . ." I watch the action on the London exchange. "Apparently, he and my father were talking about the merger for a while. I'm trying not to take it too personally."

Trevor tears his attention away from a spreadsheet that seems to be tracking some of his commodities shipments. "I think it's personal; don't you?"

I nod slowly.

He turns back to the screens and the keyboard. "Good. You can use that to your advantage."

"Oh my god. I love you." I kiss him on the cheek and stand up. "Let me get my computer and all my files, and we can prepare for the onslaught. Alexei arrives this afternoon, and I suspect Rome's going to have a deal memo for us by the end of the day."

"Sounds good." Trevor is deep in his own world as I slip out.

Margot comes out and joins us about an hour later. She might be studying seventeenth-century French history lately, but before that she was one of the best forensic accountants ever to graduate from MIT. So basically, the three of us make up this incredible group of number crunchers and data machines. Trevor is loving collating all the competitors' annual reports and shareholder reports. Margot is dissecting all the numbers like a boss. She's so much more detail-oriented than I am.

But when they start giving me their information, it's my turn to shine. I almost feel like the Sorcerer's Apprentice, bringing brooms to life and orchestrating stars and oceans. Synthesizing information has always been my strong point (despite what that loser at USC said about my being uninspired). I have the fleeting hope that I'm the Sorcerer, not the lowly apprentice summoning spirits I can't control.

Our different options sort of settle into place in my mind, and various solutions present themselves. The major assets are the thousands of acres of timber in Russia, and then the pulp and lumber plants, and then the smaller paper plants. I suspect Rome will want to sell off most, if not all, of the smaller plants; I know I would if I were acquiring the company. That will probably be a sticking point for Alexei, but he and I can play Good Cop/Bad Cop during the negotiations on those points.

It's definitely the best thing for the company to join forces with Clairebeau. The main stumbling block is my getting over the fact that Clairebeau is synonymous with Rome. I have to carve out my feelings and focus on the deal.

Around two o'clock, Lulu comes into Trevor's office with a platter of delicious sandwiches on baguettes, made from the leftover lamb and some amazing tapenade. We all eat, and I mention that Alexei's train is scheduled to arrive around three thirty. Lulu offers to go pick him up so the three of us can continue working. She trots off, and Trevor looks in her direction until she's no longer in view. The two of them are seriously adorable.

Around four o'clock, my phone rings and I see it's Vivian. I step out of the office and answer it.

"Hey, sunshine, are you back in Paris?" she asks, as if we were just talking to each other moments ago.

"Vivian, oh my god. You're not going to believe what's happened."

"Oh, tell, tell! I was wondering why I hadn't heard from you since last week."

I catch her up on coming down to Provence for Margot's wedding and how I'm now working on a possible merger.

She's quiet, especially quiet for Vivian; then she says, "Have you seen the pirate?"

I'm sitting on a stone bench overlooking the Luberon valley, and her words immediately call up a slew of images of Rome—grabbing me in the bathroom at the end of the wedding, sipping the wine yesterday. I sigh. "Yes, I've seen him."

"Oh, Miki."

"It's fine, Viv, I promise. Everything's totally out in the open. He's got shit he has to sort out, and even if he can, I'm not sure we're really a good fit."

"God . . . I don't even know what to say. How did you suddenly become the glamorous one?"

I look down at my T-shirt and cutoff denim shorts and laugh. "I'm seriously unglamorous, I promise."

"You know what I mean. My life, god, it feels so . . . rigid."

"Oh, Viv. Please don't start finding fault with your beautiful life. I've been like a chrysalis all these years, all tucked in. It's just taken me longer to break out. And here I am, I guess."

"You're right. So, tell me more about Margot's place. Is it phenomenal?"

We talk for another twenty minutes or so; then I tell her I need to go.

"All right. Call me later in the week, just to let me know you're okay," Vivian says. "I don't want to open *People* magazine and see you and Rome at Clooney's place in Como, all right?"

"You know you're much more likely to be hanging out with George Clooney than I am, Vivian."

We laugh together, and it feels good just to catch up. She doesn't give me a bunch of advice or ask me for a load of promises. "Have you heard from Landon?" I ask when we're winding down the conversation. I don't really want to know, but I guess I do.

"I'm surprised you asked. He's called Peter a couple of times, pretending he wants to set up a tennis match and then casually asking if any of us has seen you. Anything you want me to say?"

"He's left me a few messages, but I'm not sure what to do just yet. I mean, I know it's totally over, but, oh, I don't know. I just don't even want to hear his voice, for some reason."

"That's totally reasonable. He was an ass there at the end. You don't have to be buddy-buddy right away. Give yourself some time. Can I tell him you're in France, at least, so he doesn't keep sniffing around?"

"Sure. Tell him you talked to me and everything's good, and that I'll be in touch when I'm back in LA."

"And when will that be, missy?"

I take a deep breath of the dry, cool air that—Margot's right—is lulling me into staying in Provence for the foreseeable future. "It's probably going to be a while. I'm kind of falling in love with this place."

"Mm-hmm. I wonder why that is."

"It's not only Rome, I swear. It's just . . . oh, you'll probably think it's dumb."

"No, I won't. I'm almost at work, so just tell me."

"Well, I feel like I've kind of squashed down my French and Russian heritage or history or whatever, and it just feels really good, on some deep level, to go into town and speak French. This is a big part of me that I've never embraced. Does that sound dumb?"

"No, honey. It sounds beautiful. Have the best time—whether it's for a few weeks or forever."

"Thanks, Viv."

"But if it's forever, you need a big enough house so we can come for weeks and weeks every summer and Isabel can cry on your shoulder about what a despot I am."

"Done! I will buy a splendid château, and you will have your own wing. Sound good?"

"Sounds great. Okay. I'm here. I love you. Be good. Or not. You know, whichever."

We both laugh again and say good-bye and agree to touch base later in the week.

A few seconds later, Lulu is pulling into the courtyard with Alexei in the front seat, and I can tell the two of them are laughing nearly to the point of tears. I stand up and walk toward the car—I might have a family after all, even if it's not the usual one with parents and siblings. These are my people.

CHAPTER TWENTY-ONE

Rome's offering memorandum comes in about an hour later, to my Voyanovski email address. Trevor hooked up my computer to one of the monitors earlier today, and we all stare as I begin to scroll through the attachment up on the screen. The offer itself is only a couple of pages, but then there are about eighteen pages of addendums.

Alexei hisses and I start laughing when we get to the actual numbers. The bastard is doing exactly what I did to him two months ago: making a hideously bad offer, just to get our blood boiling.

"Calm down, Alexei," I say. "He's just doing it to torment you. Don't let him."

"Damn," Trevor murmurs when he gets to some of the more detailed sections about the plants and the restructuring of the timber holdings into a REIT. "He did all of this yesterday? Impressive."

"Hardly," I scoff. "I bet he's been working on it for a couple of years at least. "Half of this is probably stuff he and my father worked on together."

I have a deep, swift pang of longing for my father and try to remember that this is a pretty amazing legacy, as far as legacies go. I feel connected to Mikhail in a permanent, living way. But still, I wish he were here.

"You okay?" Alexei asks, sensing my change in mood.

I look up at him from where I'm sitting at the desk. "Just missing Mikhail."

He grabs my shoulder and squeezes. "Me, too." His face crumples slightly. "Me, too."

I smile up at him as best I can and pat his hand on my shoulder. "Like you said, this is what he wanted, right?"

Alexei nods and looks up at the screen again. "Go to the next page."

We all finish reading the document, and then I sigh and close out my email. "All right. I think we need to stop for food and to clear our heads for a bit. What do you all say? Can I take you out for dinner?"

The sound of a car pulling up sets my heart skittering, but Margot looks out the window and smiles. "Oh, it's Étienne back from work." She practically runs out of the office, and the rest of us smile at her newlywed enthusiasm.

"Dinner sounds great, Miki," Lulu says. "What do you think, Trev? Should we go to the new place over in Roussillon?"

He looks up at her. "Sure. Or we could go to that place you love over in Lacoste."

"Yes, let's go there." She turns to me. "You'll love it there, Miki. It's basically a farm. We can sit outside and watch the sunset."

"Sounds perfect. Let me change into pants, and we can leave right away." I look over at Alexei, who is going through some of the printouts I made of the offering memorandum.

"Alexei? Have you eaten?"

He looks up and shakes the paper in his hand. "You know, this is actually an excellent deal, other than the amount of money he's offering."

"I know. The management structure and the sell-offs are all totally reasonable. I've been staring at figures all day, but I'll understand if you want to forget dinner and stay to go over everything."

"No, I'll come." Alexei tosses the document on the desk and stretches up to his full height. "A nice glass of rosé will be just the thing." He puts his arm around my shoulder, and we walk out of the office.

"I'm glad we're working on this together," I say as we cross the courtyard.

"Me, too, lovely."

I kind of love when he calls me lovely now—or at least it doesn't grate like it used to—because now I feel like he thinks I'm a lovely person, not just a pretty girl.

We take two cars over to Lacoste, and Lulu is right: the restaurant is spectacular in a rustic, laid-back way. The couple who runs the farm serves the cheeses and meats they raise from their own goats and pigs, and the cool wine from the adjoining vineyard is refreshing and light.

Margot and I can't help but talk about the financials from the deal, both of us keyed up and focused on the work, even as we sip our wine under the stars. We all agree that tomorrow morning I'll send an equally offensive counteroffer and we'll get the negotiations rolling.

When we get back, I go for another long swim, needing to clear my head before I can even think about sleeping.

I slip into bed fairly early, but the combination of all the work and all the laps makes me feel like blissful sleep might actually come. My phone is charging on the bedside table next to me, and it starts to flash about five minutes after I've opened my e-reader and started to doze.

Of course it's him.

My fingers start to tingle as I decide whether or not to answer. The screen is flashing, and the phone is vibrating insistently. *Ack, fine!*

I pick it up and try to sound curt. "Yes?"

"Ah, the answer I've been praying for."

"Very funny."

"I'm not laughing."

He certainly isn't. He's as cool as can be—just inhaling a cigarette and probably taking a languorous sip of some peaking wine and trying to unnerve me.

And succeeding. My silk pajamas feel instantly sensual and provocative, instead of comfy-cozy, damn him. His voice revs me up just like he revs up the engine in his car. I want to *go*.

"What do you want, Rome?"

"Interesting question."

"Cut it out, would you? I'm just about to fall asleep, and it's been a long day. Someone's trying to take over my company, and I need to weigh my options."

He hums as if he's processing that new bit of information. "I'm pretty good at that sort of thing. Want some help?"

I want to laugh at the absurdity but manage to keep my voice steady. "Thanks, but I think I can handle it."

"You don't need to do everything on your own, you know?"

"This I do."

"I'm starting to think your father wanted us to meet. Do you ever get that feeling?"

That is so unfair. I want to shout *dirty pool*! But it has occurred to me that my father is somehow playing matchmaker from beyond the grave.

"How's Aziza?" I ask meanly.

He nearly growls, obviously annoyed that I'm no longer playing another round of We Belong Together. "Probably fine. Her so-called boyfriend is back on the scene with absurd apologies about how he thought she was trying to manipulate him or something. We're still technically engaged, if that's what you're asking." I can hear him take another sip of his wine.

We're both quiet for a bit; then I speculate, "I wonder what an apology from that man looks like."

"You'd like that, wouldn't you? Some man begging for your forgiveness." His words sound edgy, and I don't reply for a few seconds.

I exhale. "No, Rome. Just stop, all right? You call and act all flirty, and then when I—"

"A diamond necklace," he interrupts.

"I beg your pardon?"

"That's what an *apology from that man* looks like. A massive necklace from Cartier. I'm familiar with them. My mother had a vault full of similarly hollow apologies from my father." He says it with complete disgust; I'm not sure I've ever heard him speak this way.

"Okay, okay. Note to self: I'll never give you diamonds," I say, trying to lighten the tone of the conversation.

"I want only kisses from you, Miki."

My eyes close, and I slip deeper under the sheets. He's like the grand master of seduction. Honestly. How am I supposed to resist words like that?

"Rome . . ." I'm sort of breathless, and I feel like he's snaking his way through the phone and into my arms.

"*Oui, chérie?*"

I want to cry—or cry out for him. It's so tender when he speaks to me like that. So different from how he presents himself to the rest of the world. Like it's just for me.

I keep breathing, but I know he can tell he's getting to me.

"*Alors,*" he says, thankfully letting it go. "So"—he switches back to English—"are you working all day tomorrow, too?" he asks, as if he's free as a bird.

"Probably. It's a pretty complicated deal, and the offer came in absurdly low."

He chuckles at that. "Foolish man, thinking he could get you on the cheap."

My heart goes all fluttery again, and I try to breathe through it.

"Yeah. I've negotiated with him before. He's used to getting his own way, so I figure it's up to me to give him a little what-for."

He laughs, deep and pleased. "I like the sound of this *what-for*. I'm sure he's in for a real treat."

"I'm not sure he'll see it that way, but I'll let him know you said so."

"So, after you work all day, are you free for supper? You have to eat, yes?"

I exhale through my nose, wondering if I can actually separate the business from the man, or if it's all too close. Either way, I'm playing with fire. "I don't know, Rome," I answer, with genuine concern.

"I just thought I could start showing you I'm not entirely ridiculous," he says thoughtfully. "Forget I asked."

I let the silence settle and then whisper, "Yes."

"Yes?" His voice is so enthusiastic, I want to laugh-cry into the phone.

"Yes. I said yes. Dinner tomorrow night would be . . . nice."

"Excellent. Okay." He sounds so much like an eager teenager, I almost weep. "Right. I'll pick you up at seven. Is that good?"

"Sure. Just casual, okay?"

"Well, no, of course that's not okay," he replies with disdain. "What's the fun in *casual*?" He says *casual* as if the word is bitter on his tongue.

"Rome—"

"No." He's adorably huffy. "It's my date and I get to decide what we're going to do."

Infant.

"So now it's a date?" I ask.

"Of course it's a date. And if you want to ask me out on a date, then you can do that at some other time. And it can be *casual*. But this is my date," he adds.

"Fine. I'll go on your fancy date," I say, as if I'm going to be dragged through mud.

"Excellent. See you at seven."

And then the line goes dead. What an ass he is—or, more likely, a wise man, because he knew if I stayed on the line much longer I'd change my mind and back out. I set the phone down on my bedside table and turn out the light. So what if I'm playing with fire? I can handle it.

At least, that's what I tell myself until he shows up the next night in his obnoxiously expensive convertible. And drives me to his helicopter.

"We're going to Monaco for dinner on my yacht and then a spot of gambling in the casino," he informs me when we pull into the boutique hotel with the helipad, where the helicopter is starting its engines across the perfectly manicured lawn.

"Seriously? Don't do this, Rome." I'm so disappointed. He must know that the last thing I want is some splashy public-relations nightmare.

"Gotcha." He waves to the pilot, and I watch as a smartly dressed couple comes out of the hotel. They hop into the waiting helicopter, and we stay long enough to watch it lift off and veer to the south.

Rome revs the engine and leans across the armrest to kiss me lightly on the neck. I feel the touch pulse through me like the vibrations of the car. He hums his satisfaction as he inhales the scent of my skin and then pulls back and gives me a wicked grin. "I knew you'd want privacy, *chérie*, but I couldn't resist seeing the look of disgust on your face."

He pulls out of the gravel drive.

"You're an idiot." But I'm laughing.

"I got you to smile, didn't I?"

"I guess." I settle back into the comfortable leather seat and turn to look at him. "So where are we really going?"

He smiles with that satisfied air of his as he thrusts the car into a lower gear to take a tight turn. "My place."

I groan and look out my window, suddenly thinking a helicopter ride to Monaco and dinner on his yacht might be the lesser of two evils. Being alone with Rome in his château is going to be tender torture.

"So why did you ask me to get all dressed up, then?" I'm wearing a splendid confection of Lulu's—long and flowy layers of chiffon, but with a high slit that shows lots of leg, and a plunging halter neckline. Margot tsk-tsked the whole time she helped me get ready, but I can tell she's totally not sticking to her Rome-the-very-bad-man guns, even if she's still telling me all the time to be careful.

I spent the day convincing myself I can have this grown-up, fling-like relationship, or be friends, or friend-like, or something . . . manageable. I don't have to become my mother, with a string of meaningless bed partners, or my father, with some unrequited torch burning for the rest of my life.

When we get to the château, it's almost more beautiful than it was over the weekend when it was all decked out for the wedding. It feels incredibly serene: the wind swishes lightly through the trees, and the fountain in the center of the inner courtyard burbles gently.

"It's really wonderful here," I say.

"I love it, too." He takes my hand in his, as if that's totally natural. "Everywhere else feels like a stopping-off place," he confides. "This feels like home."

We go into the kitchen, and someone has set out a beautiful array of food and a couple of bottles of wine.

"Do you have a cook?" I ask.

"Yes, there's a couple who lives in one of the cottages. She takes care of all the housework, and he manages the grounds. But I made dinner."

I look down at the platters of grilled aubergine and courgettes, the slices of seared beef, and a selection of cheese and fruit. "Really?"

He nods.

"A playboy of many talents?"

He narrows his eyes as he uncorks the first bottle of wine. "I'm never going to escape the playboy thing with you, am I?"

I shrug and start to walk around the kitchen, looking at different things—antique kitchen tools and wooden pitchforks and pieces of old wine cases with the name of the vineyard branded into the wood—that have been put on the wall as decoration. I come to a small black-and-white photograph in a rough wood frame, of a boy standing between two men in a vineyard. "Is this you?"

He comes up behind me, and I manage not to shiver when he hands me a glass of wine.

"Yes, with my uncle—my mother's brother—and my grandfather."

"In Bordeaux?"

"Yes. My parents shunted me off every summer. I'm not complaining; it was bliss. Would you like to go sometime?"

I turn to face him, and he's damnably close. "Rome. Nothing has changed. Let's not talk about some imaginary future where we're spending weekends with your grandfather, okay?"

He takes a thoughtful sip of the red wine, ignoring my words, and I can feel the heat of his body a few inches from mine. "Hmm. It's not the '82, but it's quite good." He looks at the wine and swirls it around, then focuses back on me.

I take a sip and watch him while I do. "It's delicious," I say once I've swallowed. "But I hate to say, it's wasted on me. I can't really tell the difference between a forty-dollar bottle and a four-hundred-dollar bottle."

"The '82 was more like a four-thousand-dollar bottle," he says in that offhand way.

I choke on the wine in my mouth. "You're joking, right?" Between the six of us, we drank three bottles on Sunday.

He shrugs. "I mean, of course I got it for free back in '82. My grandfather always sets aside a few cases for me each year, since the year I was born. Luckily, I was born before 1982." He winks.

"I can't believe it. I was just slurping it down. It was good, but, man, is anything really that good? It's all the same, really, don't you think?"

He shakes his head slowly. "You mean to tell me—honestly— you think this is the same as what we drank on Sunday?"

"No," I concede. "But they're both just wine, you know?"

"Yes, but the one on Sunday was unique. *Un rêve.*" A dream. "Everything about that year was perfect. The sun, the earth, the grapes, the wind. Too many pieces of the puzzle to even imagine. All in perfect harmony. Even if you forget about the vintage or the cost or any of that, you can tell when something is special, yes?"

"Yes," I whisper. I know what he's doing, of course I do, but I'm sick of trying to stop him. I can have all the regrets I want tomorrow— or for the rest of my life if I want—but right now I just want to forget about REITs and $4,000 bottles of wine and playboys and billion-aires and make love to this man. Because at this moment, he is just a man. Even though all the trappings of his wealth surround him, the tenderness of his words makes him both raw and noble, somehow.

I lean forward a few inches so our hips are touching, and my body is instantly hot-wired. He takes the wine out of my hand and sets both glasses gently on the worn marble counter. Then he leans in and cradles my head in his hands and kisses me, his fingers tightening slightly in my hair as his tongue and lips search mine. He groans and leans into me—his chest pressed against mine, the wall at my back—and my mind tries to keep up as flashes of Excel spreadsheets and profit-and-loss reports flicker in a mixed-up montage of bright colors and Picasso's *Rêve* painting and the pure sensation of how his hot skin feels under my searching hands.

I've tugged his shirt from the waistband of his pants, and I'm gripping the muscled skin of his stomach and chest, clinging one second and roaming the next with light, tingling fingers across his abdomen.

"Please, Miki. Please . . ." He sounds so honest, so . . . real. All of my worries fly out the window, and I just want to give him that tenderness and warmth he so desperately needs—that we both need.

"Yes," I whisper as I begin to unbutton his shirt. "God, yes."

His hands reach around to the back of the gown, and his fingers trail up and down my bare spine. I lean my head forward against his shoulder and whimper when he unties the knot at the base of my neck that holds the halter portion in place.

When he begins kissing along my neck and shoulder, my whole body starts to quiver in anticipation.

"Miki, are you okay?" he whispers between kisses. "What do you need?"

"You know what I need, Rome. I hate how much I need it."

He keeps kissing me, and his hands begin stroking across my bare breasts—which are now blatantly exposed, the dress hanging half off me at my hips—and I feel like I'm going to explode just from those tender passes.

"I love how much you need it." He leans down and begins to kiss my sensitive breasts, and my hands are gripping his shirt around his biceps, with all my strength, my nails digging through the fabric into his skin.

"Rome . . ." I can't think of anything but his name, over and over, and how he's going to finally satisfy me—*satisfy my body*, I try to tell myself—but it feels so much deeper than that. I force myself to shove aside those thoughts of *deeper* and pretty much attack him, nipping at his neck and grabbing his thick hair in my fingers. He

MEGAN MULRY

growls and lifts me up in his arms, and we end up in the study
where we argued during the wedding, when Aziza interrupted us.

I shove those thoughts away, too, and literally pant as I pull at
his belt while he's getting my dress the rest of the way off, and then
we're both naked on the couch and he's reaching for a condom in
one of the side tables—because obviously libertines have condoms
in every drawer in a house—and then we are finally together again
and it's as if the past two months never happened and we are still in
Saint Petersburg and *together*.

"Miki . . ." He's whispering my name and looking at me with
so much intensity that I have to look away or I'll start crying. When
my gaze leaves his, I look over the couch and see his Matisse, *Interior
at Collioure*. I might cry anyway, whether I'm looking at him or not.
The woman in the painting is napping on a single bed and a red
figure stands out on the balcony and it's so beautiful and what he's
doing to my body is so beautiful and I shut my eyes so I can feel it all.

"Please look at me, Mikhaila," he says in throaty French. I open
my eyes slowly, and he gazes at me with those turquoise eyes burning into me while his body works into mine with that incredible
combination of power and sensitivity, and I can't help it—I reach
for his face and touch his cheek, and he kisses me so sweetly that I
cry out into his kiss and give myself over to the crushing waves of
sensation. Every cell of my climaxing body wants to tell him how
much I love him, how much I love this moment, but I kiss him
instead, almost angrily, to prevent myself from speaking. And then
he is following me over the edge, into oblivion.

CHAPTER TWENTY-TWO

It's just sex, Miki. It's just sex, Miki.

If I keep telling myself that over and over, I hope it will be true, as his body settles in behind mine on the couch and his big arm pulls me close against the length of his body. It's not even bed sex. *It's just couch sex, Miki.*

Within seconds, I feel like a trapped animal. Trapped is right, because I walked right into this like some stupid twitchy-nosed rabbit that bounces right into a snare in the forest.

Rome is nuzzling my neck, and I'm trying not to pitch myself off the sofa and call a cab. Are there even cabs this far out in the country? What the hell was I thinking?

I could call Margot or Lulu. Oh, god.

I take a deep breath and force myself to calm down. What am I so worried about? It's just Rome. I'm just having dinner.

And screwing the engaged billionaire who's taking over my company.

"You're freaking out, right?" he says easily, his fingers trailing lazily across the rise of my hip, to my waist, and back again. My back is cradled against his front, so at least I don't have to look at him.

"Completely."

He laughs, and his hot breath skates across the back of my neck. "You want me to take you home?"

Hell. Do I? I don't even know. Seems a bit stupid to do the deed and then run scared, but I'm just not adept at the whole let's-screw-and-then-hang-out thing.

"No. I think I can handle dinner."

"Good." He kisses my shoulder, and then he springs up from the couch behind me as if he's got all the energy in the world. He pulls on his linen trousers without any underwear and proceeds to just stand there with his hands on his hips. He's shaking his head and looking over every inch of me, and damn if I don't want to stretch and preen like a harem girl.

"Stop that," I whisper, but he can tell I'm more than halfway loving his eyes on me. He scratches his stomach lazily while he stares at my chest and then lower. I reach to partially cover myself with my inadequate hands.

He smiles wickedly. "That's even more provocative, my sweet odalisque." Bending down, he grabs his shirt. "Here—if you're feeling modest." He tosses it to me, and I grab it and slip my hands through the sleeves and try not to be too obvious about inhaling the scent of him that lingers in the fabric. Once I've got it partially on, I sit up and button it.

"Hungry?" he asks. The devil.

"Yes," I answer, not knowing how or what I feel but realizing I'm famished. "I am." I stand up with conviction; the basic human instinct to eat will have to be enough to guide me for now. I reach down and pull on his boxer briefs, then set Lulu's gown on the back of one of the armchairs. "I could have worn shorts and a T-shirt, you know."

"You're impossible," he huffs. "I wouldn't trade that moment of untying it for all the Matisses in the world. Come on." He reaches out his hand, and I reluctantly put mine in his and walk with him back to the kitchen.

We eat at the counter. He's an amazing cook (naturally), and I hum my appreciation through many bites, which seems to delight him. We drink more of the perfectly good wine while we talk about mundane things, like the book he's reading and how he found this place and decided to buy it and fix it up.

The wine is making me mellow, so when we move outside after dinner it feels really easy and comfortable to settle in next to him on a double-wide chaise longue by the pool. He grabbed a lightweight cashmere blanket from the back of a sofa as we walked through the house, and now we're lying underneath it as we stare up at the stars.

Rome touches me in an absentminded way that is almost more intimate than when he's all intense and staring into my eyes. Like I'm just there and we're together and of course he's going to be touching my arm or my neck or that sensitive spot between my fingers that shoots straight to my other sensitive spots.

I turn to face him. "Do you like to swim?"

"I love it. You?"

I smile. "Swimming's my favorite."

"Want to swim now?" The way he asks makes it sound like the dirtiest thing ever.

"Sure, I'll race you." I toss off the cashmere blanket and strip out of his shirt and boxer briefs.

"You think you can beat me?" He stands up and takes his pants off. "I'm a strong swimmer."

"Good," I call over my shoulder, taking a few extra seconds to enjoy the shadows and dips of his naked body beneath the moon, with the pool lights shimmering over his muscles. "You know I love a challenge." I dive in, and the warm water against my naked, sensitive skin is incredible, sluicing away all my worries and second thoughts, until I'm just this being in the universe and everything is right.

I totally crush him for the first few lengths, but I have to hand it to him for endurance. Rome just never stops. I finally have to pull him down by one ankle to make him give up, and then he dunks me repeatedly until I concede and beg for mercy. He obviously loves the sound of me begging and kisses me with harsh possession, his strong arms wrapped around my waist and his palms pressing into my back to keep me flush up against him as I wriggle and try to get away with the most half-assed effort imaginable. He slows his kisses and I melt into him, the warm water settling around us and making me feel as if we are joined in every way possible.

He carries me out of the water and places me on the chaise, and I'm about to joke that there aren't any libertine side tables filled with condoms out here by the pool, when he begins kissing his way down the length of my wet, trembling stomach until he's placing soft kisses between my legs. I think I'm going to die of the combination of how hot his mouth is compared to the cool night air that's making the rest of my body pebble and shiver.

"Cold?" he asks, then continues kissing and licking me until I can't think and I start quaking. "Do you want me to stop so we can go inside and warm up?" He breathes a warm stream of air against my sensitive, swollen flesh.

"Don't you dare stop," I order, pushing myself up onto my elbows so I can look him in the eye. He dips his head again, and my neck arches back in shameless pleasure, until his relentless mouth hurls me into a release that has me crying out into the night sky.

I start to doze against his shoulder a while later. He's pulled the blanket over our naked bodies, and I'm half-asleep when he whispers, "Will you stay the night?"

It seems dumb to drive back to Margot's when we're so comfortable here, so I mumble my agreement. I vaguely remember being carried up the wide stone stairs and being placed into soft linen sheets. I'm still in that half-waking, half-dreaming space when I stretch my arms above my head and reach for him. He comes into my arms and we make love again, slowly and gently, in the darkness.

We fall asleep almost immediately afterward. His chest against my back—and his strong arms enveloping me in that safe heat—lulls me into contentment.

When the wine—or my dreamy denial—wears off, I blink my eyes open into the darkness. I reach for my phone on the bedside table and remember I'm at Rome's and then see a small clock that reads 3:17. I turn back to the middle of the bed, thinking I'll get a few more hours of thoughtless intimacy against Rome's hot muscles, and see that he's sitting up at the edge of the bed, the silhouette of his body outlined by the bright screen of his tablet.

"Fuck," he mutters.

I come up behind him on my knees, thinking I'll console him, whatever it is. I wrap my arms around his neck and press my chest against his strong back and practically purr like a kitten. Then I peer over his shoulder to see what he's looking at.

"No . . ." I whisper. I'm such an idiot. I want to scratch my own skin off, or the memory of him on my skin. I pull away from him like he's my kryptonite. Because he is.

The French equivalent of TMZ has posted a picture of him kissing me in his car in the hotel parking lot last night. The headline taunts: ROMAN HOLIDAY: EVEN ENGAGED, A NEW WOMAN OF THE WEEK!

"Take me home," I say, my voice dry and brittle, not even

sounding like me. Then I realize I don't really have a home, and I hate myself even more.

"Miki, come on. It's just PR."

"Take me back to Margot's now!" I scream. I look around the darkened room and see I don't have any clothes to put on, and I'm certainly not going to put on one of his Rome-scented shirts, even for the short walk downstairs. I nearly trip on the carpet as I race out of the room and take the stone stairs two at a time to get back to the study and back into Lulu's dress. As I'm tying the knot at my neck, then closing the zipper at my waist, I want to cry so hard for how I've let myself sink this low into a pretend existence, in another woman's dress, with another woman's pretend fiancé. Rome says he wants real, but it's all still *pretend*. And I hate him for it.

He turns the corner into the room, now wearing a pair of jeans and a T-shirt. He's panting slightly, probably having taken the steps at a clip, as I did. "Miki, we have to talk. It's not that big a deal."

I blow past him out of the room and turn into the kitchen to get my small purse. I pull out my phone and begin to scroll past my text and email alerts. I open a gossip site and skim through the whole article while he stands in the doorway of the kitchen with his arms folded across his chest.

"Not a big deal?" I ask, my voice filled with disgust. "They've got a picture of me dancing in Paris with my mother—the two of us looking like we're a pair of raving lunatics! And then that damnable mouseburger picture from the USC website. They've fashioned a whole fun sidebar about how I'm also the acting head of Voyanovski Industries, with a few business-and-pleasure double entendres thrown in for good measure. Not a big deal, Rome?"

"Look, I deal with this sort of thing all the time—"

"Exactly!" I cry. I don't care about appearing sensible or keeping my voice down. If I want to shriek like a banshee, then I'm damn well going to. I shake my phone at him. "This is exactly what I told you I don't want! What I can't handle! This is what I despise about my mother! And *you*! These fucking *antics*!"

I shove the phone back into my bag and snap it shut. I'm breathing heavily from my outburst. I shut my eyes and shake my hair out and then stare at him with all the venom that is coursing through my veins. "Just let me go."

His body reacts as if I've punched him in the chest. "You can't mean that, Miki," he says from across the room. He starts to walk toward me. "After tonight . . . the two of us . . . think about what you're saying."

"Don't come near me. I mean it. Please, just . . . I can't be around you right now. Give me the keys to your car if you don't want to drive me." I hold out my hand.

"I'll take you." He stops walking toward me. I can tell he wants to touch me and make it better and hold me and make everything go away, but he is the fucking cause of everything that I want to go away.

We get in the car and ride in stony silence while I start scrolling through my emails. At four o'clock, a text pops up from Alexei.

Have you seen this yet?

It's a link to a piece in the *Financial Times*, and as I read it, my blood begins boiling in my veins.

"You fucking bastard," I say under my breath.

"What now?" He doesn't even bother looking at me. He just shakes his head and then rests it against the window to his left, after tapping his skull rather viciously against the glass several times for good measure.

I read aloud, " *'Paper Doll: Is new interim CEO of Voyanovski Industries, Dr. Mikhaila Voyanovski Durand, serious about taking over the family business or just playing house?'*"

"Aw, shit." Rome takes a tight turn and grips the gearshift.

MEGAN MULRY

"Sexist bastards. *Doll*? I'm going to sue their fucking asses. God damn it." I'm fuming. "God damn you!" I yell at him. "I am never selling Voyanovski Industries to you, you bastard. You think you can devalue the company by making me look like a fool."

"Miki, you know I would never do that."

"Liar! I've seen you do it. I've watched you take over companies for the past ten years. I know how you work. God, I was so fucking naive."

"Miki, stop."

"No, *you* stop. Just stop."

We don't speak the rest of the way to Margot's house, and I get out of the car without looking at him. It takes all my willpower not to slam the car door shut when I get out. At least he doesn't rev the engine on purpose when he leaves, but it's still loud in my ears when I open the front door and find Alexei sitting on the living room couch, looking at his computer. The sweet man is in a huge, blue-and-white-polka-dot silk bathrobe, and I smile when I look at him.

"I'm so sorry, Alexei. I'm so sorry—"

He's up and across the room and holding me in a warm hug by the time the tears come. "I thought I could do it. I thought I could run the company and be the person my father wanted me to be, and be wild and free at the same time, and I just can't. I'm so sorry if my foolishness is going to devalue the company." I'm kind of half gasping, half talking at this point.

"Shh-shh-shh," Alexei soothes. "None of that is going to happen. You are perfect, Miki. You are brilliant, and we will show them what you are. My paper doll." He smiles on that last bit and forces me to smile through my tears. "It is a wonderful name for you. We will use it to our advantage, eh?"

He's holding my chin, and I feel so young in that moment. But I also feel the fire that is still burning inside me, the fire to prevail over all of these external circumstances, to establish *my* life. I'm not going to let anyone—no matter how beautiful he looks in the moonlight—take that away from me.

"We need to go back to Saint Petersburg," I say quietly.

"Yes. That would be best," Alexei agrees.

"How quickly can we get there?"

"You go get cleaned up and pack. I'll make the arrangements," he offers.

"Okay."

I walk back to the small room and start to put all of my things into my bag. I feel like the embodiment of that George Carlin skit about "*all my stuff*"; and I think of my house in Venice, with *most of my stuff*; and then about my mother's apartment in Paris, with *some of my stuff*; and now these pieces of luggage, with *the really important stuff.* I'm done crying about all this. For some reason, I just want to get to Saint Petersburg and move into my father's apartment and go to work every day and keep that amazing company going.

And if we have to sell the Segezha plant to Durchenko, so be it. There are over five thousand employees who have come to depend on Voyanovski Industries for their livelihood, and I am done being some gadfly manager who thinks she can swan around the world while the company runs itself.

By the time I come out of the bedroom and I've changed into proper clothes, Alexei is likewise ready. "There's a helipad nearby that can take us to Nice. From there I have a private plane that will take us to Saint Petersburg. Trevor said he'll take us to the hotel where the helicopter takes off from."

I sigh. "Yeah. I know it."

Alexei manages a half smile. "Well, maybe now they'll take a picture of you leaving with your uncle and write a new story, eh?"

"Yes, maybe."

Trevor comes downstairs a few minutes later. "All set."

"Yes. Please tell Margot I'm sorry I had to leave like a thief in the night."

"She'll understand—" Trevor begins to say.

"No, I won't," Margot says as she comes downstairs, tying the knot on her bathrobe. "What's going on?"

"Too much to explain," I say as I pull her into a hug. "Everything's gone to hell with Rome and the merger and . . . just everything. I've loved seeing you, honey, but I have to get to work. Seriously." I look her in the eye, and she sees everything, I'm sure.

"I told you to be careful," she whispers.

"I know you did. I did what I wanted to do. Now I need to work. Hard."

"Okay," she says. "But call me and let me know you're all right. And don't let this sour your feelings about coming to stay with me again in Provence. I'll put an invisible fence around the place, and we'll put a chip in Rome's skin, like a pet."

I smile at the idea, then lean in and hug her again. "Thanks so much for everything, Margot. I'll be in touch about all the work you did for me on the merger, but that deal is definitely off the table."

"Oh, stop with that. Whatever you decide, just know that we're here for you. I love you. Now go." She squeezes me one last time, and then I turn to leave the house.

CHAPTER TWENTY-THREE

I never should have listened to my mother. What was I thinking, going to Paris and doing all that stupid shopping-spree bullshit? That just led to the Provence bullshit. Which led to the Rome bullshit.

I'm where I need to be now: sitting at my father's desk—my desk—where I've been ensconced for the past two months. From early in the morning until late at night. Every day of the week.

The first few days of fallout were surreal. Everything that happened in the press felt like it had happened to someone else. Everything at work feels real. Finally. The phone on my desk rings, and I pick it up with a malicious smile when I see who's calling.

"They're striking again," he barks.

"Really?" I click on my computer and quickly look at the latest news from Segezha. Sure enough, the workers have gone on strike. Again. "And that's my problem why?"

Durchenko growls into the phone, and I laugh at him—my new favorite pastime. "Be careful what you wish for, Pavel. Wasn't that what you told me? You were going to get your hands on that factory no matter what, if memory serves. You got your wish."

"Damn you, Miki. Those workers are so loyal to your family, I can't get them to do anything."

"Maybe if you started paying them a living wage—"

"I'm already paying them more than my other factory workers elsewhere."

"Don't bullshit a bullshitter. You know that factory is nearly twice as productive as any of your other factories. That's why you wanted Kriegsbeil to acquire it in the first place, so you could get in there and figure out the management structure and productivity incentives. And now that you see why, you're angry?"

"I'm not running a kindergarten or an old folks' home! Workers need to work and leave. When did I become responsible for their children and their sick grandparents?"

I laugh at him. "When you wanted a factory that produced twice as much as your other factories."

He hangs up on me—his new favorite pastime.

I know he'll be calling again before the end of the day. During the negotiations at the end of May, Pavel Durchenko and I stared at each other across the conference table, and it was as if we had some sort of Vulcan mind meld. I never looked away, just held his vicious gaze. While in Paris, I'd done a ton of research about his childhood and rise to prominence in the Saint Petersburg crime syndicate, then his transition into legitimate enterprises.

Like so many of his peers who made their way out of the sewers of Moscow, he is brilliant in many ways. He is quick-witted, able to make massive decisions in the blink of an eye, but he had a brutal childhood—and an adulthood spent compensating for it—that I can actually relate to on some very deep level.

Now that he's quite firmly entrenched in the world of international business, he can no longer get away with as much of his sledgehammer negotiating as he could in, say, Odessa—or Little Odessa, for that matter. So, three days after I came to Saint Petersburg from Provence, we all met in a conference room at the

Hermitage Hotel. Alexei, Jules, and I were on one side of the table; Durchenko and his silent attorney sat on the other side, with two massive bodyguards flanking them.

Pavel just stared and stared, baiting me. I kept thinking of my father and barely felt ruffled. The silence extended until Durchenko was satisfied somehow, and then he blurted, "Everyone out. Except you." He lifted his chin toward me on that last bit.

"Now, wait one minute," Alexei blustered.

"Go, Alexei," I said gently.

Jules slid the stack of legal papers in front of me and patted my shoulder as he left. Alexei looked into my eyes to see if I'd lost my mind, but I smiled and he saw I knew what I was doing. It was one of the best moments of my life.

Pavel Durchenko and I sat alone in that room for nearly three hours. His bodyguard brought us lunch at one point as we talked through every line of the contract. He tried to get us to stay on to manage the plant, and I told him that would have to be an entirely separate negotiation, and one that was very unlikely to end favorably. The arrangement he had with my father was a straight sale, and, after having worked on it with Jules and the others for the previous few weeks, I saw why. Dealing with Durchenko in a sale was one thing, but my father never would have entered into a long-term business arrangement with someone so volatile and domineering.

But over the ensuing weeks, Pavel and I have become—quite bizarrely—friends. He is fourteen years older than I am, but he's one of those generation-bridging types. He knows more about new techno music and Tinder and where Beyoncé is spending summer holidays than I ever will. But he's also a voracious reader and art collector; he talks about Schopenhauer and Schiele as easily as he talks about Shakira.

Usually we just argue and rib each other about business, but lately he's been a bit more sociable, most recently having invited me to a house party at his country dacha this weekend. He judiciously avoids any mention of Rome de Villiers. Clairebeau was summarily cut out of the Segezha deal when the preexisting contract came to light. I haven't spoken to Rome since I stepped out of his car in Provence.

Very cut and dried. As if Rome and I never even met. Cauterized. That's what it feels like—as if all my swirling emotions of loss and love and tenderness and frustration have been seared into oblivion. Or frozen solid.

I've got more than enough on my plate without thinking about him, and I'm thankful to be relieved of the obsession. Most of the time. Like, if he happened to be at Durchenko's house party, that would not be . . . feasible.

I finally call Pavel on Friday afternoon and confess my weakness. "Look, I hate that I even have to ask—"

"I love it when you are at a disadvantage," he gloats.

"Yes, I know that. Not that it's really a big deal, but is Rome de Villiers going to be at your place this weekend?"

"Since it's not really a big deal, maybe I shouldn't tell you?"

What a prick.

"Never mind." I'm ready to slam down the phone.

"Ah, struck a nerve?"

"Forget I called—"

"Not so fast, doll."

He and nearly everyone else have taken to calling me that absurd nickname. The publicist assures me that if I keep a sense of humor about it, it will either go away or take on a sort of endearing patina. I'm not so sure, but I'm trying to be patient.

"I'm hanging up now—"

"Fuck no!" he interrupts quickly. "Of course he's not coming to my house this weekend. Or ever. Shit, Miki. You think I'd let that slimy bastard anywhere near Azi ever again?"

I don't bother mentioning that Pavel is the slimy bastard who went out with Azi for over a year and then accused her of trying to force him into marrying her when he learned she was pregnant with *his* baby. I'm not in the mood to quibble, but I can't repress a laugh. "Really? Because you've always been so devoted?"

"Fuck you." He hangs up, and I smile at the phone, hearing the hint of humor in the supposedly bitter words. He's already told me Aziza will be in Russia for the weekend, and I suspect this might even be the occasion of their secret-wedding announcement. She's been in Saint Petersburg a couple of times—according to the newspaper and gossip rags—but I've yet to see her in person since Margot and Étienne's wedding.

Rumors of her pregnancy are starting to circulate, and rude questions about paternity are starting to crop up on some of the more salacious sites. She broke it off with Rome after the pictures of him and me made it impossible for her to turn a blind eye without looking like a doormat. She also publicly claimed to be considering her parents' wishes that she agree to an arranged marriage after all.

When the story broke that Rome and I were fooling around while he was engaged to Azi, he basically took all the heat. Not that I was paying attention, since I was too immersed in taking Voyanovski Industries—and taking myself seriously—to glance at what probably amounted to some modern act of chivalry on his part. I just couldn't bring myself to care.

If Rome wanted to throw himself onto some sort of public-relations expiatory pyre, so be it. He said he seduced me to devalue my company, and—though I had my hackles up about being depicted as some hapless victim—my new (highly paid) publicist in

Los Angeles assured me it was the least of several worse depictions. My publicist, Dani Stephens, came highly recommended by Vivian, so I trust her completely. She spins my academic background into the cause of my inability to deflect Rome's playboy wiles. I'm such a bookish genius that it is difficult for me to understand when a French pirate is making love to me.

None of it matters. In that sense, Rome was right. It's all just PR—like those teacups spinning in that children's amusement-park ride—not really affecting anything outside of a very small orbit. Dani has constructed a public Dr. Mikhaila Voyanovski Durand persona that vaguely resembles me—who goes out to dinner with clients, sponsors arts events in her new hometown of Saint Petersburg, and crunches numbers like the Hulk crunches cars—but that Mikhaila never actually penetrates my real life, my work life. My quiet private life.

I leave work on Friday afternoon, and my driver takes me to my father's apartment so I can change and pick up my luggage for the weekend. Despite my father's seriously vast wealth, I'm coming to adore the intensely private and simple way he managed his everyday life. There is an older woman who lives down the hall from his apartment who comes in every morning after I leave for work and cleans, does laundry, makes dinner—hell, I don't really care what she does, but it means I don't have to do anything when I get home exhausted and hungry every night. She's uncommunicative and bristly, and I pay her what my father paid her, and that suits us both just fine.

I swim every morning at the indoor pool at the Four Seasons. I go to work. I go to dinner with Alexei or a new colleague a couple of times a week, but mostly I'm just getting to know Saint Petersburg. I wander around the city at all hours of the night (which makes Alexei adorably protective and furious). I suspect he's hired a few bodyguards to follow me at a distance, but I've never been able to catch them. I go hear music and see student films and have even spoken to one of the local universities about teaching a few classes. I'm trying to understand the intense political undercurrents of the country, but I know it will take time.

I'm not totally isolated, despite my mother's constant griping phone calls to the contrary. She's back from Cairo and living the high life in Paris and acting like she's worried about me, when it's pretty obvious she just wants a partner in crime. She hasn't said so directly, but I think Jamie what's-his-name is also back on the scene. I do video calls with Vivian and Margot all the time, for just a quick hello or for longer calls about what they're up to. Since I don't feel like I have very much going on—other than work—I can finally be a good, listening friend again, and not the desperate mess I was in the spring.

I change into jeans and grab my weekend bag and go back downstairs to my car. In that, at least, Alexei put his foot down. He forbade me to drive around the city like a slow-moving target for any thug to rob, or worse. My company car is a massive Escalade with bulletproof, tinted windows, and the driver, Sergei, is, well, ex-FSB and a heat-packing beast.

Vivian loves all these dramatic details. She keeps calling me Natasha Fatale and wonders when I'm going to start spying. As the driver and I head out of the city to Durchenko's dacha, I pull out my phone to check emails. After I finish replying to a few important ones, I see it's after seven my time, so it's after eight in the morning for Vivian, and I decide to touch base.

"What's up?"

I love how she answers my calls like I'm still in Venice or sitting at my desk at USC.

"Nothing, just headed out to Pavel Durchenko's dacha for the weekend, and I'm riding in the back of the car for an hour and a half."

"He's totally got the hots for you."

"Trust me on this. He totally doesn't. I'm pretty sure he and Aziza are going to announce their engagement this weekend. Or even their marriage, if they've been able to keep it under wraps."

"That woman just follows you around. You need to scrape her off."

I burst out laughing. "She's pretty wonderful. I bet you'll meet her at some point and you'll fawn all over her. She's one of those people everyone wants to hug and be best friends with."

"As Isabel would say, *blech*."

I laugh and then ask, "How is my sweet Isabel? I miss her."

"You want her? She's driving me fucking crazy. She's always *bored*. Everything is *boring*. And she's dying of *boredom*." Vivian says the words with a long, drawn-out voice, perfectly imitating Isabel's tween whine.

"I would love to have her for a visit. Are you serious?"

"Well, I was kind of joking, but now that you mention it, I need to come to Italy at the end of August for the film festival. Maybe we could all meet up there?"

"Ugh. My mother's been trying to get me to meet her there, too. She's renting a villa and then going to the film festival in Venice. Is that why you're coming?"

"Yes. You should come. It's a lot closer than LA."

"I don't know. The last week in August is pretty busy for me."

"You sound like you're hedging. Please come. For me?"

"You are such a pain. You know I don't want to see my mother—and Jamie is back in the picture, by the way."

"Yeah, I saw something about that in *Variety* or something. I think that independent movie he was making in Mexico last year is actually up for some awards. Who knew?"

I sigh. I don't know why I'm still blaming my mother for having set so much of the Rome nonsense in motion. It's obviously not her fault. Maybe I just don't like being reminded that I have that same reckless streak inside me and I need to keep it on a very tight rein.

"Yeah, and my mom was a producer, so I guess they kissed and made up and they're tooling all around Europe together for the movie."

"Well, that's better than having her whining to you, isn't it?"

"I guess. I don't know."

"Look, we're never going to solve your mother. Just don't even tell her you're going. I'm staying in a huge villa on the Grand Canal, and there's plenty of room. You and Isabel can tour the city while I kiss movie-star ass."

I start laughing again. "I thought they had to kiss your producer ass."

She starts laughing, too. "No. It's the directors who have to kiss my producer ass." By that point, we're both laughing happily, and I realize I want to see her in person and hang out in a big hotel bed with Isabel and watch movies and ride around in a gondola and just be silly for a few days.

"Okay, I'll do it. I'd love to come. Email me your dates, and I'll meet you in Venice. If you can get there a few days early so we can all hang out together, I'd love that."

"This might put Isabel in a better mood for a few weeks . . . or a few minutes. It's impossible to tell these days. Okay, I'm at work— I've got to go. Bye, sweetie. Can't wait to see you!"

As the call disconnects, I pull the phone away and smile at the screen. Then I scroll through my messages and see a few from my mom that I've listened to but haven't returned. It's been only about a week since we last spoke, but she's in bizarrely attentive mom mode, so I know she's going to be all dramatic about not having heard from me in *ages*. I click on her number and gird myself to be verbally assaulted.

"*Finalement!*" she cries into the phone.

"It's only been a few days—"

"Never mind that. I'm just dying to see you. I have big news!"

Oh, dear. This can't be good. "What news?"

"Jamie and I are engaged."

I try to think of something to say, but a few beats of silence pass.

"To be married," she adds needlessly.

"Wow." I'm watching the city gradually turn into countryside out the darkened window to my right. My mother is finally going to get married. How messed up is it that I have basically zero response, other than *Please tell me you're going to sign a prenup*.

"*Wow?*" Now she's pissed. "That's all you have to say to me after all these years of begging me to settle down and be a mature adult? You know what, Miki—"

"Mom! I'm thrilled for you. I'm just surprised, okay? The last time we saw each other, you told me everything was over between you and Jamie—"

"Well, sort of. I was distraught by your father's death, and that upset Jamie, but, you know, he loves me and I love him. Oh, Miki. I wish you would change your mind and join us in Italy at the end of August. We're going to do a small wedding the weekend before the film festival. Please say you'll come."

That at least I can give her. "As it turns out, that's why I'm calling. I'm definitely coming to Venice after all. Vivian is renting a villa, and I'm going to meet up with her while she's there, so I'll just come in the weekend before and stay with you."

"That's fabulous! Darling, I can't wait to see you. I've missed you." Her voice lowers, and she sounds sweetly hesitant. "Do you think next month is too soon to get married?"

"No," I finally laugh. "I think after fifty-three years, next month is absolutely perfect."

"Oh, wonderful!" She turns her mouth from the phone and calls into the distance. "Jamie, love, Miki is going to come to Italy for the wedding."

I can hear him in the background, and he actually sounds sort of genuine when he says, "Excellent!"

"Okay." Simone is sort of breathless now that she's once again got everything her way. "So why don't you fly in that Friday afternoon and we'll go for a small dinner at Le Calandre, just the three of us, and then I'll wear a simple white suit or something on Saturday and you can be our witness and we'll have lunch at the house with a dozen or so friends? Does that sound good?"

"It sounds divine. I'm really happy for you, Mom. I'm sorry I was taken aback at first. No one can ever accuse you of being rash— in this, at least."

I can hear the smile through her words. "Yes, in this, at least. In many other things, perhaps I *have* been rash."

"Well, haven't we all?" I ask kindly.

"Yes. Yes we have." She's silent for a few seconds; then we wrap up the call. "So we'll see you in a month?"

"Yes, I'll see you then."

We end the call, and I take a deep breath and realize I just shouldn't take my phone out when I'm riding around in the back of my car, feeling open-minded. In less than an hour, I've managed to get myself roped into ten days in Italy. Leaving Russia feels sort of unnerving all of a sudden. I sink lower into the backseat and shove my phone into the bottom of my bag. I promise myself I'm not initiating or answering any calls for the rest of the weekend.

CHAPTER TWENTY-FOUR

Durchenko's place looks more like a summer palace than a dacha. My father and Alexei's dacha is the old-fashioned kind, a rustic log cabin where men go to drink and beat each other up for fun, or to swim in the freezing water of the Gulf of Finland and then beat each other up. Like everything about him, Durchenko has taken the idea of a traditional dacha and pumped it full of steroids, or, in his case, money.

It has to be at least ten thousand square feet; the rustic log exterior stretches in two long wings from either side of the large, double front doors. A huge bear head hangs above the outside entry, beneath the roof of the covered porch that extends around the whole perimeter of the house. As my car pulls up, Durchenko himself comes out the front door to greet me. I grab my weekend bag and my computer case out of the car, tell my driver to pick me up at noon on Sunday, and follow Pavel into the house.

There are ten or twelve people hanging out in the sunken living room. Some of them look remotely familiar and wave to me without getting up. The high glass walls on the far side of the room have an unobstructed view of the gulf, and the summer evening is bright. It's a beautiful space.

"It's gorgeous, Pavel. I didn't even realize I was sick of being in town." I smile up at him, and he nods.

"Good. This is good. Let me show you to your room so you can put your things away."

He takes me down a long, wide hall that's lined with hunting and fishing photographs, of Durchenko, of course—often accompanied by some easily recognizable famous companions—holding up a marlin or a large deer or some other animal I'm pretty sure is not meant to be hunted anymore.

We turn into a smaller hall, and he leads me into a large, simply furnished room with rough-hewn wooden furniture and another pristine view of the gulf through a set of French doors to the covered porch. "This is truly spectacular. Thank you again."

"I am glad you came." He pauses, then looks at me carefully. "Aziza is looking forward to seeing you again."

I look up from where I am setting my bag on a luggage rack at the end of the large bed. "Oh. It will be nice to see her, too."

"No, it won't," he says in that brusque, half-scoffing way of his. "It will be awkward and uncomfortable, but it has to be done. Drinks at eight thirty. Come out and join us whenever you wish." He leaves the room, shutting the door behind him to give me privacy, and I am left standing there hoping it's not going to prove *that* awkward or uncomfortable.

I unpack my things and then step out onto the porch and sit for a while, taking in the bright northern evening and listening to the expansive quiet of the forest. Alexei and I have gone on several site visits over the past few months, and, as much as I miss the ocean, it's been incredible to hike in the forests and other natural areas of this country. It could easily become home, for at least part of the year.

Getting up reluctantly, I put on my imaginary social armor and head into the living room.

"Mikhaila!" Aziza's voice is high and excited. She walks across the large room and pulls me into a tight hug. "How are you?" she asks after she's released me but is still holding on to my upper arms.

"I'm fine. How are you?"

"No, no, no." She shakes her head, and her long earrings swing. "I mean, really, how *are* you? Let's go sit outside." She slips her arm though mine and leads me out to the enormous back porch. "Pavel, we'll be back soon."

He blows a kiss to Aziza and I want to make fun of him, but then I realize he's actually in love with her. The flash of pride or adoration or whatever is unmistakable. He can't really take his eyes off her as we walk outside.

"Sit," she orders, gesturing toward a large, comfortable sofa. She stands in front of me for a few seconds; she's wearing tight black pants and a fitted boatneck top that clearly outlines the round curve of her stomach between her narrow hips.

She sees the direction of my gaze and begins to rub her stomach lovingly. "I'm having a baby."

"I heard." I look up, and she smiles and takes a deep breath, then sits down next to me.

"I owe you every apology, Miki. May I call you Miki?"

Awkward does not even begin to describe how I feel. The last thing I want is some heart-to-heart with this woman I barely know.

"Aziza, please. Of course you should call me Miki. I mean, we met at Margot and Lulu's—"

She swipes her hand impatiently in front of my face. "No. We have to speak the truth. Rome cares for you so deeply, Miki. You must know that?"

My stomach drops a few inches, and I want to squirm off the sofa and run back to Saint Petersburg in my strappy sandals if I have to. I do not want to sit here like a trapped creature and listen to this blissfully happy woman tell me why I should be with someone who is so entirely ill-suited to who I really am.

Even though she looks far younger, I know Aziza is in her thirties. I have no doubt she has seen her share of life's ugly side, between her childhood in Somalia and the work she's done to help refugees since then. Lulu and Margot genuinely like her, and she is probably a wonderfully insightful and charming woman. Still, I don't want to hear what she has to say.

"Aziza. Please listen to me. It's all in the past and—"

"No!" She sounds really angry, and I realize I've underestimated her, misled by her dazzling smile. The smile is now distinctly absent. "I will not listen to you."

Well. Okay, then. I sit back and rest my hands on my lap, the picture of a schoolgirl ready to receive her punishment.

Aziza grips her hands together and groans. "I have a horrible temper. Pavel told me I should hold my tongue, but I cannot."

I should have known if she could take on the likes of Pavel Durchenko, she's someone who knows how to manage stubborn people.

"Fine. Say what you need to say," I respond rather coolly.

Then she looks as if she might cry. "I'm so emotional with the pregnancy. I can't stand it!" She smiles and her face softens. "I am not an overly emotional person by nature. That's probably why Rome and I became such good friends at university in Lausanne. Stone-cold hearts, the both of us."

I hate when she says Rome's name. I don't want to think too hard about why it bothers me so much.

She sighs again. "Okay. So, I won't go on about Rome. But I hope you know that everything he did for me was . . . for me. I asked him to get engaged when things fell apart with Pavel after I told him about the baby." She looks through the plate-glass window back into the large living room, where Pavel is now laughing hoarsely with one of his cronies. When she turns back to me, it's all in her eyes. "I just love him so much. How does such a thing happen?"

I want to like her, I really do, but this woman is driving me bananas. I don't want to get drawn into why she's in love with Pavel or any of it. "I don't know," I answer honestly.

She narrows her eyes at me. "You are tougher even than Pavel, aren't you?"

I shrug. "Look, Aziza, I don't want to be rude. I know you're friends with Margot and Lulu and everything. But what happened with Rome . . ." I hesitate because I'm not sure how to say it, exactly. "Well, it's over. That's the bottom line."

"But what if—"

"Please." My voice is slightly more shrill than I'd like. I take a breath and continue. "You seem like a person who respects other people's decisions, Aziza. I'm happy for you and Pavel, I really am. I bet we'll spend a lot of time together over the years. But it doesn't need to be rainbows and butterflies for everyone, all right?"

I can tell she's insulted, but I don't really care. Who the hell is she to tell me about Rome? Fuck her.

She sits up straighter and blinks once. "Okay, then. I just wanted to apologize—"

"Accepted," I interrupt again. "Again, not to be rude, but it's private. And it's over. But mostly it's private."

"I totally respect that. I shan't bring Rome up again—"

Stop saying his name! I want to scream.

"As long as you know he was acting entirely on my behalf, as a gentleman, to defend my honor."

Now not only does she want me to forgive him, but I'm supposed to elevate him to some chivalric hall of fame? I take another deep breath. "Thanks for letting me know. I really appreciate it." I so desperately want this conversation to be over, I will say anything just to make it end. I look over my shoulder, back into the living room, and manage to catch Pavel's eye. I widen my eyes at him, silently begging him to rescue me from emotion central, and I see him excuse himself from his conversation and head toward the porch to join us.

He comes outside and stares down at Aziza. "I told you it would be awkward and uncomfortable," he says bluntly. "Miki doesn't give a crap about any of that emotional bullshit. Just drop it, Azi. All right?"

"Well, all right, but—"

"Azi." His voice is implacable.

"Fine!" She jumps up and goes to stand next to Pavel. He pulls her into a one-armed hug and kisses the top of her head. The way her eyes slide shut and she presses her cheek against his chest is almost despicably adorable. I stand up to go back inside with them.

"Sorry about that, Miki," Pavel says.

"No need to apologize—"

"Since I've apparently apologized enough for all of us!" Aziza says with a laugh. We go back inside and join the others for an obscenely large and indulgent supper.

Aziza totally respects my boundaries the remainder of the weekend. She never mentions Rome again, and the rest of the people at the party turn out to be an entertaining mix of business associates and old friends of Pavel's. Over dinner on Saturday, Pavel and Aziza announce they are officially engaged. They'll be getting married in a private ceremony within the next few weeks. Lots of champagne and bawdy toasts follow, and I go along with the festivities as much as I can.

MEGAN MULRY

When Sergei arrives Sunday at noon, I practically run out to my car. Note to self: *No more house parties. Ever.*

Sergei takes me to the office, instead of home. I spend a few hours doing work, then book my flight to Venice. Vivian has sent pictures of the villa she's rented on the Grand Canal, and I start to get excited about spending time with her and Isabel. I've been to Venice only once, and it was with my mother when I was a surly teenager. I trailed around behind her as if she were leading me to jail.

I send Isabel a text letting her know how excited I am to see her and for the two of us to hang out. She replies in about seven seconds with lots of Emojis, telling me she's excited, too. I shut down my computer and look around the office. I picture Rome handing me that first cup of coffee and my skirt slipping and my shirt coming undone. I'm not sure how it could have gone any differently for the two of us. Crossed wires and all that. I sigh and get up from my desk and head home.

The following week, Aziza and Pavel get married in a top-secret ceremony in Cyprus; he even manages to get her recalcitrant parents to come. When vast amounts of money are involved, even Pavel can save face.

I keep all my attention on work, putting a new deal together with an Indonesian group. We are going to acquire a few thousand acres, but I also get to sit on the board of a conglomerate that is fighting deforestation in that country. I now realize this is how I should have started back in March—testing the water gradually instead of diving into the deep end of the pool with the likes of Jérôme de Villiers and Pavel Durchenko.

As the Venice Film Festival approaches, I start to feel giddy with excitement. I haven't really allowed myself any frivolous pleasures for months, and the idea of drinking a Bellini at Harry's Bar with Vivian while we look at beautiful people stroll by is very appealing.

She's also got passes to some of the superstar-studded receptions, so Isabel and I can join her and gawk at Michael Fassbender and Benedict Cumberbatch up close.

I'm also fortifying myself against the fact that Rome might be there and I'll just have to be a grown-up and speak to him politely if we do meet. I'm fortifying myself with serious fashion. I've got one red gown in particular that is being shipped in from Lanvin. It's a splurge, but I figure what the hell. I'm spiteful, apparently, because I want to look stunningly beautiful when Rome sees what he's missing.

After I board the flight to Venice, I realize I'm having a bit of a panic attack. Only a bit, but still. Alexei got all doting and protective this week and wanted to make me travel with at least one bodyguard, and I refused, so here I sit in first class, and I feel a little unmoored. I relax after we take off and after a glass of champagne, and I begin to make a leisurely pass through the latest issue of *Paris Match*. Rookie mistake.

Rome and some young French actress are holding hands and smiling for the camera. I stare at the photo of the two of them walking into an opening at the Louvre. If I had a magnifying glass and a loupe, I couldn't be any more obvious. The steward asks if I'd like more champagne, and I hold up my empty glass without looking at him. "Keep it coming."

I look at the pictures a while longer and then flip the page and almost throw up. Rome and my mother are laughing like they are the oldest best friends at some cocktail party, and I want to call out to the captain to turn this plane around and take me back to Saint Petersburg immediately.

I force myself to keep reading and learn it is actually an engagement party for my mother and Jamie. And Rome is producing Jamie's next movie.

My stomach is in knots. I hold up the champagne glass again before the steward has to bother asking. I chug it.

Why won't he get the hell out of my life? It was bad enough worrying about whether he was going to be at Pavel's stupid house party a few weeks ago; there's no way I can sit through my own mother's wedding if Rome is going to be there, hovering. I open my tablet and send her a text.

Is Rome de Villiers going to be at your wedding?

She responds in a few minutes.

Of course not. Where are you?

I let her know I'm on the plane and I'll see her in a few hours, then put the device back in my bag. I shut the magazine and lean back into the large seat and try to breathe evenly. I'm obviously going to have to see him at some point, but I'm not sure I'll ever be ready.

I have to change planes in Zurich; I pass through the airport in a fog. I end up dozing off for the one-hour final leg. I wake up when the plane touches down at Marco Polo with a jarring screech. I'm disoriented from the champagne and a rather graphic dream involving Rome in a helicopter, naked. I sit up straighter and pull my hair back into a severe ponytail. I'm off the plane and through customs quickly. My mother has sent a car and driver to pick me up.

Simone and Jamie have rented a beautiful house about thirty minutes outside the city. When I arrive, Jamie answers the door and holds his arms wide for a hug.

"You want to call me Dad?" he volleys.

CHAPTER TWENTY-FIVE

For some reason, it strikes me as hilariously funny and I hug him, despite the past few years of thinking he was a complete jackass. So what if he's thirty-five and my mother is fifty-three? Maybe there's some sexy synergy there. I should stop being such a judgmental bitch.

"I think I'll stick with 'Jamie what's-his-name,'" I reply lightly when I pull away from the hug.

He smiles, a sweet, happy smile that I've never seen before, or never bothered to look for. "That sounds about right," he says. "I'm glad to see you, Miki. It's been too long."

"It's good to see you, too, Jamie. How is she?" I set down my bags and look meaningfully toward the sweeping staircase as I follow him into the living room. He's set up a small bar with an ice bucket and few glasses on the sideboard.

"She's wonderful. Want a drink? How was the flight?"

"I'd love a drink. Whiskey, please. The flight was fine. By the way, congratulations—I saw an article about Jérôme de Villiers and your production company."

Jamie looks up at me from where his hands are putting a few ice cubes into a lowball glass. "So you know he's producing my next documentary, and that's cool with you?"

"Of course. I'm fine with it." What else am I going to say?

Jamie hands me my glass and sits in the chair to my right. "His foundation contacted my production company, and I didn't know who he was. I mean . . ." He looks into his glass and shakes the ice, then looks back up at me. Jamie's a handsome guy, no question, with dirty-blond hair that's very California-surfer long and dark eyes that have an intensity that somehow never feels too serious. "I mean, I knew about the Clairebeau Foundation, but I didn't know about any of your . . . dealings with him."

I shrug. "Look, it's been a hectic year. With my dad and . . ." My voice falters.

Jamie is holding his glass with two hands, his forearms resting on his thighs. He's in jeans and a dark button-down linen shirt. I see how his fingers tense on the glass at the mention of my father.

"Jamie, she loves you."

He looks up at me. "I know you've disliked me for ages—"

"I saw too many jerks. I'm sorry I judged you based on all her past . . . missteps."

His lips quirk, and he looks up when my mother swans into the living room in some Moroccan-looking white caftan thing. Her short hair is slightly messy, and she looks beautiful. I stand up and hug her. "Congratulations," I whisper.

She looks into my eyes. "You're happy for me? For us?" She peers over my shoulder to include Jamie.

"Of course I'm happy for you!" I exclaim.

The three of us stay at the villa while we finish our drinks. They ask about my life in Saint Petersburg, and I ask where they're going to be living for the next year. Then we go out to dinner at my mother's new favorite restaurant, in Rubano. As I watch her and Jamie interact, I realize what a wonderful effect he has on her—a settling patience, it seems to me. He doesn't try to tamp her down, like some of her older boyfriends used to do, nor does he simper and hang on her every word, like some of the previous boy toys.

Over coffee, he turns to me. We've had a few bottles of wine, and we're all feeling happy and relaxed. "So, what are you going to do about Rome?" Jamie asks easily.

My mother's eyes widen at him as she takes a sip of coffee, like that subject is Off-Limits and Jamie has broken some code.

"Sorry, are we supposed to pretend he doesn't exist?" Jamie laughs.

I smile, too. All the wine and the delicious food, and seeing my mother happy and content, makes Rome seem distant and easy to discuss. "No. We don't have to pretend he doesn't exist." I pick up the teaspoon and stir my coffee. "What do you want to know?"

"Was it just a fling, or do you think about the future?" Jamie asks.

I start to see why he's growing into an award-winning documentary filmmaker. He gets right to the point. He's sprawling against the sleek chrome-and-leather chair with one arm slung casually across the back of my mother's chair, and he's just asking a straightforward question. I can answer it or not. He makes it sound like it doesn't have to be some bloody mess.

"Both, I guess." I put the teaspoon down and keep staring at the table. "You've met him." I look up, and both my mother and Jamie nod but don't say anything. "He's pretty great."

"Yes," Simone adds, slightly breathless, as if she's been dying to enumerate Rome's stellar qualities. "He is quite fabulous—"

Jamie places a gentle hand on her forearm, and I want to hug him so hard. He's not shutting her up or anything, but he totally understands how her enthusiasm might hurt me. She looks at him quickly, kisses his cheek, and then turns to me and says, "Yes, Rome is pretty great. Go on."

"What I mean is, I'd be a total liar if I said the idea of a future with him hasn't crossed my mind. But he's just so . . . assertive."

I shake my head sadly and look back down at the table, dragging my fingernail in straight lines across the white tablecloth.

"He's a pretty forceful character. I hear you." Jamie sounds like he knows from personal experience.

I look up and see he's smiling ironically.

"But so are you!" Simone blurts, no longer able to hold her tongue. "Who better for a man like that than a woman like you!" She extends one long, elegant hand to encompass my existence. "Beautiful. Brilliant. Stubborn as an ox."

Always with the backhanded compliments.

"I mean that in the best way possible," she backtracks.

"I know, Mom. Let's move on to another topic, okay? That's about all I can handle for the moment. If I happen to cross paths with Rome at some point this week, so be it, but I'm not going to pursue him."

Simone looks like she wants to add something, but Jamie simply says, "Fair enough." And that's the end of it.

I fall asleep in the Italian countryside that night thinking my mother and Jamie are probably going to make it after all. Not that I have any idea about that sort of thing.

The next day, their wedding is exactly as Simone predicted: Small. Quiet. Beautiful. The two of them are completely at ease with one another, without any of the bickering and sniping I used to associate with my mother and her boyfriends *du moment*. They are nearly always together, but I never see them being annoyingly touchy-feely, either.

The wedding reception is a casual dinner party with a few of her older friends and some of Jamie's younger friends, and it is wonderful. We all sit under a very large tree in the expansive formal gardens. A cook came with the rental, and she and my mother have become best friends, as is Simone's habit. I want to warn the poor Italian woman that she will never hear from my mother again (while my mother promises they will see each other forever and always, as the innocent woman teaches her new best friend how to make pasta from scratch from her secret family recipe that's been passed down for generations). The pasta is delicious and the wine is local and simple and the fourteen or so people at the table, including me, are enjoying themselves.

A young producer, George Kendall, is sitting to my left. He lives in LA, and I sort of grill him for local details. I love hearing the neighborhood updates—he also lives in the Abbot Kinney area—and I realize I'm missing it less and less, to the point where I mention I might be willing to rent out my place in Venice, or eventually sell it.

"Oh, I'd love to take a look," George says, with a hint of something more suggestive in his tone. I think he's kind of checking me out, and it feels fun to flirt.

"You should," I encourage. "It's close to the beach. Do you surf?"

"I used to. Who has time anymore?" He turns his chair slightly, giving me his full attention.

"I always made time to do it," I say, twisting my wineglass as I remember, and I make a silent promise to go to Biarritz or even Cornwall to catch some waves here in Europe. "It's definitely what I miss most about living there. But Saint Petersburg is pretty amazing. I feel like I've landed on Mars and I need to do a lot of exploring."

"Sounds fascinating."

"You should visit sometime."

"Are you inviting me?" He looks genuinely interested.

I smile at the memory this invokes. The Rome memory. I promise myself I will not carry a torch for the rest of my life, like my father did, but I realize in that moment that I am not willing to give up entirely on Monsieur Jérôme de Villiers just yet. Because when Rome said the same thing—nearly those exact words—I remember feeling like a long fuse was being lit and the sparking cord ignited me from the tips of my toes to my tingling scalp.

I smile easily, but with no promise whatsoever. "I know some wonderful bilingual guides who could show you around the city and take you out to the Catherine Palace and the Summer Palace. The Hermitage is wonderful also."

He smiles and gets the hint that I'm not interested in pursuing anything more. "Sounds good. Maybe when Jamie and Simone are there, we could all meet up?"

"Oh," I say, after I swallow another sip of wine. "My mother has vowed never to step foot in Russia. It's a long-standing family argument, you might say."

Simone overhears me from the other side of the table and interjects. "Never say never, darling. Now that you're actually *living* there"—she shudders dramatically—"I'll have to come and see in person how deplorable it really is."

"See?" I say to George. "Russia is *deplorable.*" I do a fair version of Simone's breathy voice when I say it with her sexy French accent, and Simone and a few other people sitting near us laugh at the imitation. The rest of the evening passes in that same breezy way, and I feel like I might be able to have a proper social life again at some point.

I stay with them a few more days, and on Thursday a car comes to take me into Venice. I hug my mother and Jamie good-bye. We've got plans to sit together at one of the gala dinners on Saturday night at the festival, so we don't have to have one of her usual dramatic farewells.

The car drops me off at Piazzale Roma, where I hop on the vaporetto to Vivian's rental house. I knock at the front door, and when it swings open, Isabel is there to greet me. She has grown so much in the past few months, I barely recognize her. She's leggy and her hair is longer. She is going to keep Vivian on her toes for the next ten years at least.

"Miki! You're really here!" She hugs me quickly and then stands aside to show me into the villa. "Isn't it fantastic?"

I look up and see it is indeed fantastic, from the ornate tile work on the walls to the frescoes of cherubs three stories above us. "Phenomenal!" I drop my bags and turn to look at her. "Where's your mom?"

"Meetings." She rolls her eyes.

"Good! More time for the two of us! Let me take a look at you." She smiles and appears awkward while being inspected.

"You're so grown-up."

"No, I'm not," she despairs. "I'm only eleven. It's so bor—"

I hold up my hand. "I forbid you to use that word while we are here. In this magnificent place!" I throw my hands wide, and she smiles at me.

"Okay. Fine." She gives in. "So what should we do first? Gelato? A gondola ride? The museum? I can't wait. My mom was so bor—I mean, she was really busy on the flight over, so I'm really excited to see you."

"Me, too." I pick up my bags again. "So where are we sleeping?"

"This way. You won't even believe it. The windows open right out onto the canal, and I just can't wait for it to be nighttime. We can get in our pajamas and sit by the window. It will be so awesome."

I follow her up the large stairway that hugs the walls of the central portion of the grand house, until we reach the fourth floor. She opens the double doors to our room with a flourish. "Ta-daaaaa!"

"Look how lucky we are." There are two queen-size beds against one wall, and they each face out two arched windows with stone window seats. I put my bags in the corner and walk toward one of the windows. It's the middle of the day, and the ornate wood shutters with leafy fretwork designs are closed to keep out the heat and sun. Patterns of shadow and sun speckle the terrazzo floor.

When I open one shutter, it's like pulling aside a curtain onto some magical world. The city, with all of its turquoise waterways, the island of Giudecca in the distance, the water taxis and gondolas and vaporettos, is spread out before us. "Oh, Isabel," I whisper. She is standing right beside me.

"Thanks so much for inviting me, Miki. I think it's going to be really special."

We stand there with one arm around each other's waists and just stare out at the bejeweled city as it gleams and sparkles beneath the glittering summer sun.

All I can think is, *Rome is out there somewhere.* I can feel him.

I squeeze her quickly. "Okay. I think lunch first, then a gondola ride, then—"

"Oh, I forgot! Mom hired someone to take us around. I made her swear it wasn't going to be, like, a horrible tour guide with an orange flag, and she promised me it would be cool. She should be here at one o'clock."

I look at my watch and see it's ten 'til. "I'm sure the guide will be stylish and fabulous if your mom hired her. Let's get our stuff together so we're ready when she gets here." I pull out my cell phone and see that Alexei has sent me a couple of messages about the Indonesia deal. I reply quickly and then slip the phone into one of the pockets of my casual green sundress. I grab my small credit-card holder and put it in the other pocket. After I put my sunglasses on my head, I turn to Isabel. "I'm ready!"

Isabel is rifling through her backpack, trying to decide what to bring. "Do I need my iPad?"

"What? No! We're in Venice, silly! Bring your phone to take pictures, and forget everything else. Come on!"

She laughs and puts her cell phone into the back pocket of her far-too-tight-but-I'm-not-saying-anything shorts. We walk down the grand staircase holding hands, and there's an older, white-haired butler type waiting for us in the front hall.

"Signora Voyanovski?" he asks formally.

I extend my hand to greet him. "Yes."

"I am Signor Moretti." He shakes my hand, then clasps his hands behind his back. "If you have any requests while you are here, please let me know."

"Thank you. Everything looks perfect, but if we need anything I'll be sure to ask."

There's a knock at the door, and Mr. Moretti pulls the door open.

A tall woman with long, dark hair smiles at us. She is probably in her midtwenties and positively beams enthusiasm. "I am Teresa. The guide?"

"Excellent!" I'm so excited not to have to stare at a map all afternoon, I want to hug her. She's very smiley, and she's already chatting with Isabel, asking what my young charge is most interested in seeing and doing. I turn to Mr. Moretti. "We'll see you later. Thanks again."

He shuts the door behind us, and we begin walking down the narrow *via* that runs alongside the house. "I do have one fixed appointment, to take you to a private art collection. Your mother mentioned you both like Matisse. Is that right?" Teresa asks. "Would you like that?"

"Yes!" Isabel cries. "Right, Miki?"

"Of course—that would be fabulous."

"*Perfetto!*" Teresa says in her charming Italian. We walk for an hour or so and end up at a villa on the Grand Canal, not far from the villa where we are staying, but on the other side. It's in spectacular condition, beautifully renovated but retaining all of its original, five-hundred-year-old details.

"How incredible!" I look up at the ornate facade and stretch my neck to see the intricately carved stonework at the roofline. "Who is the owner?"

"He's very private," Teresa explains, "so we're not permitted to say. He allows three special tours each day during the month of August, through the public areas only, of course."

"Of course," I agree. It's probably some Russian oligarch of my acquaintance. The cultural connection between Saint Petersburg and Venice has a long history, and many of the nouveau-riche Russians have places here.

We walk in, and a guard answers the door, looking like a cross between an Armani model and an assassin. "*Benvenuto.*"

He speaks to Teresa in rapid Italian. She opens her well-worn messenger bag and extracts a printout of our confirmation form. The killer Italian nods and returns the piece of paper.

"This way, please." He leads us into a spectacular drawing room overlooking the canal, then steps into a corner and touches his ear, obviously using a security system to let command central know we've entered the inner sanctum.

Teresa starts telling us about the collection. I realize the guard is going to accompany us throughout the tour, and I quickly return my attention to what Teresa is saying. I just sort of sigh into the whole experience when I see we're looking at a Titian. Isabel has the same reaction. We hold hands and listen to Teresa tell us about the history of the family who built the palazzo to house their art and sculpture collection. For generations, they filled the house with exquisite pieces, until the family gradually fell into financial ruin. The palazzo was shut down for many years, and most of the artwork put into high-security storage, until, about ten years ago, a philanthropist negotiated a long-term lease with the Italian government. The agreement, Teresa explains, allowed him to purchase the place and restore it to its former splendor, on the condition that it would revert to the Italian nation upon his death.

We go into the next room, also vast, and begin looking at the antiquities. Isabel is slightly less interested in the sculptures and urns, so I suggest we continue to the next painting gallery. Teresa agrees and leads us upstairs to an expansive gallery with about ten windows on one side and an equal number of twentieth-century modern masterpieces on the other. Picasso's *Rêve* is there, and I gasp at the sight.

"How . . . ?"

"It is so beautiful, isn't it?" Teresa smiles. "It's new this summer. Several of the acquisitions in this gallery are from the past few months. I love getting to see them up close." There's a bench in front of the painting, so the three of us sit down and just stare at it for a while. I'm holding Isabel's hand again.

"So *not* boring, right, Isabel?"

She looks at me, then back at the canvas. "It's awesome."

I've heard that the Wall Street mogul who bought the painting from a Las Vegas mogul sold it recently, but the new buyer's identity has been very hush-hush. The colors that I've seen many times in art-history books are much more vibrant in real life: the red of the chair, the bright yellow of the sleeping woman's pearl necklace, the primitive pattern on the wall behind her.

After a few more minutes of admiring silence, Teresa recollects that she's supposed to be telling us things and starts informing Isabel about the history of the painting and why it's important. We move to a Matisse next, and, out of nowhere, I start crying.

"What is it with you and the Matisses?" Isabel asks impatiently. Teresa pulls a packet of tissues out of her magical satchel, and I take it gratefully.

"You are heartless, Isabel. One day you're going to have a crush on someone and I'm going to make fun of you, and you can see how it feels."

"I'm sorry, Miki." She looks genuinely contrite, so I give her a watery smile.

"No worries, sweetie."

"Is it still the same crush from when we were in LA?"

When she says it like that, I realize it must seem like light-years have passed in her world since then. I nod resignedly. "Yes. Same crush. Can't quite seem to shake it."

"Well, maybe it's not just a crush after all?" *Oh, Isabel of my heart.*

I dry my eyes and we continue around the room. I realize the entire collection is really a symphony of beautiful women. The Picasso, the Matisse, a Modigliani nude, a Léger. I am starting to lose my breath. I ask Teresa if we can sit down again at the end of the gallery.

"Of course. Are you unwell? Shall we cut the visit short?"

"No. I'm fine. I just . . . I guess all these paintings remind me of someone, and I'm a little overwhelmed."

Teresa smiles. "It's a very seductive gallery, eh?"

"Yes," I answer. Teresa takes Isabel over to a Bonnard, and I keep looking at the Modigliani. It kind of washes over me, all that love. There's no question that the man who put this collection together adores women, or one woman in particular; it's in every brushstroke, every dab of color.

A few minutes later, I take a deep breath. "Okay. Whew!" I laugh briefly as I stand up. "I think that bit of drama has passed."

"Good!" Isabel says with relief. "I'm not sure how much more of that I could take."

"Oh, cut it out." We finish hearing about the rest of the twentieth-century modern pieces, and then Teresa and the assassin lead us up to the next floor to see the jewelry collection. There are ancient Roman and Etruscan earrings and cuffs; and then some Buccellati, Verdura, and Bulgari twentieth-century pieces; and everything in between. When we've finished looking, we make our way out of the final gallery and walk down the large circular staircase behind our silent escort.

At the second-floor landing, a door swings open and a woman walks out holding a pile of papers, speaking in rapid French. She nearly bumps into me but scoots around me quickly, saying "excuse me" in Italian. Then she looks up, catches my eye, and bursts out laughing. "Miki! Is it you?"

It's Zoe Mortemart, Étienne and Jules's cousin. I'm stunned into silence, and she reintroduces herself.

"Zoe! Zoe Mortemart? From Margot and Étienne's wedding, remember?"

Of course I remember! I want to yell.

"Zoe, how great to see you again," I manage. "This is Teresa, our guide, and my goddaughter, Isabel Travkin." Zoe turns to Teresa and Isabel and gives them a big smile.

"Nice to meet you both." She turns back to me. "So, what are you doing here?"

"We just finished having a tour of the art collection."

"Really? I'm surprised you would darken the door!" She's speaking, as always, as if I have any idea what she's talking about, as if the two of us are part of some secret society of knowing females.

"Well, Teresa was able to get us a private tour, so we—"

Zoe starts laughing again. "You mean you don't even know whose house it is?" She wheezes between the words, she's laughing so hard. "Priceless!" She shakes her head when she gets hold of herself. "Come with me." She grabs my upper arm, and there's nothing I can do but follow her back into the room she's just emerged from. I look over my shoulder and widen my eyes at Teresa and Isabel to let them know I haven't a clue.

After shoving me into the large room, an office of some kind, Zoe shuts the door behind me. She's left me standing alone in the middle of a book-lined library with a large partners' desk in the middle. I'm staring at the back of Rome's head.

CHAPTER TWENTY-SIX

Jesus, Zoe. Do you ever fucking knock?" he asks, without looking up from the document he's working on. "Seriously. I'm not going to give you any more information. Just run the story about the Matisse and leave me alone already—"

He swings around to face my direction, and I try to stay standing as his expression goes from peevish to confused to adoring.

"Miki?"

"Hi." It's the only stupid thing I can think to say, and it sounds sort of breathless to boot.

He tosses his pen onto the desk and stands up. I'd forgotten how tall and strong he is, how he pulses in real life. I feel like I'm starting to tilt backward when he slowly approaches me, like he's the heat of the sun or something and I should be shielding my eyes. He reaches out to touch me, and my whole body goes into some weird defensive mode. He senses it immediately and drops his outstretched hand.

"How are you?" he asks, with so much tenderness and concern. I'm still holding the used tissue in my right fist, and I feel like I'm going to start crying again. He's so beautiful, just like the Matisse and the Modigliani, all that love and . . . and . . . something I can't describe, but it feels sweet and peaceful. It feels like what I imagine home feels like, to people who have a home.

I miss you, I want to whisper, to just let it come out like the tears before—to let the words and the feelings and everything just fly out of me. But what if—oh, I don't know—what if there's a blond woman under his desk or he just had sex with Zoe or hell knows what else? "I'm good," I answer.

"Good," he agrees too quickly. If I didn't know better, I'd say he was nervous. But this is the world-renowned playboy billionaire; he doesn't have nerves. Oh, but he does. I know he does. He's looking at me and he licks his lips quickly, and I feel my heart start to pound, and not just in my chest. "Are you free . . ." His voice falters. "Are you free for a drink? Or dinner?"

I remember Isabel. "I'm here with my goddaughter . . . I should probably go."

He strides past me to the door and pulls it wide. Zoe is standing there, grinning, with the silent guard and Teresa and Isabel behind her on the landing. "Zoe, go away," Rome says bluntly, barely looking at her.

"Don't say I never did anything for you, Rome!" She laughs and skips down the stairs, showing herself out.

"Vittorio." Rome starts speaking to the guard in fluent Italian. I don't understand what he's saying, but I hear the words *prosecco* and *antipasto,* and the next thing I know Vittorio is gone and Isabel and Teresa are standing in the library with us.

"Will you please stay for a drink and some appetizers on the roof terrace?" He directs the invitation to Isabel, and I think she's finally met her match. He's so effortlessly charming.

"Uh . . ." She looks to me for confirmation. I nod my agreement. "That would be awesome." She turns back to me. "Should we call my mom? I think she finished her meetings at five."

Teresa is staring around the room in stunned silence, trying not to gape, then remembers she's supposedly working. "Oh, yes!" She looks at her watch. "I promised Ms. Steingarten I would have you both home by five."

I look at my watch and see it's already a few minutes past. "Thanks for the kind invitation, Rome, but—"

"Miki! Mom will totally understand!" Isabel widens her eyes at me as if I am the stupidest girl in the fifth grade.

Rome smiles at his new accomplice, then looks at me. "Isabel is a very wise girl. It's best not to pass up spontaneous invitations to a Venetian rooftop at sunset."

The way he looks at me, well, I actually sway. "Okay." I clear my throat because I can't seem to get that breathiness to go away. He keeps staring at me.

"So?" he asks.

"Right," I say, snapping out of my may-I-stare-into-your-eyes-for-the-rest-of-my-life reverie. "Teresa, we're fine to see ourselves home. Thank you so much." I reach out and shake her hand.

"The pleasure has been mine." Her eyes twinkle as she smiles and shakes my hand. "Please let me know if you want any more tours." She hands me her card.

"I definitely will. Thanks again."

Rome opens the door and leads Teresa out to the landing. Another guard is standing there, and Rome instructs him to show Teresa out. I imagine his Armani assassins popping up like mushrooms—anytime one is called away, another one appears.

When he comes back into the study, the sun is slanting through the beveled windows behind me and he looks insanely gorgeous, sporting his typical casual uniform of a white oxford shirt—rolled up to reveal his strong, tan forearms—and beautifully tailored linen trousers. The easygoing cut of his clothes somehow makes him appear even more powerful. "So, Isabel, do you want to call your mother from my landline—"

"I've got it!" I interrupt, pulling out my cell phone and dialing Vivian.

"Where are you guys?" she asks without preamble. "I thought for sure you'd be back by now."

"We ran into a friend . . ." I'm dreading her impending shriek and hoping it won't be too obvious across the room.

"Really?" she asks doubtfully.

I think she already suspects.

"Yes," I speak quickly. "Jérôme de Villiers's art collection . . . It's such a funny coincidence . . . The tour guide made arrangements for us to visit this anonymous collection . . . and it turns out . . ."

Vivian is laughing hysterically, just like Zoe did. Apparently, my botched love life is sidesplitting. I keep talking over her gasping fit.

"So, he's invited Isabel and me to have a drink on his rooftop terrace . . ."

"Of course he has!" she nearly guffaws.

"So, we'll be home in about an hour."

She stops laughing immediately. "Absolutely not!" she cries. "What's his address? I'm coming over."

Isabel and Rome are laughing about something out the window, as he points across the canal.

"I'm not sure that's—"

Rome calls over from the other side of the room, "Please tell Vivian I'd love to meet her if she'd like to join us." Of course he says it loudly enough that Vivian can hear.

"Oh, thanks, but—" I try.

Vivian yells into my ear, "Yes!"

"She'd love to," I answer lamely.

"Great." Then he's looking at me again, and it's like Isabel and Vivian and his bazillion-dollar Venetian palazzo and the whole universe all evaporate and he's just looking at me. "Great," he says again, more softly.

"Okay, that's fine," I say to Vivian. Then I look back at Rome. "What's the address here?"

He gives me the details and I tell Vivian, and she tells me she'll be here in five minutes. I'm tempted to tell her not to trip on the cobblestones in her haste, but I refrain. I put the phone back in my side pocket as Rome and Isabel begin walking toward me.

"All set?" he asks.

"Yes, she says she'll be here in a few minutes. Should we wait for her?"

"We can if you like, but one of the guards can also show her up."

"Okay," I answer, getting a little buzzed just standing near him.

We start to go up the stairs, Isabel and I walking in front of Rome. "So, how many guards do you have?" Isabel asks enthusiastically. I look over my shoulder and see Rome looking at me again, and I stumble on the edge of one of the stone steps. He reaches up quickly to steady me, his palm at the base of my spine, and I feel it like a brand through the thin fabric of my dress.

"Thanks," I whisper.

He pulls his hand away once I'm steady, and I can feel the outline of where he touched me for many seconds afterward.

"There are about twenty guards, Isabel," he continues smoothly. "But they're not mine, really. They belong to the palazzo, because of all the artwork."

"Cool."

When we get to the top floor, another guard is standing by glass doors that lead out to the roof terrace. He touches a button and the doors slide open.

"Wow!" Isabel beams. "This place is seriously awesome."

"Thanks," Rome says, and it sounds like he really means it.

There's already a bottle of prosecco in a silver ice bucket on the stone side table, and a platter of salamis and cheeses and small pickled vegetables for us to nibble on. Isabel walks straight to the edge of the roof, craning her neck to get a better view out over the canals.

"Be careful!" I bark.

"Seriously, Miki! You have to see this." Isabel's perfectly safe, with the half wall coming up above her waist.

"I'll be there in a second," I tell her. I'm staring at Rome while he's looking in Isabel's direction and opening the prosecco. I love his hands on the neck of the bottle and how he's twisting the large cork. My gaze travels up to his face, and he totally nails me fantasizing about his hands, having turned back at some point to focus on what he's doing. We are looking at each other like idiots when the cork explodes from the bottle. I jump, and Rome smiles and pours two glasses for us.

He finishes making the drinks, then walks over to where I'm standing and hands me one of the flutes. He's added a bit of fresh peach juice, and I can smell the summery, intoxicating scent as he holds it out for me to take. When I wrap my fingers around the stem, he still doesn't release his hold, and I look up into his eyes.

"Miki, I want—"

"There you are!" Vivian cries as she explodes onto the roof deck. Rome releases the glass and takes a few steps away from me to introduce himself to Vivian and offer her a drink.

"Perfect timing," he says with that dastardly hint of his French accent. "I haven't taken a sip yet, so here's a Bellini for you. I'm Rome. You must be Vivian."

"Why, yes, I must." She's such an easy mark, honestly. I bet if he asked her about her husband, she would reply, "*Who?*" with complete sincerity.

I watch as she flirts with him and he spars easily. He pours another drink for himself and makes a nonalcoholic version for

Isabel. The four of us sit down on the large outdoor sofas and enjoy the early evening, chatting about the film festival and some of Vivian's more high-profile deals, all while my insides are turning into something resembling panna cotta.

Rome talks to Vivian and Isabel like they're old friends, but even though his words are directed toward them, it's as though his energy is somehow directed at me. He doesn't look at me too much or do anything overly obvious, but I feel hot all over and start to get fidgety in my seat whenever he talks.

After the second round of drinks and more platters of food casually arriving, I catch Isabel yawning and know she must be feeling the jet lag. And I need to get out of here. I feel flushed and overwhelmed by the rush of all the old, unresolved emotions, and there's nothing Rome and I can discuss in front of Isabel and Vivian, in any case.

"Getting sleepy, Isabel?" I ask.

Isabel looks like it's the last thing she wants to admit, but she nods. "I am. A bit."

I stand up and Isabel does, too. I want to laugh at Vivian, who looks as though she's considering a longer visit with Rome while I take her eleven-year-old daughter back to the villa. "Vivian?"

"Oh, fine, I'm coming. But it's just so magical here. I hate to leave."

Rome is now standing as well. "Come over anytime. Please feel free."

"Really? How wonderful." Vivian may be blushing.

If we were sitting at a table with a tablecloth, I would totally kick her shin right now. "Vivian?"

"Yes?" She turns to me like she barely knows me.

"Let's go."

"Oh. Right." She puts her glass on the Etruscan stone table and smiles at Rome. "Thanks again. The prosecco, the delicious food—"

"Viv," I interrupt softly. Isabel is leaning into me, and it really is time for us to leave.

"Come this way," Rome says, leading us back into the house as soon as he sees how exhausted Isabel is. He presses a button and opens a door to reveal a small elevator. "At your service." He smiles at Isabel.

"Thank you," she says with a yawn, and the four of us get into the narrow cab. As the elevator makes its smooth descent, it's basically torture standing a few inches behind Rome. Isabel and I are at the back, and Vivian and Rome are standing right in front of us. When it mercifully comes to a stop, Rome pushes open the door to allow Vivian to exit; Isabel follows her mother into the front hall.

"Miki, may I call you?" he asks in a low voice, but politely, as if he's some country gentleman hoping to pay me a visit.

I look up at him as I turn to fit through the cramped door of the elevator, my hip skimming his. "Yes . . . please." I'm frozen there for a second.

He exhales, and I feel the warmth of his breath against my neck. He turns quickly to see that Isabel and Vivian have gone toward the front door and are no longer visible, then kisses my lips with a fleeting tenderness. "*Jusque-là*," he whispers in his sinful French.

Until then.

CHAPTER TWENTY-SEVEN

As soon as I'm out of his range, I start to breathe normally again. Isabel is dozy and sweet, leaning into her mother as we walk to the bridge and cross back to our side of the canal. When we reach our place, Isabel looks up at me and says, "If anyone can help you get over your crush, I bet that man Rome can. I think he likes you."

Vivian smiles at me over Isabel's soft blond curls. "I agree."

"Well, you are both exhausted," I say. "So why don't you go to sleep and we'll see about crushes tomorrow?"

"Okay," Isabel answers easily. We are up in our room by then, and Vivian is helping her out of her shorts and T-shirt and putting her into her pajamas. She's asleep within seconds.

I'm sitting in one of the stone window seats, looking out at the city. Vivian comes over, and I stand up to give her a hug.

"I love you, Miki."

"I love you, too, Viv." I hold her close. "You're the best."

She pulls back and looks into my eyes, making sure I'm all right. "You okay with everything? With him?"

I nod. "More than okay. Whatever happens."

"You want to talk about it?" she asks.

"No, I'm good. I'm going to stay up and read for a while."

She hugs me one more time, then turns to go. "Sleep well."

"You, too."

A few seconds after she leaves, I feel my phone vibrate in my pocket with a text alert. I pull it out and smile.

What are you wearing?

I smile at the screen, then type back.

The same thing I was wearing ten minutes ago when I saw you.

A few seconds pass with the cursor blinking, so I know he's composing a reply. He texts:

Want to meet up for a late supper?

I look at Isabel asleep and then out the window at the magical city.

I'd love that.

His reply is there in a few seconds.

Casual?

I smile at the memory of our last "date" and think of my Lanvin gown. Why should I save it for the gala?

Formal. I'm in the mood to get *dolled* up.

Touché. Be ready in thirty minutes. I'll be down in front of your place.

I smile at his familiar determination, then put the phone away. I try to be quiet as I rustle around in the bag, feeling like the teenager I never was—sneaking out to meet a boy. I find the dress in the white tissue and shake it out. After I hang it up, I stroke down the sensuous fabric for a few seconds, imagining the feel of Rome's hands through the silk. I quit my reverie when I remember the real man is on his way over and I need to jump in the shower.

As I quietly get ready, I think back to that first night in Saint Petersburg and how willfully careless I tried to be. All this time, I thought I was protecting myself from Rome and the wildness of his passion, but the truth is so obvious now. I've been afraid of my own voracious appetites, tamping myself down, shying away from my own power.

- 273 -

After I put on some mascara and lip gloss, then pile my hair into a loose knot with a few clips, I do my usual *oh, well, that's good enough* assessment of my appearance in the mirror. But this time I stop short. I realize that my good-enough life is very, very good. If Rome wants me as much as I want him—as much as his tender kiss by the elevator seemed to indicate—what the two of us have is so much more than enough.

I slip into the red dress, the sheer layers of long, diaphanous silk caressing my bare legs, and zip up the side. I go through my suitcase until I find my small silver clutch and silver heels. I carry the shoes in one hand so I don't make a click-clacking racket as I go down the stairs, but my heart beats too fast for me to think about anything beyond getting to the ground floor without tripping.

Signor Moretti is there when I reach the front door. "Will you be returning late?" He gives me a quick, complimentary appraisal.

"Oh, I'm not sure, but most likely yes. May I take a key?" I slip on my heels as I speak to him.

"That's not necessary; it's on a code." He gives me the four digits and then shows me how to make sure the door is double-locked when I return.

"Thank you."

He smiles, obviously knowing I'm embarking on some romantic rendezvous. He opens the door for me, and when I step out, I see Rome walking toward me in the deep shadows of evening. It's not quite full night, and the light makes his sleek hair look velvety and his skin take on a coppery hue.

When he has nearly reached me, he pauses a few feet away and puts his hand over his heart dramatically. "*Bellissima*," he whispers.

I hold the dress fabric slightly away from me and do a half twirl. "I wanted to get your attention."

"You've got it." His voice is rough and strong.

I go still and stare into his eyes; he doesn't look away. I close the distance between us and kiss him lightly at the edge of his mouth, that small spot that lifts up slightly when his smile is at its most devilish. He groans and pulls me up against him, both of his hands around my waist so our hips slam together, and I bend into him easily. Then I'm circling his neck with my eager hands and his lips are on mine and we are kissing in the shadows. I'm ravenous for him, as if I can finally enjoy a delicious meal that I've forbidden myself to try for my entire life, forbidden for reasons that I now realize were anchored in fear.

Still, kissing has never been our problem. I pull away slowly, caressing his smooth cheek with my fingertips. "What did you have in mind for dinner?"

He stares at me for a few more seconds, looking like he has plenty to say but knows we will get to it eventually. "This way."

He holds my hand as we walk back toward the Grand Canal. When we turn off the narrow *via*, there is a glorious motorboat waiting for us at the edge of the canal. The polished teak gleams in the dusky light. Two of his guards are on board, one at the wheel and the other holding the line and waiting to help us get on.

"Your chariot," Rome says. He has that sweet eagerness that I noticed earlier on the rooftop, like it really matters to him what I think.

"I love it," I whisper as I slide past him and take the guard's hand so I don't slip on the edge of the boat. Rome's eyes glitter with pleasure. Has it always been this easy to fill him with that bubbling joy?

Once he jumps aboard, the line is untied and the motor revs and we pull out into the canal at a smooth pace. There's a built-in leather couch at the back, and Rome gestures for me to have a seat. "Do you mind taking your shoes off?" he asks. "The spiky heels are hell on the wood."

"Oh, sure." I bend down to undo the tiny buckle, but he reaches for my wrist.

"Allow me." He kneels down, and when his fingers touch my bare ankle, I gasp. He smiles up at me. "You like that?" He traces his finger on the sensitive skin and smiles.

"You know I do. We've never disagreed about that."

His face clouds slightly. "Yes." He finishes taking off my shoes, and then he's sitting next to me.

He reaches for my hand, and I feel like that teenager again, the one who never got the memo about making out in movie theaters or how to talk to boys. But then his thumb is gently rubbing the back of my hand and I simply give myself over to how good it feels to be with him, just to sit next to him. I let my head rest on his shoulder as the two of us look at the beautiful buildings drifting past, and he hums his pleasure at the contact.

"Rome?"

"Mm-hmm?"

"I'm pretty sure I've loved you since the first time you walked into my office in Saint Petersburg."

His breathing stops while he waits for me to continue. "But?"

I look up at him and smile. "No buts."

His eyes are gleaming with hope and tenderness. "Tell me you love me."

Of course that's the bastardy way he would tell me he loves me. "You're impossible," I say instead, but I'm kissing his neck and his jaw through the words.

"Tell me you love me," he whispers again, sounding deliciously strained, as if he's about to lose control of . . . everything.

He leans his forehead against mine and shuts his eyes. I can feel his heart pounding beneath the palm of my hand where it's resting against his chest.

"Do we need to start over?" he asks. "I'm happy to court you and prove it all. I want to earn you, Mikhaila. Everything I did before was so"—he moves his forehead slightly, right and left, against mine—"impulsive. And I want everything from here on out to be filled with purpose. I want you to know it." He touches my chest over my heart. "To feel it here."

"I already feel it, Rome. You've been inside me since the first time I heard your voice, the first time I laid eyes on you."

He's kissing my neck and bare shoulder and I'm melting against him.

"Would you move to Saint Petersburg?" I ask, considering practicalities for a moment, before the spell of his kisses pulls me back under.

"Yes."

I pull his face up so I can look into his eyes.

"Yes?"

"Of course. Turns out I have a bit of money and I can live wherever the hell I want." His lips are swollen, and his turquoise eyes are gleaming with happiness. "I don't care where I live, as long as we're together."

I can see the boy in those eyes, the child who was never told how wonderful he was, never praised for being himself. I get to tell him those things for the rest of my life. "I love you. I love your impetuous nature, your generosity, your thoughtfulness, your loyalty . . ." His eyes try to track away, as if it embarrasses him to be praised. To be loved. "Look at me, you beautiful man." His gaze returns warily. "You are mine, damn it."

"I've always been yours, Miki. Always." He leans in and kisses me again, and I feel it like a vow, a touch that binds us to each other completely.

We spend the rest of the night floating around the city—holding hands, kissing under bridges, eating caviar, touching each other as we glide along ancient canals. He assures me that the public-indecency laws are far more lenient here than they are in the States, but we definitely come close to breaking a few.

As the sun starts to rise over the lagoon, my head rests in the crook of Rome's shoulder while he reclines next to me. I pull a blanket over us as we stare up at the morning stars. The sound of the water against the side of the boat lulls me into a lovely half sleep.

I'm not sure how much longer we ride around, but the sun is definitely above the horizon when the boat pulls up in front of Vivian's villa. "Time for Cinderella to go back to her evil stepsister," Rome jokes. I look up into his eyes with obvious desire, but we're both exhausted.

"Tonight," I promise. "Will you come to the gala with us?"

"Yes, if you like. I was going to avoid it, thinking you wouldn't want me there, but now . . ." He leans down and kisses me again, and, god, it feels so damn right. My body begins to heat up immediately. "You need sleep," he finishes.

I groan at the truth of it, wanting him in my arms and wanting sleep. "I would love it if you came to the party. I even packed a special dress with a bare back just for you. But it might be wrinkly." I look down at my happily disheveled self.

"I'll send over a new gown this afternoon," he offers easily. My little fixer.

"I can get my own dress."

"I know you can," he smiles, touching my jaw. "But will you let me?"

"I'm afraid it will be something totally over the top."

"Of course it will be over the top. I don't think I ever misrepresented myself with false promises of being run-of-the-mill, did I?"

I laugh and kiss him again. "Certainly not." The two of us walk back to the front door of the villa, then make out in the narrow *via* for another twenty minutes. "Why am I not going up to your bed, again?" I ask.

"Because you're tired . . . and on vacation with Isabel," he answers between kisses. "Or something."

"Right. Tired." I kiss him one last time, then hold his face in my hands again. "Mine."

"Yours," he whispers.

"Forever."

He nods solemnly. "Forever." He kisses me one last time. "Sleep well, my paper doll." He winks.

"You're going to pay for that." I wink back and tap in the code to open the door.

"I want to pay and pay," he replies suggestively, touching my back with a single finger while I reach for the door handle.

"I know you're good for it. Now go get some sleep. I'll see you tonight." I shut the door slowly, but not all the way, so I can watch him walk away until he's turned at the end of the *via* and I can't see him any longer. I push the door shut, and soft tears of happiness trail down my cheeks. Walking up the stairs, I can feel everywhere he touched me, every kiss, every light caress. My body is covered with him.

When I get up to the bedroom, Isabel rolls over and mumbles something in her sleep. I tiptoe across to my side of the room and pull off the dress and throw on an oversize T-shirt. I crawl into bed, and as my eyes are drifting shut I hear my phone vibrate on the floor, inside my clutch. I fumble for it and pull it out.

You are my perfect.

I fall asleep with the phone cradled to my chest.

EPILOGUE

Two Years Later

H urry up, or we're going to be late to our own wedding," I call up the large stone stairs of Le Cloître. Rome and I have spent the past two weeks in Provence, being very lazy and keeping the world at bay, but now it's time for the big day.

He appears at the top of the stairs, and I'm tempted to call off the whole damn thing just so I can push him back into bed and spend the rest of the day in his arms. "You're so disgustingly handsome."

He smiles like the devil and walks down the stairs toward me. He's in a dark suit with a crisp white shirt that's a glinting contrast with his tanned complexion, and his silvery-gray tie reflects the morning sun.

"What took you so long, anyway?" I ask.

"I needed to get something out of one of the safes, and I couldn't remember which one it was in."

I shake my head. "I can't believe I'm marrying someone with so many safes he can't even keep track of them."

He shrugs. "They'll be your safes within the hour. You can keep track of them after that. Turn around," he orders.

I sigh. "Rome. We *have* to go."

He raises one eyebrow. "Turn. Around."

I'm wearing the red Lanvin gown I wore in Venice two summers ago, and I know how much he loves its low, exposed-back. I turn slowly, for full effect, and feel him put on a long double strand of pearls. He fastens the clasp, then wraps his strong fingers around my neck, adjusting the necklace so it rests like a choker in front and falls to the middle of my back. He kisses my nape, and a shiver runs down my spine.

"Remind me why we're getting married?" he asks, his voice husky.

"Because you want our baby to have your name?"

"That's easily accomplished without a wedding. Why else?"

"Because you are mine," I whisper hotly. "And I'm a possessive witch who loves you."

"Yes," he whispers. "You love me."

"I do." I turn in his arms and kiss him on the lips. "Now let's go, already."

We walk out to the car and are driving down the curving road soon after. I rest my hand on his forearm. I love the feel of his muscles tensing and relaxing as he works the gearshift. My mind is busy thinking about a big deal I've got going in Brazil, and then I'm thinking about my house in LA, which is finally going to be sold. And then for some reason I am reminded of Landon Clark. I see a copse of trees and a small lane up ahead.

"Say, Rome?"

"Yes, love?" He's concentrating on the road, but I love how he always concentrates on me when we're talking, whatever else he's doing.

"See that lane up there on the right?"

"Yes?"

"Even if it meant we were going to be late for our own wedding, if I were to suggest we pull over and—"

Before I even finish, he slams on the brakes and fishtails into the shady lane.

We are only about fifteen minutes late arriving at Margot and Étienne's house, where about a hundred of our closest family and friends have gathered for the ceremony. No one seems to notice or care about our tardiness, except to remark that we look so particularly happy today.

ACKNOWLEDGMENTS

Love and thanks to everyone who helped make this book a reality: to my agent, Allison Hunter; to my editors, Krista Stroever, Maria Gomez, and Kelli Martin; to my reader/writer heroines, Janet Webb, Anne Calhoun, Miranda Neville, Alexandra Haughton, Mira Lyn Kelly, Lexi Ryan, Alison Kent, and Jeffe Kennedy; to my beloved family and friends, Peg, Jeff, Helen, Jeb, Electra, Bobbi, Maté, and Dorothy. Finally, a special thanks to everyone who hangs out with me on Twitter. This book underwent extensive revisions and major overhauls during the past two years, and the random "you can do it" or "can't wait to read it" in my Twitter stream at two in the morning meant more than I can adequately convey. Most of all, thanks to you, gentle reader!

ABOUT THE AUTHOR

Wheaton Mahoney, 2011

Megan Mulry writes sexy, stylish, romantic fiction. Her first book, *A Royal Pain*, was an NPR Best Book of 2012 and a *USA Today* bestseller. Before discovering her passion for romance novels, she worked in magazine publishing and finance. After many years in New York, Boston, London, and Chicago, she now lives with her family in Florida.

31901055885992